*To Glouces[...]*

*I hope y[...]*

*adventur[...]*

*Best Wishes Paul*

# AFGHAN BOY

## THE IMPOSSIBLE DREAM

*by*

## Paul Gait

**Grosvenor House
Publishing Limited**

The right of Paul Gait to be identified as the author of this
work has been asserted in accordance with Section 78
of the Copyright, Designs and Patents Act 1988

The book cover is copyright to Amy Bennett

This book is published by
Grosvenor House Publishing Ltd
Link House
140 The Broadway, Tolworth, Surrey, KT6 7HT.
www.grosvenorhousepublishing.co.uk

This novel is entirely a work of fiction.
The names, characters and incidents portrayed in it are the
work of author's imagination. Any resemblance to
actual persons, living or dead, events or localities is
entirely coincidental.

A CIP record for this book
is available from the British Library

ISBN 978-1-78623-549-7

# DEDICATION


To Chris and Sue


And
Canine friends
Smudge and Dusty

# THANKS

To my wife Helen, for allowing me to spend countless
hours to develop yet another story.

To family and friends for continued support
and encouragement.

To Janet for again spending many hours proof
reading my manuscript.

# Prologue

Millions of children worldwide, suffer the consequences of adult's erroneous activities; whether through tribalism, war, ideological fanaticism, social ineptitude, addiction or greed.

Children are frequently deprived of their right to a happy, carefree childhood, by becoming the innocent victims of the transgressions of 'grown-ups'.

Some are fortunate enough to break away from their troubled environment, and the depressing, self-perpetuating, downward spiral of negativity.

Mohammed has been orphaned in a suicide bombing and was subsequently rescued, from the debris of his family home, by his Scout Leader, a British Army soldier and his search dog.

Following the end of the soldier's posting, Mo, a Scout, dreams of being re-united with him. The boy believes that the soldier is the only person that cares about him and wants to adopt him.

But the boy's dream seems improbable. For, how could a fourteen-year-old orphan, from an impoverished background, travel to England and then find that same soldier?

Ironically, a terrorist kidnapping, gives Mohammed the opportunity to break away from his dangerous environment. But his journey to a 'safer' life is far from easy.

During his pilgrimage, Mo finds that being a Scout, has a currency for friendship, that is accepted worldwide, which helps him and his companion, Abdul, on their way.

Together, Mohammed and Abdul, tackle the seemingly impossible challenges that confront them, involving thousands of miles on foot, through sandstorms, braving armed gangs and in overloaded trucks, a sinking dinghy, and the menacing refugee camp in Calais.

Their story is not unique. For each day, countless thousands of people leave their homes in pursuit of their own dreams for a better and peaceful life.

Sadly, thousands also perish in pursuit of that dream.

But, sometimes, given the right circumstances, all dreams are possible.

Can Mohammed's determination, turn his conflict affected life around, and achieve that 'impossible dream'?

This is Mohammed's story

# PART ONE

# Afghanistan

# Chapter One

Mohammed was teasing his young sister, Aryana, as they were sitting down at home for a family meal, when their world, literally, caved in on them.

A suicide bomber had driven a heavily laden Isuzu D-Max truck, packed with high explosives, through the outskirts of the village towards an army checkpoint.

Alerted by the screaming engine of the speeding vehicle, an alert army sniper, shot the driver dead before he could reach his target.

Unfortunately, as the driver's hand no longer maintained pressure on the 'Deadman's switch', the explosives detonated prematurely. A deep crater marked the bomber's bloody end.

Although short of his intended target, his bomb had a catastrophic effect on the community. The explosion was devastating.

Fragile, shanty, buildings within a twenty-yard radius of the bomb were flattened by the percussion wave.

A mushroom dust cloud rose up from the carnage, blotting out the sun and casting a dark evil shadow over the scene.

Sergeant Tom Bow heard the distant explosion while he was still in Camp Bastion.

'Here we go again,' he thought, as his radio burst in to life.

'*Sierra One, Sierra One. This is Sierra Control.*'

The soldier pressed the transmit button on the radio strapped to his webbing.

'*Sierra One receiving over.*'

'*Sierra One, we have a job for you, Over.*'

'*Go ahead Control, over,*' the soldier replied, pen in hand.

'*Category one; Large explosion, truck bomb, houses destroyed, people trapped.*' The controller then relayed the coordinates .

'*Roger, all received. On our way,*' the Sergeant answered, quickly getting his Arms and Explosives (AES) search dog out of his air-conditioned kennel.

'Come on Jersey, we've got some work to do,' he said, clipping the lead on the dog's collar.

Within a few minutes, in a well-rehearsed process, his protection team quickly grabbed equipment bags and weapons and boarded their heavily armoured transport.

A convoy of vehicles 'steamed out' of the military fortress, heading to the site of the reported explosion.

Ahead of them, rising above the scene of devastation, they could see the column of black smoke, a demonic sign of the malevolent deed.

As they got closer, the adrenaline of being despatched to assist at yet another scene of disaster was replaced, by apprehension. Concern etched on the faces of the soldiers.

It was worse for the dog handler, for he knew that the explosion had occurred in the area where some of his Scouts, from the ad hoc Scout Troop he had created, lived.

As they arrived at the Afghan police roadblock, he realised that to his horror, his worst nightmare had come true.

The house of his eldest scout, Mohammed , had been completely obliterated by the blast.

The soldiers in the convoy, well versed in conducting similar rescues, erupted out of their transport and immediately set up a protective cordon around the area.

Shortly after, a heavily armed army air corps support Lynx helicopter landed, sending up a dust cloud.

A soldier dashed from the helicopter to speak to the Sergeant.

'What's the score mate?' the helicopter's young air gunner shouted, over the noise of the Lynx's still turning rotors.

'Just arrived ourselves, Jezza, but it looks like it was another suicide bomber on his way to paradise. As usual, I'm afraid he's taken some of his countrymen with him,' the Sergeant replied.

'God, where do you start in this mess?' Corporal Jeremy Hopson, the helicopter gunner said, looking around.

'I think we'll start over there,' the dog handler decided, pointing to a pile of rubble where Mo's house lay in ruins.

Several men were already frantically 'shuffling' lumps of masonry from the heap that used to be a home.

'Right. Let's get this lot organised then, the Corporal said and strove off purposefully to get more villagers organised in a human chain to hasten the clearance of debris from the collapsed buildings.

Anxiously the Sergeant looked around at the crowds of bystanders, hoping against hope to see the Scout amidst the group. But sadly, to no avail.

'Come on then girl. Time to go to work,' he said to the dog, with great dread at what they might find.

So, after putting special protective leather boots on Jersey's paws, the soldier led his dog up on to the pile of rubble and took her off her lead with the instruction to 'find.'

# Chapter Two

Mohammed's family home had been flattened by the blast; the lightweight breeze block construction was no defence from the fearful explosion.

As the jets screamed overhead, more shocked locals and uniformed rescuers materialised and helped, frantically digging at several of the large rubble areas.

Although well used to the regular carnage of the, seemingly endless, conflicts that plagued the country, they still hoped, that by some miracle, they would find survivors underneath the demolished buildings.

The dog handler and his search dog were no strangers to this type of devastation. For as well as detecting the presence of arms and explosives, they had successfully rescued scores of people from bomb and earthquake damaged buildings.

The working cocker spaniel loved her job and had an excellent record of success.

So, after a short while, working with the frantic villagers, the dog indicated 'a find' by pawing the ground and barking.

The Sergeant instructed the rescuers to remove the debris in the area where the dog was barking.

Shortly after, the rescuers uncovered the body of a man, Mo's father.

The Sergeant quickly checked for vital signs, but unfortunately, his injuries were catastrophic, and he was dead.

'Good girl,' the Sergeant encouraged and rewarded Jersey with her toy, allowing the dog to play with it for a few minutes, then he took the toy off her and instructed her again to 'find.'

The dog wandered over the debris and sniffed around until she made another 'find,' and barked her success.

The Sergeant made his way to the new site and with his heart in his mouth, checked the body as they uncovered it, dreading that it would be the boy. But it was a woman, Mo's mother, sadly also dead.

The soldier rewarded the dog again and after a few minutes urged her to another 'find'. As they dug deeper into the ruins it became obvious that there would be few, if any, survivors.

A short time later, the dog indicated that she had found someone else.

As the rescuers moved the debris, the dog handler could see they had uncovered a child's hand.

As they moved more debris, they found a young girl. But it was obvious that the child had suffered severe head injuries.

However, when the Sergeant checked her vital signs, to the delight of the rescuers, he confirmed that she was still alive. He quickly called in an army medic, who had arrived in the convoy with him, to render first aid.

The dog handler rewarded the dog again and then urged her on to find Mohammed.

But by now, working in the unrelenting 50-degree heat the rescuers were exhausted. The soldier had to keep sprinkling water on Jersey to try to cool the panting dog down

So when the dog indicated another 'find', it took the soldier sometime to motivate the helpers, so much so, that he started frantically moving the debris himself.

The demoralised villagers were not optimistic of finding anyone alive, but Jersey's sensitive nose had locked on to this latest scent. She was getting more and more excited as the masonry was moved out of the way.

'Mo can't be alive under all this, the dog handler thought. 'Let's just hope that he's lying in a void.'

And then amidst the rubble the soldier saw a small hand with a friendship bracelet on the wrist.

He knew then, that it was Mo. He recognised the colours of the plaiting from when the boy had made the bracelet at one of the Sergeant's scout meetings.

Mohammed was one of the group of young Afghans to whom the soldier had been teaching Scouting skills; part of a 'hearts and minds' campaign, aimed at breaking down the suspicions of the locals about the army's intentions.

The sergeant shouted at the others. 'Hurry, here look, he said, kneeling by the hand.'

Shortly after moving two large blocks of concrete, they uncovered the boy completely.

The dog handler's heart skipped a beat as he confirmed that the dust covered face belonged to Mo. 'Oh damn, why him?' the man thought.

The boy was, mercifully, unconscious and hopefully had not experienced the claustrophobic effects of being entombed under the debris.

Laying across his chest was the boy's pet dog, Nipper, who the soldier could see immediately had been killed by the falling masonry.

As they moved the body of the dog off the boy's chest, the Sergeant's heart stopped. Underneath, Mo's chest was awash with blood.

With trembling hands, the soldier quickly checked the boys vital signs and, considering the amount of blood, was surprised to detect a strong pulse. Puzzled over this medical contradiction, he checked the boy for the extent of his injuries, then with great relief realised that it was the dog's blood, not Mo's.

The boy's dog had taken the brunt of the collapse and had clearly saved Mohammed's life.

The Sergeant felt sad at the dogs demise as Nipper and Jersey had been doggie friends, they loved chasing each other and enjoyed play fighting.

The dog handler had allowed the two dogs to play together, although it was against standard operating procedures, aimed at preventing search dogs getting fleas or rabies from the local canines.

Jersey nuzzled her playmate and pawed at its lifeless body to try and get it to move. But obviously to no avail. The dog looked at the soldier and whimpered as if to demand help for her friend.

'Sorry Jersey. Your friend is dead I'm afraid. You'll have to find a new playmate from now on,' the Sergeant said quietly, stroking her.

Slowly, Jersey moved to the battered figure of the boy and licked his ashen face.

The soldier spoke gently, 'No Jersey, Mo is very ill. He doesn't need your kind of attention.'

But the dog persisted and to everybody's joy, the boy stirred. Mo sneezed, and a small cloud of dust fell off his face.

Immediately, the soldier called in a helicopter to medivac them out of there.

'*Control from Sierra One; We have two red casualties for immediate evacuation,*' the sergeant said into his radio. '*Two children need to be flown to Bastion. Over*'

The military hospital there dealt with all major trauma, including, bizarrely, treating injured Taliban fighters.

'*Sierra One; Any other casualties? Over,*' the controller asked.

'*Sadly not. Over*' he said looking around at the forlorn rescuers at the other piles of debris. '*The rest of Mo's family didn't make it.*'

In the meantime, the soldiers conducted first aid treatment to the children, and stabilised their conditions.

Within 15 minutes the twin rotor evacuation Chinook was creating a dust storm as it landed nearby.

As the medical crew rushed out of the tailgate, Jeremy, the young Corporal had been waiting near the landing site and led the medics to the injured children. The medics quickly made an initial injury assessment and connected drips to them. The children were carefully put on stretchers and loaded into the waiting helicopter.

As a father himself, Tom was upset by seeing the awful injuries of the children, but, not wishing to show his emotions to the rescuers, he held it together, although his dust goggles hid the tears in his eyes as the helicopter lifted off.

'What an awful world we live in Jersey,' he said, addressing the dog.

The dog looked back at him as if giving an acknowledgement. 'What had they done to hurt anyone? Anyway, you did a good job again, girl. Here's a treat,' he said, taking a chicken snack out of his pocket and giving it to the dog. 'You're a very good girl,' he continued, rubbing the dog's chest. 'A very good girl.'

# Chapter Three

Over the next few weeks the soldier and Jersey visited the now orphaned children every day in the military hospital.

'How are they doing today, Nurse?' the dog handler asked, as he and Jersey arrived for their daily visit.

'I have some bad news I'm afraid. Unfortunately the boy's sister, Aryana, has just succumbed to her head injuries.'

'Oh...sod,' the Soldier said, holding his true feelings in check. 'What about the boy?'

'Oh Mohammed's doing as well as can be expected, considering the extent of his injuries. Although his breathing is a bit erratic as he inhaled a lot of dust, however we were worried most about his concussion and chest injuries.'

'Poor kid.'

'The X-ray of his badly broken arm shows that it is healing.'

'Well at least that's one positive thing going for him. Does he know about his sister?'

'Yes, and he was obviously very upset.'

'Poor kid. So now he's all alone in the world?' The soldier observed sympathetically, glancing at the sleeping child lying in the hospital bed.

'I'm afraid so,' the nurse confirmed.

'And obviously his family have all been buried now. So, he couldn't even attend their funerals,' the soldier revealed.

'He looks so pathetic, poor kid. I presume the injuries to his face are just superficial?'

'Yes, they should heal very quickly. But I'm not so sure about the psychological ones.'

'Thanks Nurse,' he said, walking to the boy's bedside and sitting down.

'Hello, Mo,' the Sergeant said, gently touching the boy's arm. 'How are you feeling today?'

Jersey immediately leapt on to the bed and lay on Mo's lap, much to the nurse's concern, but she held back from ordering the dog off, as she recognised the therapeutic effect the dog's presence had on the traumatised child.

The boy stirred from his nap. 'Oh, hello Jersey,' Mo said, enveloping the dog in a hug with his un-plastered arm and stroking his canine 'saviour'. 'Hello Sergeant Tom,' the boy croaked. 'I'm getting better, thank you.'

'Good news. I'm pleased to hear it,' the Sergeant smiled. 'I'm sorry to hear about your sister.'

'I shall miss her,' he said, a tear running down his battered face. They said she never regained consciousness,' Mo paused and then asked. 'Is my dog Ok? 'Who is looking after him?'

The soldier had been withholding the bad news from Mo but knew that one day he'd have to tell the boy.

'I...I'm sorry Mo. He didn't make it.'

'Do you mean that he's dead too?' Mo tried to be brave about this latest devastating news, but he could not control his tears which cascaded down his battered face.

'Yes, I'm afraid so. But you can be very proud of him though.'

'Why?' he sobbed.

'He saved your life.'

'How?' More tears streamed down onto the bedclothes.

'By protecting you from the falling debris,' the soldier explained.

Mo buried his face in Jersey's coat and hugged her even tighter.

The dog seemed to know what Mo needed and nuzzled into the boy's neck and lay still.

The Sergeant had to turn away, for he too was filling up. The gut-wrenching wailing of the boy cut through his tough soldier veneer and had got to him. 'Life can be so cruel,' the soldier cursed under his breath. 'The boy has lost everything.'


Over a period of several weeks as the boy recovered from his ordeal, the soldier brought him sweets and spent time talking to him about Scouting and football. The two exchanged some friendly banter about the performance of the boy's favourite team, Manchester United.

'What is going to happen to me when I leave hospital?' Mo asked fearfully.

'Do you have any relatives living nearby?'

'I have an uncle. But he is very strict. I don't like him very much,' the boy explained. 'He does not like me doing Scouts either.'

'I'm sure he will be kinder to you under the circumstances. Anyway, I want my star Scout back in the team, so hurry up and get better.'

'Can I stay with you instead?' the boy pleaded, looking at the soldier with doleful eyes.

'As much as I'd like to help you out, you know that I live on an army base. Civilians aren't allowed, unless they are doing a special job.'

'I could do a special job for you,' Mo said enthusiastically. 'I could look after Jersey...clean your boots and...'I could be your interpreter.'

'Sorry Mo, but as much as I'd like that, it can't happen.'

'Perhaps you could adopt me?' the boy suggested desperately.

'Sadly, I will be coming to the end of my tour shortly and going home,' the Sergeant announced, his voice tight with emotion. '

'Oh!' The boy said quietly, crestfallen. 'Tell me what it is like, your home. Are there bad people there too? Is there any bombing?'

'There are bad people all over the world Mo. But we must make sure they do not stop us living as we want to live, in freedom,' the dog handler replied. 'But no, there is no war where I live.

Here, I have a photograph of my family,' Tom said, pulling a picture out of his wallet.

'Is this your house?' the boy said, gazing at the family gathered in front of the four-bedroom red brick house.

'Yes.'

'And you have two children and there is another dog.' Mo said, pointing at the group in front of the building.

'Yes, the dog's name is Shadow. He used to be like Jersey, but after working with me for nine years, he is retired now, and so he lives with my family.'

'How old are your children?'

'My daughter is now thirteen and my son is ten.'

'I think I am thirteen,' the boy volunteered. 'Could you take a photograph of us, here, now?'

'Yes, I think that's a good idea,' the man said, pulling out his mobile phone. 'Let's do a selfie. Ready? Smile.' Mo lifted Jersey up, so she could be in the photo too. The pair smiled at the phone.

'Is that it?'

'Yes.'

'Let me see, let me see,' the boy demanded excitedly, reaching for the phone.

The soldier quickly moved to the photograph section on his phone and showed the boy.

'Ha, that's brilliant. Look at Jersey, it looks like she is smiling too.'

# Chapter Four

The two soldiers were off duty, and sitting in the relative cool of the Sergeant's tent, in the centre of the fortified camp.

'I hate to say it, but today's been very qu....' Jeremy started to say.

'Don't say the 'Q' word, or all hell will break loose,' Tom interrupted.

'Yes, strange how that seems to jinx things. Anyway Lottie, I don't think much of your hospitality,' Jeremy said, smacking his lips. 'It's a bit dry round here isn't it?'

Tom's nickname had been given him, through some strange army tradition that distorted his name, from Tom Bow, to Tombola, then to Lotto, and finally to the endearment of Lottie.

The Sergeant was tall and wiry, with blue green eyes. His short haircut helped with the extremes of temperatures, exacerbated by having to wear heavy body armour. He was known for his even temperament, cool head and friendly nature.

'Sorry, Jezza, have a tinny,' the Sergeant said, digging in to a small fridge behind him and retrieving a couple of cans of beer.

'Talking about tinnies, I'm thinking of going to New Zealand to live when I've finished in the army,' Jeremy divulged.

'New Zealand! Why New Zealand? That's the other side of the world.'

'Yeah. But it's a beautiful country. The pace of life is slow, probably several decades behind England.'

'What will you do? Join their army?'

'No. I was thinking of joining the Police Force. They use helicopters to drop in on drug farms apparently, I'd say doing this job makes me a prime candidate, don't you?'

'Yes, sure does.'

'So, will you be going home soon yourself?' the army air corps gunner queried.

'Yes. And I won't be sorry to see the back of this hellhole.' Tom confirmed.

'How's that kid that you and Jersey rescued? What was his name?'

'Mohammed. Yeah, he's OK. He should be coming out of hospital soon. Poor little sod. He's only got an Uncle left now...unfortunately there appears to be no love lost between the two of them. I wish I could adopt the kid and take him away from all this crap.'

'Yeah, I know how you feel, but if we went around adopting every little kid who has been orphaned here, we'd be overwhelmed by the sheer numbers.'

'It's tough, and if losing the family wasn't bad enough, when I told him his dog had died too, the kid broke his heart. God that was awful.'

'I know it's hard. But, there's no room for sentiments here. You don't need me to tell you that we are soldiers first and foremost not welfare workers. No offence to your Scouting activities.'

'None taken.'

'You know the golden rule – leave your family emotions at home.'

'It's difficult though isn't it? When you have a family yourself, your perception changes. You have a different perspective on kid's lives. They have a certain 'energy' and enthusiasm about them. That's probably why I like being a Scout Leader, too.'

'Over the years, I've become a bit of a Jekyll and Hyde character by developing two personalities. Tough Army, soft family,' the young gunner explained.

'Easier said than done though, mate. I think of what I would want someone to do with my kids if Helen and I died.'

'Come on chap. You've done enough tours now to know how it goes,' Jeremy counselled.

'You're right of course. But it's going to be hard to leave him here with no family. He's a great Patrol Leader and most of all, he's a cheeky chappie and I can't help but like him… like a son,' Tom explained.

'He'll be alright. But I'm not sure that I know him.'

'Mo is short for his age, brown eyes, black hair and is sporting a fine moustache on his top lip. Got an infectious smile.

'Yes, now I think of it, I do know him.

'Yes once seen, never forgotten, is Mo,' the Sergeant reflected.

'If his uncle doesn't look after him, the Red Crescent will. If all else fails, they are the best option for him for his future.'

'I know. But it doesn't make it any easier.'

'Anyway, he'd probably have difficulty fitting in to our western culture.'

'No, I don't think so. He's a pretty savvy kid, very astute and speaks English really well too.'

'How come?'

'Don't know. I assume he's been taught it at school and picked up a lot from all the soldiers that have been posted here. You got to remember, that us Brits and Yanks have been over here for some time now. Kids are like sponges; they pick things up pretty quickly.'

'Yeah, I suppose you're right.'

'I've even used him to help me translate with some of the villagers. Nothing that would get him in trouble with the Taliban mind.'

'Anyway the country needs youngsters like him to rebuild itself.'

'You're probably right,' the Sergeant agreed, lost in thought. 'You're probably right. Another beer?'

'I thought you'd never ask.'

# Chapter Five

It had taken some time for the Sergeant to persuade his army 'boss' to allow him to work with the local Afghan youngsters and possibly create a Scout Troop.

Like many others, Tom Bow was convinced that 'bomb and bullet' wasn't going to achieve anything other than continuing the conflict. Whereas working within the community, would help to plant a few seeds of hope, that would possibly, germinate to make a brighter and more stable future.

Some of his colleagues were sceptical about his 'hearts and minds' philosophy, but by working with the children, he hoped that he had made at least a slight improvement to their lives.

He recognised that the youngsters that he saw on the streets of Afghanistan were no different to the ones back at home, except that they lived in a war zone. The psychological effects of being confronted daily with the horrors and trauma of the conflicts, inevitably had a detrimental effect on them.

So, it seemed quite natural for him, while he was serving there, to continue his Scouting and to develop a bond with the local youth.

One basic humanitarian guideline that Tom particularly favoured was about international friendship:- *A scout is a friend to all and a brother to every other scout, no matter where the other comes from'*. Which has been modernised to:- '*A Scout belongs to the worldwide family of Scouts.*

He knew from his own experiences and feedback from former Scouts that belonging to the Scouting movement was indeed a currency for friendship that was accepted worldwide.

So, he'd successfully engaged with the Afghan youngsters, who were always hanging around the soldiers anyway, looking for handouts of sweets and pencils.

Although football wasn't his first love, he knew that he could attract youngsters to random knockabouts and hopefully gain their trust and break down barriers of suspicion.

So he 'obtained' some footballs from army stores and brought them to the usual street corner gatherings.

At first the games consisted of a random group of youngsters having a knockabout on a street corner with a ball. But eventually it evolved into proper' games of competitive football. He organised a mini league table and started recording scores and created a lot of interest.

After the matches, while they cooled down, the Sergeant decided to show them how to do some craft work, hoping to maintain their interest.

He took along some paracord and showed them how to plait the cord into friendship bracelets. That was when Mo really came to his attention, for while the other youngsters were only mildly interested. Mo was very keen to learn.

'Can I do that?' he'd asked.

'Yes of course you can. I'll show you how.' The soldier showed Mo the technique.

And Mo was very quick at catching on to the method and produced several multicoloured versions which he proudly displayed on his wrist.

'Now you've mastered that, would you like me to show you how to make a Turks Head woggle?' the Sergeant asked, and was faced with a lot of hysterical youngsters, laughing at the strange name.

'What's a Turkeys head wobble?' Mo asked, trying to contain himself.

'It's not a Turkeys head wobble,' the soldier laughed. 'It's a Turks head woggle and it is used for keeping neckerchiefs around your necks.

'Ha, ha,' Mo giggled even more. 'What is a knicker-chief? Is it made from somebody's pants?'

'No nothing as daft as that. Ok, let me explain,' the soldier smiled. 'I am a Scout Leader and in my Scout Troop we have a neckerchief, which we wear around our necks. It is black and yellow, and it's how people know that we are Scouts and what troop we belong to. It is unique to us.'

'Oh, that sounds good. Can we have one?' Mo asked. 'And then we can put our turkeys head wobble on it .' he said, dissolving into another fit of giggles.

'Right, watch me carefully,' the soldier said, cutting a length of single core electrical cable about three feet long.

Slowly he wove the cable around his fingers and showed the boys the technique of creating a plaited woggle.

Holding the completed woggle on his thumb,' that's where you put your neckerchief to hold it together,' he informed them.

'Can I have a go,' Mo said enthusiastically.

'Yes, here you are, here's a length of cable for you. Don't worry if you go wrong,' the soldier told him.' I will help.'

But Mo didn't need any help. He completed it successfully by himself.

'Look, I've done it,' he said, proudly holding it up.

'Well done,' the soldier said, impressed with his abilities.

'And I can make my woggle wobble,' Mo said attracting laughter from his friends as he wobbled it on his hand. 'Can we have a neckerchief of our own?' Mo went on eagerly.

'Yes, I see no reason why not,' the soldier agreed. I have some special material back at base that we can use. I can guarantee it will be unique,' he informed them.


The following day, the dog handler arrived with ten large triangular pieces of camouflage material. 'This will be our special neckerchief,' he told them and then demonstrated how to roll it

'This is one way of making your neckerchief look smart. You grab the two ends and flick it round and round until it's like a tube. You need to leave a peak on the back of about 10 centimetres, or you can just put it on a surface and roll it in a long sausage shape, ' he explained.

After Mo had produced his camouflaged sausage neckerchief, he put it around his neck.

Excitedly he slid his Turks head woggle up the neckerchief, but as soon as he took his hands away, it immediately slid off.

'Oh, it doesn't work,' he said picking the woggle up.

'It's OK. It's just that the hole in the woggle is too big,' the sergeant advised. 'You can either make a smaller one or redo that one. Up to you.'

'Please may I make another one.'

'Yes of course. Do you remember how to do it?'

'I think so.'

And within ten minutes Mo had made a perfect woggle which was tight enough to stay on his neckerchief.

Confident in his abilities Mo consequently helped the others to make theirs.

The Sergeant was satisfied that the early signs of a blossoming Scout troop was starting to materialise, as one by one the boys all put on their neckerchiefs and secured them with their homemade woggles.

Like a lot of the youngsters at his meetings there, Mo led a life where violence, war and destruction were his norm. The conflicts had been going on for all his thirteen years. He knew nothing different.

Despite living in a war zone, his father scraped a subsistence living from a small holding. It was hard work. The parched soil gave very little goodness into the vegetables that he grew and sold.

Mo's sister, Aryana, was two years younger than himself and, like siblings the world over, they squabbled but were extremely loyal and protective of each other.

Until now, the family had been fortunate not to have been involved in any collateral damage of the conflicts and had gone about their daily life unhindered.

The various armies, who had been brought in to tackle the terrorist situation, held a fascination for the children.

The soldiers from the different nationalities had commodities that the children had never seen before and tempted them like 'bees around a honey pot'. Even simple things like sweets, pencils and small note books attracted large groups of youngsters in the hope of receiving a hand out.

Always in demand, of course, were the different types of sweets that the children had never seen or tasted before.

The Americans always had the biggest varieties of gifts, but the British were friendlier and spent time talking to the children. And so it was, that Mo became friendly with Sergeant Tom Bow and his dog Jersey.

# Chapter Six

The sergeant's life, before he joined the services, had always been centred on his love for Scouting.

Becoming a soldier was just an extension of his passion for everything outdoors and adventurous.

His enthusiasm for doing enterprising activities like kayaking, caving, climbing, long distance hikes and wild camping all over the British Isles was infectious. Many of the young people in his care, continued doing the activities into their adult life.

As a Scout leader, his regular weekly meetings of ten and half to fourteen and half year olds had given him a privileged insight into the minds and expectations of young people.

He loved planning expeditions for them and gained a great deal of satisfaction from seeing the youngsters develop their self-confidence and self-belief.

When he left school he was, as most young people are, unsure of what to do, so he took, what he thought at the time, was an easy option and decided to join the army.

After his basic training, he joined an infantry regiment for a couple of years and was posted to Iraq and Afghanistan. Here he experienced the traumatic effects of armed conflict on his fellow human beings.

It was while he was there that he saw Military Working Dogs in action. Their ability for sniffing out

Improvised Explosive Devices (IEDs), arms caches, tracking down bombers, finding trapped people and even identifying drug dealers, was highly prized. The canine sniffer was literally a life saver.

So, irrespective of the increased dangers, it quite appealed to Tom to be at the forefront in this type of activity, as a dog handler.

Hence, he reviewed his credentials for a possible change of service career and felt confident that he had enough background canine experience.

As a child, he grew up with dogs. There was always a very much loved, and often spoilt, dog in the house.

He remembered fondly that during his early childhood, the family pet was a three-legged black and tan terrier called Judy.

The dog had sustained it's injuries when she dashed out into the road and decided to, unsuccessfully, 'take on' a car.

When the young Tom took the dog out walking, it's strange three-legged gait always attracted comments from people like...'what's the matter with your dog? Has she hurt herself? You should take her to the vet!'

Tom's well-rehearsed answer was; 'No, she had an accident and she's not in any pain. She can run faster on three legs than she could on four.'

Judy was twelve when she eventually died of 'old age'. He'd buried her in the vegetable plot in the back-garden. He'd said a 'home-made' prayer over her grave.

Consequently, he decided that, yes, he was sufficiently qualified to at least apply for the Military Working Dog regiment to do a dog handling course.

Fortunately, the army also considered that he was suitable, and he was 'over the moon' when he was invited to undertake the selection process.

During the assessment at the Defence Animal Centre in Melton Mowbray, he was observed interacting with several dogs, to ensure that he had the presence and command to work them. He successfully passed this strict scrutiny.

Shortly after, he was introduced to his first Military Working Dog called Shadow. Shadow was an adorable black Labrador who proved to be a good 'sniffer'.

They bonded straight away and had worked together for the full nine years considered to be the working life of a military working dog.

Shadow was trained as an Arms and Explosives search dog and had a high detection rate. Through the dog's abilities, countless lives had been saved.

When Shadow was considered too old to carry on his duties, and after living day and night with his trusty companion, Tom was understandably reluctant to say goodbye to his work mate, so he adopted the dog as a family pet and was given a new working dog called Jersey as a replacement.

# Chapter Seven

Jersey was a chocolate brown working cocker spaniel with trusting brown eyes and a sturdy white chest. Her long floppy ears were covered in masses of unruly brown fur, like 'puffed out' sideburns.

The Sergeant immediately fell in love with his new work companion when they were introduced to each other at the Defence Animal Centre, in Melton Mowbray; the home of the Royal Army Veterinary Corps.

However, before the pair could enter any conflict arena, they had to be evaluated together to prove that they could operate effectively as a team.

For, in operational circumstances, if the animal failed to detect an explosive device, it could lead to potentially deadly consequences.

So, together, they spent many hours undergoing the comprehensive and structured training regime.

This training method, of hiding her favourite toy with some PE4 explosive, was just another game to the dog.

The association of the smell and instant reward when she was sitting down, indicating the find, worked well. But Jersey added her own 'find' indication as well, by joyfully barking about her success.

Training also included exposing Jersey to the sounds of battle such as  explosions, gun fire, mortars and the noise of jets and helicopters.

To ensure she was not frightened and could stay focussed, she was tested in all forms of transport that they could use, including tree skimming helicopters, armoured vehicles, lorries and landrovers.

She was adjudged to be suitable and passed with flying colours, becoming another 'wagtail' in the large community of Military Working Dogs (MWD).

Jersey was trained primarily as an Arms and Explosives Search (AES) dog, like Shadow before her, but so successful was she, that she was also upgraded and trained for searching bodies, both alive and dead.

Just like her master, who had to wear protective gear, Jersey had to get used to wearing a harness and small leather 'booties' to protect her paws when searching over rubble strewn areas.

She was also equipped with special goggles, amusingly called 'doggles', in case of operating during dust storms; and ear defenders, if operating in a constantly noisy environment.

Jersey soon learnt that the moment her collar came off and the harness went on, that was the signal that she was going to work.

The Sergeant also found that she was controllable, at distance, with a silent dog whistle.

However, when Jersey was off-duty, she occasionally disgraced herself by demonstrating her kleptomaniac tendencies, for any food left unattended was fair game for the scavenging dog.

Jersey was a good natured, friendly dog and proved to be good for morale with the soldiers on base.

Despite the heat, she would often be seen engaging someone to endlessly throw a ball for her to chase and retrieve in the dusty fortress.

Mohammed's dog, Nipper, was usually not far away from Mo's side, so that when the Sergeant was having a training session with his Scouts, Jersey was sometimes allowed to accompany him, rather than staying in kennels.

Consequently, the two dogs played chase and play fighting together. Each in turn rolling over on their back to play the underdog and then seeking shade as they panted to cool themselves down.

The Sergeant wasn't so 'uptight' as some of his American dog handling colleagues, who prevented the locals touching their dogs and definitely preventing any mixing with the Afghan dogs. Fear of catching rabies and fleas was their apparent reasons.

Jersey attracted constant fuss from the Scouts and fascinated her audience when she joined in a game of football, using her snout to dribble the ball.

But the most important aspect of Jersey's relationship with Mo was that when the rescuers were about to give up, she had persisted and effectively saved the boy's life.

# Chapter Eight

Finally, the boy was discharged from hospital and, reluctantly, went to stay with his uncle.

Within weeks the Sergeant's posting came to an end and his, seemingly endless, third tour of duty in Afghanistan was over at last.

The soldier went to Mo's Uncle's house but was immediately sent away by the old man when he saw the uniform.

'No soldiers here. Go away,' he shouted, waving a long-handled spade at Tom.

Hearing the shouting, Mo came out of the building. 'It's OK Uncle, he is the one who has been visiting me in hospital,' Mo explained.

'Go away,' the old man continued. 'No soldiers. No soldiers.'

Mo grabbed the soldier's arm and led him away.

'You see. He is not a nice man,' the boy reiterated.

'It's alright Mo. I understand. He is probably frightened that he will be seen by the Taliban talking to me.'

When they were clear of all the buildings, the soldier explained his reason for being there.

'Mo, I have come to the end of my posting here. I am flying home tomorrow. I want you to carry on doing your Scouting with your friends. OK?'

'Do you mean that I will never see you again?' Mo asked fearfully.

'I don't know if, or when, I'm likely to be posted back here,' the Sergeant admitted.

'But who will keep an eye out for me? Like you used to do?'

'Your Uncle?'

'He doesn't like me,' the boy said miserably.

'You have lots of friends and what about your Scout patrol?' the soldier suggested, wanting to leave Mo with a positive way forward.

'In hospital, you said that you would adopt me if you could.'

'Yes, well... I didn't actually mean...anyway, Afghan laws are different to UK laws,' the Sergeant stuttered, wrong footed by the boys reminder.

'So if I came to England...could you adopt me there?' the boy probed.

'I don't know...probably yes. But you can't leave here,' he directed. 'You must look after your uncle and help to rebuild your country.'

'What if I could get to England?' the boy persisted.

'No, forget it Mo. Don't torture yourself with that idea. It's not going to happen,' the soldier said firmly. 'Now I need to go.'

The soldier stood, and as if coming to attention, offered Mo his left hand. 'Always remember our special Scout handshake,' he reminded the boy. 'It will help you all your life.'

Mo shook his left hand, then leapt into the others arms and hugged him tightly, sobbing.

'Please, please take me with you Sergeant Tom. I will work for you and do jobs,' Mo pleaded.

'I'm sorry Mo, but as much as I'd like to, I can't. Besides your skills would be better used here as an interpreter.

You must stay here and help your country recover from this terrible time. You have an important future ahead of you, I can tell.'

The soldier hugged the boy, then, with a lump in his throat, released him and turned away. Suddenly he stopped and went back to the distraught boy.

'Oh, Mo. I meant to give you this,' he said, taking a small parcel out of his pocket.

'What is it?' the boy asked, wiping his tears with the back of his hand. And staring at the neatly wrapped parcel.

'It's a small birthday present. You can open it when it's your birthday. OK?'

'I don't know when my birthday is. But I've never had a present before. Thank you.' Mo beamed and gave Sergeant Tom another hug.

'I hope you like it,' the soldier said, and quickly turned away so that the boy wouldn't see his tears. 'Be safe. Mo. Be safe,' he whispered under his breath, as he returned to his Foxhound armoured vehicle.

Mo couldn't wait to open the parcel. As his mentor was getting into his transport, his eager hands ripped open the brown paper from the small box. With great excitement he reached inside and found a long black plastic tube.

Immediately he recognised it as a flint, used for lighting fires, that he had seen the Sergeant using. Also in the parcel was a small red handled multi-bladed penknife; both practical items that he could use.

Finally in the bottom of the box he was overjoyed to see a photograph. It was the one that they had posed for while he was still in hospital, of Jersey, Sergeant Tom and himself. He gazed lovingly at it, a small tear trickled down his cheek.

These were the first real possessions that he'd ever owned, and he knew that he had to keep them hidden or they would 'go missing'.

'Hopefully these will be the start of many other things I will own,' he thought.

He had been so preoccupied with his present that he hadn't noticed the soldier's vehicle leaving or his tearful farewell wave.

'Goodbye Sergeant Tom,' he said at the departing dust cloud.


The following day Mo heard a plane take off from the military airport and assumed that the Sergeant was on board.

Mo watched as the huge twin engine Airbus 320 Voyager lifted off from the Afghan runway, its steep ascent, designed to quickly distance itself out of the range of any shoulder launched missiles.

'Someday soon, I will see you again Sergeant Tom and repay your kindness,' he whispered to himself, his eyes misting over as the plane disappeared behind the clouds.

# Chapter Nine

On board the plane, the soldier looked down at the parched land below him and wondered how Mohammed would cope living with his 'grumpy' uncle.

'Oh well, there's nothing I can do to change things,' he thought.

He picked up his book and tried unsuccessfully to read it. And as much as he tried to push the thought of the boy to the back of his mind, he was still thinking about him as the plane touched down for their brief stop in Cyprus.

Quickly, he retrieved Jersey from the hold, made a fuss of her and took her for a walk around the airfield.

'Come on Jersey, I think we could both do with stretching our legs, couldn't we?' he said, putting the dog's lead on.

As they walked around the perimeter fence, Jersey kept looking behind them as if waiting for someone to join them.

'No, Mo and Nipper aren't going to join us, this time.... and never again either mate,' the soldier said, sadly.

Eventually, they re-boarded the plane for the final hop to the Oxfordshire military airport at Brize Norton.

After touchdown, Tom said a temporary goodbye to Jersey as she was taken away for a short period of quarantine back at the regiment's headquarters.

Duty done; he joined the line of soldiers making their way from the plane to the runway apron.

Tom could see his wife, children and his former search dog Shadow waiting in front of the crowd at the edge of the tarmac.

As they spotted him, they waved frantically, the children jumping up and down and the dog joining in barking his welcome.

The soldier rushed over to them and enveloped them all in a group hug with his powerful sun-tanned arms.

'Hello family. It's nice to be home. Let me look at you two,' he said, looking at his eleven year old son Paul and thirteen-year-old daughter Angelina. 'My, how you've both grown. You're now quite a young lady,' he said looking at her.

Angelina blushed at her father's compliment.

Shadow, not to miss out on the show of affection from his master, leapt up excitedly and barked his welcome too. The soldier bent down and lifted the dog up into his arms.

'Oh, you want some fuss too, do you?' he said, smothering the dog with love. In return the dog licked his face, it's stubby tail telegraphing its pleasure at seeing his master again.

With the emotional greeting over, they walked toward the terminal building, the children carrying their father's hand baggage, hoping that he had brought them a present from his latest trip.

Tom slipped his arm round his wife's slim waist and pulled her to him.

'Steady Tiger. You'll have to wait a bit longer or you'll have us arrested for a public decency offence,' she said, gently pushing him away. 'I'm so glad you're home safely. How was it this time?'

'Six months of the 'same old, same old'. Nutters blowing themselves up and trying to take as many others with them as possible.

We had a particular nasty one. Took out a whole block of houses, lots of casualties including the whole family of one of my youngsters, Mohammed, who was in my Scout troop.'

'What happened?'

'The suicide bomber in his pickup truck, was shot on his way to blow up a compound and unfortunately it resulted in the explosives detonating early.

It blew up Mo's house. There was nothing left but a pile of rubble. But good old Jersey found him under the debris, just as they'd given up hope of bringing anyone out alive.'

'Poor kid.'

'Unfortunately, his parents, little sister and dog weren't as lucky as him. So, he's all alone in the world. Makes me realise how lucky we are living here, without the constant fear that the boy experiences daily,' the sergeant reflected.

'War is awful isn't it?' Helen said, tightening her grip on the soldiers hand.

'Tell me about it. There are no winners, that's for sure,' he confirmed.

'What will happen to him now?'

'Well, he's got an uncle. But Mo thinks he's a bit of a tyrant. Although I met him once, and he appeared to be OK to me …just a frightened old man.

The boy pleaded to come back with me, so I had to check my kit to make sure he hadn't smuggled himself into it,' the Sergeant joked, trying to make light of the situation.

'I must confess, that I had a lump in my throat when I said goodbye to him though.'

'You big softy,' she said, standing on tip toes and giving him a kiss on the cheek. 'I'll see if I can't take your mind of things later.'

# Chapter Ten

Several days after Sergeant Bow's departure, Mo rounded up his Scout patrol.

'Right guys, I'm sorry to have to tell you, but Sergeant Tom has gone home, so we won't be seeing him or Jersey anymore.'

The five other members of the patrol groaned their joint disappointment.

'But I'm going to keep us Scouting together, as Sergeant Tom would want us to do.' Mo continued.

The patrol welcomed Mo's intentions.

'Yeah but doing what?' one of the patrol asked, sceptically.

'I went to the army base this morning,' he continued, 'and asked if they could find us a new Leader,' Mo explained. 'But they told me it was unlikely. So, we are going to have do it ourselves,' he enthused.

'Well, it isn't going to happen then,' the sceptical one said, pessimistically.

'There is a Scout group at my orphanage,' Abdul added. 'Perhaps we could join them?'

'Let's see how we get on running our own group first,' Mo suggested.

'It won't happen,' the pessimist warned.

'Ok,' the others agreed, overruling the gloomy prediction.

'I have a list of things that we used to do with Sergeant Tom, ' Mo told them. So, we won't be short of ideas for the programme.'

'But who will be the Leader?' Abdul queried. 'We need someone in charge.'

'Me.' Mo announced firmly. 'I will carry on as Patrol Leader (PL) and you, Abdul, will be my Assistant Patrol Leader (APL),' he added. 'We will continue to wear our special neckerchiefs as before. So nothing really changes.'

'Except, the Sergeant isn't here anymore,' Abdul pointed out.

'Yes of course,' Mo said quietly.

After a short game of football, they broke up and went home.


When Mo got home, he was met by his Uncle who was furious.

'Well. How much money did you earn today?' Mo's uncle demanded.

'Sorry Uncle, I have not been working.'

'Why?'

'I have been organising my Scouts.'

'You come here begging to live with me. You eat my food and you don't work,' his Uncle exploded.

'Sorry Uncle, but my arm is still very weak from the...from the bomb.

'Nonsense. You have enough strength to do this... this Scouts.'

'Sorry. But...'

'You bring danger to my house by going to the army too. The Taliban will think we are giving them information. They will think we are spies. Do you know what happens to spies?'

Mo shook his head.

The old man slid his hand across his neck in a cut-throat gesture.

'I am truly sorry uncle,' the boy, replied nervously. 'I was asking about getting a new Leader for our Scouts, that was all.'

'You should be out on the streets selling or cleaning shoes. Bringing money to pay for your keep. Not playing around.'

'We aren't playing. We are Scouts.'

'Scouts! More like Police spies.'

'No.'

'Don't backchat me boy. I was there when your Scouts became Policemen and Border guards during the Russian invasion.'

'We aren't...we're not the same.'

'That's another thing. You are upsetting the neighbours with your uniforms. Those things on your necks. Are you forming another army?'

'No Uncle. They are part of the uniform that Scouts all over the world wear. It is a sign of brotherhood.'

'I owed it to my brother, your father, to give you a home after his death. But you are creating problems for me. I have had enough. You must leave my house,' the old man demanded angrily.

'Leave! But where shall I go?" Mo said, shocked at the sudden turn of events.

'The Red Crescent have an orphanage. I will hear no more from you now. You have caused me great problems in my community. Now, get your things and go.'

The boy looked at the old man who was trembling with rage and decided that further pleas would fall on deaf ears.

'I am sorry for displeasing you Uncle. I will go now.'

The boy picked up his few belongings and retrieved the presents that the soldier had given him from their hiding place.

'Thank you Uncle, for giving me shelter. I am sorry that I have disappointed you and brought sadness to your house.'

The old man said nothing.

Distraught, Mo left his uncle's house.

The Afghan Red Crescent Society (ARCS) runs a large orphanage, sometimes known as an Marastoon or Social Welfare Centre; it has been operating since 1930 in different towns across Afghanistan and were designed to serve as public institutions serving those in need.

In 1965 they were handed over to the Afghan Red Crescent and to this day they continue to provide temporary shelter for vulnerable individuals, particularly orphaned children, the poor, the disabled and the elderly.

The need for such a facility now, more than ever, is a sad reflection on the death toll during the unrest and the seemingly never-ending conflicts.

Mo knew about the orphanage from his APL Abdul, who had been living there since his parents had also died in a suicide bombing.

Abdul had told Mo about his daily routine.

'My day begins early,' he told him. 'I wake up, pray, and repeat my lessons until breakfast time. After breakfast, I go to a normal school outside the Marastoon and after lunch, I return to attend a tailoring workshop.'

'But what if I don't' fit in,' Mo had asked.

'You will. Initially I found it difficult to come to terms with the loss of my parents but as the months passed, I began to adapt to life at the Marastoon and was able to focus on my studies and make new friends,' Abdul had reassured him.

Mo walked through the hot dusty streets, with his few possessions, to the orphanage.

He looked at the Red Crescent emblem, a red moon set on a white background, and stopped outside the large austere building, frozen by his anxiety of what was to come. What if they sent him away? Where would he go? What would he do?

'What would Sergeant Tom say,' he wondered. 'He would probably remind me of the Scout Law. '*A scout has courage in all difficulties*'.

'Yes, that's all I need to do it, courage,' he convinced himself. 'Just go in and ask.'

So, with great trepidation, he summoned up his nerve and entered the building.

He walked down a long corridor and approached an elderly grey bearded man sitting behind a desk.

'Excuse me Sir. My name is Mohammed. I am am… an orphan.' The words caught in his throat. 'My… my family have all been killed. Can you take me in, Sir?'

The man greeted Mo with kindly eyes. 'Of course my son. The door is always open to such as yourself.'

Mo relaxed. It was going to be alright after all.

The man looked through a large notebook on his desk. He ran his finger down the entries and got to the bottom of the page before he looked up again.

'You are lucky Mohammed. There is a place available for you now, as one of the older children has left,' the administrator informed him. 'I will just take some details and then I will take you to the dormitory. You will also be registered for schooling here as well.'

'Thank you. I am truly grateful.' Mo replied quietly, a tear of relief blossoming from his eyes.

Mo's emotions were all over the place. The homeless orphan was unsettled by the new 'topsy – turvey' world he had been forced to enter.

# Chapter Eleven

Mo had been in the orphanage for three months and had acclimatised to his new life, thanks to help from his friend Abdul.

The Scout Patrol meetings were going well with Mo running the programme of activities.

Tonight they had been doing fire lighting using Mo's flint, which the Sergeant had given him.

But now the meeting had finished, and all the others had dispersed for the evening. But Mo and Abdul were still wide awake and not ready to go to bed. Instead, they were sitting around the dying embers of the fire, chatting and  bemoaning their life and prospects.

'The trouble is, nothing will ever change here,' Mo observed, pessimistically. 'There will always be war.'

'Yes, our Leaders are all corrupt.' Abdul added, looking around, ensuring no-one was listening.

'Nobody cares for anyone but themselves.'

'Except the orphanage, that is.'

'Yeah, but you cannot trust anyone.' Mo reminded him.

'I heard a teacher the other day say; 'The only way to teach a child is through a beating.' Abdul volunteered.

'Yes, I've had several beatings myself,' Mo confirmed. You know, there's no war or beatings in England,' Mo told Abdul for the twentieth time.

'I know, you keep telling me,' Abdul yawned, not interested.

Mo had never given up on his hopes of going to England to be reunited with the Sergeant and dreamt about it every night, consequently boring Abdul with his repeated stories.

'Well if you really want to go to England. You need to get some money,' Abdul informed him.

'Money? What for?'

'I've heard of a way to start a new life in Europe, away from all this fighting,' Abdul said, enthusiastically.

'How?' Mo demanded.

'People smugglers.'

'People Smugglers?'

'Yes. You pay them money and they smuggle you into Europe.'

'Is England in Europe?'

'Yes, I think so.'

'So if we go to Europe, I will be able to get to England? And find the Sergeant?'

'Yes. They have things called open borders; so, when you are there, you can travel to whatever country you want.'

'Wherever you want?' Mo repeated, dreamily.

'Yes. And they feed you and give you shelter, clothes and money to live on.'

Abdul had fired off Mo's vivid imagination.

"The smugglers told me: 'You will be able to drive taxis and make hundreds of dollars each month.'

'We could make a good living in a new place away from war,' Mo said excitedly. 'Why didn't you tell me about this before?

'Because I only spoke to the Smugglers today and they told me to keep it quiet otherwise the authorities might stop it.'

'Ok,' Mo said suspiciously, not convinced that the other was telling the truth. 'How much money does it cost for these people smugglers?'

'One thousand five hundred dollars.'

'One thousand five hundred dollars! Where will I get that sort of money from?'

'After school, I am working for the Americans. They pay good money and tips. I've got $500 so far,' Abdul volunteered.

'No you haven't,' Mo challenged.

'Yes I have.'

'Show me then.'

'I can't. It's hidden. And I don't want you to see where I've hidden it. OK?'

'Oh! You can trust me, Scouts honour,' Mo said, making the three-finger salute.

'No.'

'Oh,' Mo said, still unsure about the truth of Abdul's story... Do you think I could get a job there too?'

'Well I suppose so. I will pass your name on to them.'

'Ok thanks.'

Eventually they left the campfire and returned to the orphanage. When they went to bed that night, Mo smiled in his sleep as he dreamt of going to England and the euphoric meeting he would have with the Sergeant.

The dream was so vivid that he was able to remember it clearly when he awoke.

In the orphanage the children were encouraged to expand their skills, whereas Abdul enjoyed tailoring, Mo chose art.

Lack of art materials restricted what Mo could create, however, undaunted, he decided to use his artistic skills to paint his dream.

Mo worked diligently in reproducing the images that he saw in his dream and proudly showed Abdul the following day.

Abdul was surprised at the image, which consisted of the silhouette of a soldier and a small boy stood in front of him, on the side was a silhouette of a dog. He asked Mo what the painting meant.

To be honest, I'm not sure, but the Sergeant is the black shadow with his dog Jersey and I am the ghost, the white boy standing in front of him.

'Why are you a ghost?'

'I'm not sure, perhaps it was because I nearly died when our house was blown up.'

'Why the two stripes of red and green?'

'I think it must be something to do with our country's flag.'

'Then the soldier is the third colour of our flag. That's why he is black,' Abdul pointed out.

'Yes of course. Black, Red and Green,' Mo agreed, 'the colours of our national flag.'

'I understand that famous painters give their paintings a name,' Abdul observed, showing off his limited knowledge of the art world. What will you call yours?'

'I...don't know. What do you reckon?'

'Well, as much as I know you want to – I don't reckon you'll ever be going to England. It's an impossible dream Mo,' Abdul counselled.

'That's it then. The Impossible Dream it is,' Mo beamed. 'You're a genius Abdul. Thank you.'

# Chapter Twelve

Mo was woken from his wonderful dream by a disturbance. People were running around shouting in panic. An automatic gun was fired nearby. Someone screamed.

'Quick Mohammed. Wake up. It's the Taliban. We must hide,' Abdul shouted, shaking his sleepy friend.

But before they could do anything, several heavily armed men came into the dormitory and rounded all the boys up.

Roughly they were all shepherded outside and into the back of a large truck. When the truck was full, the fighters climbed into the back themselves and pulled the canvas doors shut.

The truck immediately raced off into the night.

Where are we going?' Mo whispered and was immediately hit on the head by the butt of an AK47.

'No talking,' the terrorist barked.

Mo was shocked by the sudden violence. He felt something warm and sticky trickling down his face. He put his hand to his head and realised it was blood.

Having heard Mo yelp as he was hit, nobody else spoke.

It was a hot and very uncomfortable ride. Despite a sandstorm raging outside, the driver was going at breakneck speed to escape any pursuers.

They seemed to be driving for many hours before suddenly it slowed.

The hostages could hear talking outside and it accelerated again briefly, before coming to a complete stop and the engine was switched off.

The tailgate of the lorry was yanked open, and the curtains thrown back.

It was still dark outside as the hostages were ushered out and forced to stand in a line against a wall.

A floodlight was switched on and shone at them. The hostages blinked at the sudden brightness, putting their hands up to shield their eyes and were immediately ordered to put them down or be shot.

A large bearded man strode forward. In his hand was an AK47 with spare magazines taped to it.

'You are sons of Afghanistan. You are now going to become soldiers of the Taliban,' he informed them. 'If you try to escape you will be punished before you are killed. Do you understand?'

The hostages gave a muted 'Yes.'

'You have been chosen to become Jihadists. This is a great honour for you to die for such a important cause. You will be trained and if you fail the training you will be shot. Do you understand?'

'Yes,' the hostages chorused.

In the meantime, as soon as the news of the kidnapping had got out, a rescue mission had been initiated.

Unfortunately, a sandstorm blew up suddenly and not only grounded the helicopters but also obliterated the kidnappers tracks. The hostages were on their own.

Jeremy, the Lynx air gunner, was initially part of the team who were going to track down the kidnappers but because of the adverse weather his flight was grounded.

Coincidentally, Corporal Hopson was just going out of the base when a distraught old man stopped him.

'The Scout man is he here?' the old man demanded.

'No, he's gone home.'

'It is Mohammed. He has been kidnapped, the old man said. I should have been looking after him.' 'He is my brother's son. I sent him away to the Marastoon and now I have lost him, I have lost him,' the old man repeated, smacking his forehead in anguish.' My brother will haunt me. You must find him, you must rescue him.'

'When the sandstorm has ceased, we will be out there don't worry,' the Corporal said, trying to reassure him.

'Please. I have broken my pledge with my brother. You must help.'

'Don't worry, we'll find him.'

But, unfortunately, subsequent search missions failed to find where the kidnapers had taken the boys.


Over the next two weeks the orphans were given endless lectures about the terrorist's ideology.

They were forced to do interminable physical exercises, undertake hand to hand fighting; stripping down and shooting an AK47 and taught how to fire a Rocket Propelled Grenade (RPG). Making IEDs was also on the curriculum.

Mo struggled with his arm, weakened by the injuries that he sustained in the bomb blast, but kept going, never complaining once.

Those who were deemed not to be trying were beaten and, if they continued to fail, were considered unsuitable...and they 'disappeared'.

With the lack of initial success in tracking the terrorists down, Jeremy eventually decided to ring the Sergeant to relay the information about Mo being kidnapped.

'Hi Lottie, it's Jez. How's the weather with you in England?'

'Hi Jezza, Oh it's cloudy and raining.'

'We could do with a bit of that over here to cool things down.'

'This is an unexpected pleasure. To what do I owe your call?'

'Not sure how to tell you Lottie, but that kid you were pining over has been kidnapped by the Taliban.'

'What?'

'Sorry to be the bearer of bad news, but your friend Mohammed was one of the kids kidnapped by the Taliban from the Red Crescent orphanage.'

'What? I thought he was living with his Uncle. Are you sure?'

'Yes. His Uncle came here, very upset and told me. And I saw his name on the list. Apparently, it didn't work out with the old man and the kid, so the old man sent him away. Now he feels guilty about it.'

'How long had he been there?'

'Soon after you left. Reckons he was in the orphanage for a few months apparently,' the air gunner explained.

'If his life wasn't already bad enough. Now he has to deal with this,' the dog handler said in exasperation.

'It's not fair is it?' Jeremy concurred.

'The kid must wonder what he's done wrong to deserve all this crap.'

'Yeah, poor little bugger.

'Perhaps I should have adopted him after all,' the Sergeant reflected. 'How long is it since he was taken?'

'About two weeks I reckon.'

'Not long enough for him to be turned then.'

'No, hopefully not.'

'Do you know what, if anything, is planned?'

'Confidentially, I would expect some active response before too long. If you know what I mean?' Jeremy suggested confidently.

'Let's hope it's not too long in coming then,' Tom added.

'And worse still that he doesn't end up as a casualty of any collateral damage if they do a rescue mission.'

'God no.'

'I'll keep you informed. Cheers Lottie.'

'Thanks for letting me know Jezza.'

Tom was devastated at the news and felt guilty about Mo's situation. He had left Afghanistan with a heavy heart anyway but hoped the kid would grow up and be safe from the conflicts.

But being kidnapped, with the possibly of being 'turned' into a terrorist he hadn't even considered.

# Chapter Thirteen

The fierce demands of their kidnappers during their training sessions in battle craft, escape and evasion techniques, climbing ropes, crawling under barbed wire and digging tunnels had taken its toll on the boys.

Unused to the noise and dangers of battle, the boys were terrified when told to run ahead of people firing live rounds over their heads and laying low when real grenades were exploded near them.

Mo and Abdul were just about coping with the physical aspects of the energy sucking exercises, but it had aggravated Mo's injured arm, so Abdul helped him, wherever he could, when the Taliban weren't looking.

Despite the nagging pain in his arm, Mo had fallen into a deep exhausted sleep, after relentless training all day in the gruelling 50-degree heat.

Mo was so fatigued that the first explosion failed to wake him.

The Reaper drone's first missile exploded but failed to destroy the targeted ammunition store.

However, the second missile hit its target and set off a white-hot sympathetic explosion that lit up the night sky.

The colossal detonation created a mini earthquake which woke Mo instantly, the ground shuddering from the force of the exploding rocket propelled grenades and high explosives housed in the store.

Seven thousand five hundred miles away in California, the drone pilot whooped her joy as her monitor screen picture overloaded from the brilliance of the explosion.

'That's what I'm talking about,' Captain Kim Seng beamed to her 'co-pilot,' sitting next to her.

In their comfy, air-conditioned office, divorced from the sounds and smell of the battlefield their explosive success was just so surreal, just like playing a computer game.

The pair 'high fived' their achievement.

'Mission accomplished,' she said, smiling. 'Now for the boys on the ground to sort the Taliban out. In the meantime we'll get our baby safely back home to Bastion,' she said taking control of the drone again.'

The Special forces 'intel' had been spot-on. From the moment the terrorists had kidnapped the orphans, despite the sandstorm, they had been finally tracked by painstaking analysis of satellite surveillance to their secret desert base.

Under the cover of darkness, the squad of eight soldiers had taken up positions around the camp and confirmed that the kidnapped orphans were indeed in the camp. Clandestinely they monitored the comings and goings of the terrorists and their prisoners to plan the best time for a rescue mission.

After a few days of surveillance, lying in shallow holes in the baking desert heat, the special forces had calculated a window of opportunity and called in the night-time drone strike.

For maximum impact, the team carefully 'painted' the ammunition store with lasers to guide the missiles accurately to their target, thus reducing the risk of collateral damage occurring to the hostages.

The sound of the major explosions stunned the frightened occupants of the hut.

'Was this another exercise?' they wondered.

Fearfully, they gathered in a frightened huddle wondering what to do, when shortly after, a local explosion blew down the locked door.

The room filled with smoke and several men entered the darkened hut. Like some dreamlike disco, torches and red laser beams were highlighted in the smoke,

'Special Forces.' Stand Up and put your hands on your heads.' A balaclava wearing soldier demanded.

Several others took up defensive positions near the doorway.

The group of hostages did as they were ordered, wondering if they were going to be killed.

The Taliban had told them that if they were captured, they would be tortured, before being killed.

'Move into the centre of the hut, in a line,' he shouted.

The group shuffled as a frightened pack into the centre of the room.

'Now put your hands together in front of you,' he commanded.

Immediately, another soldier went along the line of hostages and secured their hands with cable ties.

When they were all securely bound, the soldiers placed themselves amongst the line of youngsters and led them out of the hut.

'Follow us and keep your heads down,' the leader ordered.

In the ensuing panic of diversionary explosions, the hostages were led to safety by the Special Forces team.

Nevertheless, they had to dodge the incoming crossfire from the Afghan army, with tracer bullets flying over their heads from the insurgents.

The frightened crocodile of hostages shuffled out from the hut, through the ramshackle buildings, carefully stepping over the debris from the destroyed watch towers.

As they passed the blasted metal camp gates, which were hanging drunkenly on their remaining hinges, their apprehension eased. Perhaps they might be regaining their freedom after all.

Each hostage's identity was quickly checked before being hastily loaded on to lorries for fast evacuation.

While the Afghan army dealt with the insurgents, the lorry carrying Mo and Abdul escaped under the cover of darkness. Their vehicle, escorted by a Special Forces team, drove at breakneck speed for several hours to the fortified army base.

In the safety of the army base they were able to discard the rag tag 'uniforms' that they had been forced to wear and put on clothes from the army store.

All of the released hostages were interviewed by the military intelligence team to glean any information from them about their kidnappers.

As Mo and Abdul were interviewed, the administrator glanced at her paperwork and noticed a reference to indicate that Mo's Uncle had been in touch and wanted to hear any news about Mohammed.

'Could we go and see him?' Mo asked.

'I'm not sure,' the administrator said .'let me talk to the major first.'

At first the major was reluctant to let them leave, as they intended to repatriate all the children back to the orphanage from where they had been kidnapped.

But after further questioning and happy that they had not been 'turned', Mo and Abdul were allowed to go to Mo's uncles.

'On the understanding that you return to the Orphanage within a week,' the administrator emphasised.

'Yes we will. Thank you very much,' Mo said gratefully. 'If we leave now while it is still dark, we will be safe.' Mo suggested.

'But what if your uncle doesn't want you?' Abdul pointed out. 'After all he made you leave his house.'

'He must want me, if he's asking about me,' Mo said hopefully. 'And you must come too Abdul.'


At his home in Gloucestershire, Sergeant Tom was beside himself with worry.

For, as promised, Jeremy had advised him of the planned drone attack on the Taliban training camp.

'I'll let you know how it goes Lottie,' Jeremy had reassured him.

'Thanks Jezza.'

As he hung up Helen asked. 'Any news?'

'No nothing yet. I just hope he's alright,' the Sergeant said quietly.

To help take his mind of events, the Sergeant took Shadow, the family's dog, for a walk, all the while pondering the likely outcomes.

'Would Mo survive any collateral damage?' he wondered. 'Or worse still, had he been 'turned' whilst he was there and was he now fighting as a jihadist against the very troops that had been sent in to rescue him?'

The waiting was interminable. Finally, the call came through the following day from Jeremy.

'All the hostages have been safely rescued; Mo included. No injuries,' he was able to advise.

'Thank God for that,' Tom breathed a sigh of relief. 'Let's hope from now on that they give the orphanage some better protection. If you see Mo, give him my best wishes.'

'There's just a little snag to that,' Jeremy relayed. 'Mo and his mate, Abdul, left the army base and I can't find out where he is. I thought he was supposed to be going to the orphanage. But he's not there.'

'God, I hope he hasn't been turned and gone back to join them,' Tom wondered aloud.

'I know his uncle had a guilty conscience about putting him in the orphanage. I wonder if he's gone there? I'll see what I can find out.'

'Cheers Jezza.'

# Chapter Fourteen

In fact the boys had returned to Mo's Uncle's house in their village and as there was no lock on his door, they crept in quietly and woke the old man.

'Uncle, uncle. It is me, Mohammed,' Mo said quietly, touching his uncle's arm.

'What...what is it?' the old man said, startled.

'Uncle, I am sorry to disturb you, but I don't know what to do. We have escaped from a Taliban training camp and need to hide.'

The old man roused himself slowly. 'Just a minute. Let me make sure that I am not dreaming.'

He stretched out his calloused hand and touched Mo's arm.

'Yes Uncle. It is not a dream. We are really here,' Mo confirmed.

'Thank Allah you are safe. After I heard that you had been taken by the Taliban, I haven't been able to sleep. I kept thinking, what would my brother say if you were killed when I should have been looking after you?'

'What can we do?' Mo pleaded.

'You need to go away from here, to where nobody knows you,' the old man said, now fully awake.

'Yes, but where?' Mo asked.

'We could always go to Europe, Abdul suggested.

'Don't be silly. Where will we find the money? You said it would cost fifteen hundred dollars each.'

'Do you really want to go to Europe?' the old man asked, earnestly.

'Yes. Sergeant Tom says there are no wars there and we would be safe.'

'Then you shall both go.' Mo's uncle directed.

'Both!'

'Me too?' Abdul queried.

'Yes, yes of course. It will be safer if there are two of you. You will need to protect each other on the journey. It will be difficult. There will be lots of challenges.'

'But where will we get the money?'

'I have some money, but it is at the Orphanage, hidden,' Abdul revealed.

'I don't think it is wise that you go and collect it. I have some money which I can give you.'

'But Uncle...'

Don't worry. You can repay me...when you have made your fortune and are rich men,' he laughed.

'Thank you, uncle. But uncle how will you afford it?'

Mo was wrong about his uncle, he was far more thoughtful and generous than Mo had given him credit for.

'I want you to turn to face the far wall,' Mo's uncle told them.

'Why?'

'Just do as you are bid,' the old man said firmly.

Satisfied that they had complied, he went to a large stone near the fireplace and rolled it aside. He took out a large quantity of US dollars and put the stone back in place.

'You can turn around now,' he said.

'Mohammed, I have been saving a long time to leave and start a new life myself,' he said, showing the large wad of notes in his hand. 'But I am too old to take the long journey to Europe.'

'But Uncle...'Where did you get all that American money from?' Mo asked, flabbergasted by the amount.

'I have been selling certain products to the American GI's for some time,' the old man confessed.

'Oh, I see,' Mo said knowingly.

'I've thought about making the trip for too long. It is now too late for me. But you are young, with dreams to dream.

So, I want you to have the money to buy your way there instead. At least, if you go, there is chance for a future for you. And who knows, one day it will be safe for you to return and help rebuild our country.'

Mo couldn't believe his ears. This was the same man who had berated him for not bringing money into the house, but who already had a hidden fortune.

'Uncle my thanks seem so inadequate for your wonderful generosity.'

'Yes, yes.' The old man dismissed Mo's expressed gratitude and instead talked about how they were going to make it happen.

'You must hide here, until you are ready to leave. You must NOT leave the house until you are ready to go, do you understand?'

'Yes. Thank you so much Uncle, I will repay you somehow,' Mo said humbly.

'By the way Mohammed, the orphanage brought your possessions here after you were taken.'

The old man went to a shelf and gave Mo a small wrapped bundle. Inside Mo found his precious knife, flint and more importantly the selfie photograph.

'Now let us all get some sleep. We have a busy few days ahead of us,' his uncle suggested.

As the two boys laid down under a blanket, the old man returned the money to it's safe place.

Over the next few days they were busy preparing for the journey.

Using a tailoring skill that Abdul had learnt at the orphanage, they sewed money into their clothes behind double layers of material. And hid Mo's precious things in a false bottom of his rucksack.

Finally they were ready to go, and Mo's uncle dug out, from his secret hiding place, a map of the world that he had ripped out of a newspaper.

They talked about the possible routes that Mo and Abdul could travel. Unfortunately, although the map showed the countries and capitals it lacked any real navigational detail.

'I was thinking of going through this way,' uncle explained, using a stick to trace the route on the newspaper. 'Iran, Turkey, Greece, Italy, France and then England. But there are other routes too. It will depend on many things that you meet on the way.'

'What sort of things?' Abdul queried.

'Police, Politics and borders. So, it is important that you know where you are going. Some people give up because they can't navigate and get lost.'

'We did map reading with the Sergeant and I have a compass in the knife that he gave me. So, we should be ok,' Mo said, naively.

'It is a big and dangerous world out there. The first part of your journey is to get to Kabul bus station. Just be careful and look after each other.'

'We will Uncle, we will.'

So, having said a tearful goodbye to Mo's Uncle, the boys fearfully set off, uncertain about what lay ahead for their long journey into the unknown. Was it an impossible dream after all?

# PART TWO

# Pilgrimage

# Chapter Fifteen

In the late afternoon, Mo and Abdul wandered the busy streets of Kabul, Afghanistan's dusty capital, looking for the bus station.

Eventually, Mo worked up enough courage to ask, and was directed to the bustling terminus near the university, in Kabul City

Nervously, they joined the queue for the ticket sellers, and bought a one-way ticket to take them to Zaranj, the capital of Nimruz, near the border with Pakistan and Iran, for the second leg of their long journey.

As the daylight faded, the place came alive. The boys were amazed to see scores of young men starting to arrive, each carrying large backpacks.

Mo and Abdul settled down to keep their place in the queue and dozed fitfully during the night.

At 0600hrs the 'big bus' rolled into the bus stop and, after checking in their tickets, they boarded the ramshackle 53-seater, which was soon overloaded with passengers and their luggage.

And, after what seemed like hours of waiting in the hot cramped conditions, the bus finally left the bus station on its long journey.

Mo and Abdul exchanged nervous grins as they started their pilgrimage to a new life.

Kabul, wedged between the Hindu Kush mountains, along the Kabul River is in a narrow valley. The boys marvelled at the stunning views as they cut through the narrow valley roads, descending from the high altitude capital city, 5,876 feet above sea level.

The bus made its way, cautiously along the three hundred miles of rugged, twisting, mountain roads.

After seven uncomfortable hours, they reached Kandahar, at the south of the country, on the Arghandab River, at an elevation of 3,310 ft.

Here they stopped for a change of driver, and an exchange of some passengers. Half the passengers leaving and being replaced by a new set.

Mo and Abdul took the opportunity to get off and bought some food from one of the stalls in the bus station.

After another, frustratingly, long wait in Kandahar, the big bus finally left the former capital and crawled its way along another, 300 miles of steep and precarious mountain roads.

Here and there the dusty desert areas were occasionally punctuated by the greens of well irrigated crops, hugging the banks of the Helmand river. Oasis's in an otherwise arid desert landscape.

Enroute, they were temporarily delayed by a blazing taxi blocking the road. The vehicle had apparently run over a mine, planted by the side of the road. The driver had been killed, but amazingly, the three passengers, although injured, had survived the explosion.

The carnage was a traumatic reminder for the boys, if one was needed, of the reason that they were leaving their unstable homeland.

As they finally left the site of the explosion a sandstorm blew up and the road and horizon was lost in a thick beige mist.

Fortunately, the bus driver's knowledge of the route helped to keep them on the road, but at a snail's pace.

Finally they arrived in Zanarj during the evening; the passengers, exhausted by the hot 15-hour journey, tumbled off the bus, bleary eyed by the marathon trip.

Mo and Abdul gathered their meagre belongings together, glad that the seemingly hot, endless bus ride had at last ended.

The boys sought out a smuggler straight away and soon found a swarthy looking man talking to someone and heard the words Turkey and Greece in their conversation. After the other person left, they approached the man.

'Excuse me Sir, are you able to make arrangements to get us to Greece?'

'Who's asking,' the man said suspiciously, looking around.

'My name is...' Mo started to say.

'I don't want your names. Have you got money to pay me?'

'Yes Sir,' Mo said, feeling the money padded into his jacket.

'It's fifteen hundred dollars...each. I want half now,' the man demanded.

'If we give you the money now, how will we know you will turn up to take us?' Mo asked suspiciously.

'You don't! You're the ones who wants to go to Greece. It's up to you.'

The boys looked at each other and nodded. 'We will come back in a little while. We need to get the money,' Abdul informed him.

'I shall be here,' the man replied.

The boys went into a deserted alley and cut a small hole in their jackets and took out some money.

'Let's just give him five hundred, then if he doesn't' turn up, we haven't lost everything,' Mo suggested.

'Ok,' Abdul agreed. and put some of the money back into the lining.

Within a few minutes they were back to where they had met the man. But he wasn't there.

'Oh, we've lost him. Now what do we do?' Mo said, desperately looking around.

'I don't know,' Abdul said, his spirits dashed.

'We could go looking for him.'

'I'm tired and hungry. Let's try again in the morning, there might be someone else who could help,' Abdul suggested.

# Chapter Sixteen

The pair rested in an alley near to a restaurant; delicious smells wafted from the open kitchen door, but as tempted as they were, they knew it would be foolish to waste money on a good meal so early in their journey. Instead they chewed on flat bread that they had brought with them.

They slept fitfully, knowing that in the morning they would have to find the smuggler again and if successful, might be attempting the dangerous journey across the border into Iran.

Their uncomfortable night was disturbed in the early morning when they were unceremoniously kicked awake.

'Wake up, wake up.' They were urged by the large swarthy individual whom they had met the previous night.

'Money, I need your money. If you want to get in the truck,' the large man demanded.

'I heard you charging only five hundred dollars to some people.' Mo said bravely. 'Why are we paying three times that amount?'

'Because they are only travelling to Iran for work. You are going to Greece to get to England, I suspect.'

'Oh,' Mo exclaimed, 'his hope of negotiating a lower price derailed.

'Don't worry. I will make all the arrangements. It costs a lot in bribes,' he continued. 'I will get you there, no problem.'

Although they initially, planned to give him only five hundred dollars, they didn't want to lose the opportunity of booking their place , so they gave him the full amount as wanted.

Mo and Abdul had taken the precaution of binding the three thousand dollars together, which Abdul surreptitiously removed from his jacket, and gave it to the man.

Quickly the smuggler counted their payment and satisfied it was all there, stuffed it into his jacket pocket.

'Alright ,' he said. 'Now you wait.'

'What do you mean? Mo said, apprehensively

'The convoy will be going at two o'clock this afternoon. You must wait.'

As the morning wore on Mo and Abdul were on edge, nervous that they might have been fleeced out of their money by a scam. However, they went to the place that the smuggler had told them to wait at and were amazed to see over a hundred other migrants waiting too.

'Hopefully this is the right place,' Mo said.

'We'll soon find out whether we have been ripped off,' Abdul said pessimistically.

But, at two o'clock, a fleet of old dilapidated pickup trucks arrived in convoy and pulled to a halt. The drivers popped their bonnets and checked water and oil levels before closing the hood and getting in.

The boy's smuggler suddenly arrived at their side. 'Get in that truck, quickly,' he ordered.

The boys ran down to the red Toyota truck that he'd pointed out.

At the same time, there was a general stampede, as the other refugees, anxious not to miss out on this trip, ran to other vehicles.

Having now paid a large amount of money for the trip, the boys were disappointed to find that they would be crammed into the open back of an old dented pickup.

With great apprehension they clambered in and joined a group of ten others already in the back.

Mo looked around the motley group of fellow refugees, most wearing headscarves and scarves across their mouth and noses.

Their fellow travellers consisted of an assortment of people of all ages and sexes, ranging from, a girl of similar age to himself, to an older looking man, whom Mo estimated to be his Uncle's age of about 55 years.

He thought about his uncle and conceded that he was right in his decision not to undertake the exhausting journey, at the same time wondering how this older man would cope.

Before they set off, they were given a pair of goggles and a bottle of water each.

'What's the goggles for? Mo asked, one of the other migrants.

'Dust. You can get massive dust storms in Nimruz. The 120 days wind will suddenly whip up a sandstorm. Hence the face scarves too,' he revealed.

'Yes, we experienced one on the way here, yesterday,' Mo informed the other.

'Let's use our neckerchief for a face scarf,' he suggested to Abdul. They dug into their rucksacks and duly retrieved their camouflage coloured neckerchiefs, tying them around their neck in anticipation of needing them.

As the last refugee climbed in, the driver fired up the overladen truck, it's suspension bottoming out with the weight of its human cargo.

The truck sped out of the square and weaved his way through the Zaranj community.

The boys were feeling excited, but apprehensive, about the next part of their adventure.

Mo was surprised to see that they drove past a sign that indicated 'IRAN 5Km' to the right.

'Where are we going?' he asked, suspiciously. 'The sign indicated that the bridge over the Helmand River to Iran is that way. Back there.'

'Yes. But only to those who have the proper paperwork. We must go around all the border control checkpoints,' the other advised him.

Within a short space of time the dwellings were left behind, and they entered the treacherous Baluchi desert.

After several hours under the blazing sun and choking dust, Mo and Abdul were exhausted, their spirits plummeted, and wondering how much more of the bone jarring journey they could take.

Just as they thought that they couldn't take anymore, the convoy stopped. But only while the pick-up trucks were refuelled at a collection of dilapidated huts that went under the misnomer of a petrol station.

Gratefully, they were allowed to get out to stretch their legs.

'Where are we?' Mo asked the sweating driver.

'In the Nimruz province,' he grunted and continued filling up the fuel tank.

'How much further do you reckon?' Mo quizzed Abdul.

'I don't know. I didn't know that there was so much desert,' Abdul replied. I think I've eaten half of it.'

However, their hot dusty journey continued for several more hours through the rough arid Nimrozi landscape along with a convoy of other pick-up trucks.

To Mo's amazement the convoy also passed people making the risky trip into Iran on foot; Young single travellers and families walking relentlessly towards their goal, were left behind in a swirling cloud of choking dust as the convoy zoomed past.

After six hours driving at breakneck speed, the vehicles crossed the Pakistani border along an ancient smugglers route.

Then to their consternation the trucks pulled up and everyone was ordered out.

'What's going on?' Mo asked his smuggler

'We are going through Taliban controlled area. We will have to go on foot for a while,' he replied, getting a large rucksack out of the cab and gave them packets containing flatbreads and dates. 'There will be more, when we get to the cars in Iran, he advised them.

'How far?' Abdul asked.

'It will take us a full day before we reach the cars in Southern Iran. They will take us onward into the centre of Tehran, and we will pick up different transport to take us on to Turkey.'

'At least we aren't being bounced around in that truck anymore,' Abdul added.

The group set out on foot through the arid heat of the desert, keeping an eye out for the Taliban, gangs of robbers and trigger-happy border guards from both Pakistan and Iran.

'Most of the guards have been bribed to turn a blind eye. But some of the police also want a payment, too. Now do you see where your money is going?' their smuggler grunted.

Halfway into their journey, a sandstorm blew up. Navigation was impossible with visibility down to a few feet, so they huddled together while the wind sandblasted them.

Eventually, it stopped and, after 24 hours on foot, their challenging trek finished, as they reached their next lot of transport.

Without ceremony, the hot, exhausted and anxious passengers were quickly crammed into the waiting cars.

The convoy, of overloaded cars, pulled away at breakneck speed. The drivers exhibiting delusions of immortality as they drove dangerously fast over the desolate landscape.

Mo and Abdul were petrified, especially when one of the cars in front of theirs, ran off the road and overturned, throwing the occupants across the desert floor.

Their driver didn't stop or ease up to see if they could help the injured people. It was as if the devil himself was chasing them.

Fortunately, they arrived safely, then their smuggler directed the exhausted and shell-shocked boys into the back of a waiting lorry, where they hid behind the load of wooden packing cases.

The twelve-hundred-mile journey through Iran seemed like eternity. Frustratingly, they were constantly having to stop and queue at checkpoints manned by armed militia.

Fortunately, the driver was obviously well known to the guards and the bribe paid to them ensured minimal delays.

Abdul was nearing the end of his resilience. The jolting journey had created sores on the back of his legs and although he was used to high temperatures, he was becoming dehydrated.

'I'm not sure if I can take any more of this,' he croaked to an equally exhausted Mo.

'You can do it. Remember, *a Scout has courage in all difficulties*,' Mo reminded him.

'I've had too many bad things happen to me to be courageous about them anymore. I'm just worn out,' Abdul croaked.

# Chapter Seventeen

Eventually, the lorry that they had hidden in went through the Iranian - Turkish border  and it arrived in Van, eastern Turkey.

Their smuggler got them out and booked them into an overcrowded hostel, where they spent a sleepless night.

In the crowded lounge area, Abdul overheard a concerning conversation.

'Did you hear that Mo? Some people left their home in northern Afghanistan three years ago and spent two years in Iran working to raise the smugglers' fee to take them onwards?' Abdul relayed, appalled at the implications.

'Yes but we are here already. So we don't have to worry about that,' Mo counselled, trying to placate his worried friend. 'Anyway, I hear that eventually, they got refugee status, and their aim is still to move to Europe.'

'I heard them say too, that many migrants get stuck in Turkey.' Abdul continued pessimistically.

'Yes, because jobs for them are scarce here,' Mo explained patiently.

This news further blackened Abdul's mood.

'We're never going to make it.' Abdul groaned. 'Let's forget it and go home before it's too late.'

'No. Why would we? We have travelled so far now to think of going back. Anyway, we don't need to worry about all that because we are travelling on,' Mo reminded him. 'Surely there are houses for them to wait in?' Mo suggested.

'Yes. I heard them say that there is an apartment run by smugglers in Zeytinburnu.'

'Where's that?'

'It is another neighbourhood of Istanbul. But the apartment is already crammed full. The place is only fit for a small family, but it is home to up to 30 young Afghans each night.'

'But we don't have to raise any more money,' Mo reminded him.

Not having to work to get additional funding, reminded Mo of the debt of gratitude he owed to his Uncle, which he vowed to repay sometime, somehow.

The following morning the smuggler shepherded them into another lorry, where again they hid under the load, and travelled six hundred miles to a small community of Afghan families in Konya, Turkey.

Here they spent another night recovering from their long, hot and uncomfortable journey.

Eventually they moved on to their final truck stop three hundred miles on reasonable roads to the outskirts of Istanbul. Having bypassed the capital itself, the convoy drove quietly, showing no lights, down minor roads until they reached a gravel track and parked up.

It was night when they arrived. The full moon made everything take on a ghostly and sinister appearance.

It was warm but very windy as they alighted from their surprisingly reliable truck.

'Thankfully that is the last we see of the inside of a truck,' Abdul groaned. 'I think every bone in my body is bruised.'

'You can't bruise bones,' Mo pointed out, unsympathetically.

'I have,' Abdul moaned.

'Perhaps we should stay here for a while for you to recover?' Mo suggested unrealistically.

'No, I'll be alright now that we are out of the truck.'

Mo spotted a group of people on the other side of the road.

'What are they waiting for?' he asked the big man.

'They are waiting for their organiser. He is making sure that the Police aren't around I expect,' the big man clarified. 'They will be on the sea trip too.'

'Where are we going next?' Mo asked.

'The next part of your journey is crossing the Aegean Sea to Greece,' the Smuggler informed him.

'Brilliant. But is it safe?' asked a fearful Abdul.

'Of course it is. We have had many trips before tonight,' the Smuggler replied.

What he didn't say, was that not all the trips had had successful outcomes.

# Chapter Eighteen

Neither of the boys had been in a boat before and were very apprehensive.

As they followed their Smuggler down towards the shore, behind them more and more people were silently joining the crocodile. Men, women and children of all ages were heading for the boat that would facilitate their dream; the great escape to Europe.

'What's that smell?' Abdul asked, sniffing the air.

'I think it must be the sea,' Mo replied.

'There's a strange noise too.'

'I don't know, perhaps it's the sea too.'

As the migrants weaved their way through the dark narrow pathway, they had their first glimpse of the sea, its white foam skirt-like waves crashing and retreating on the beach.

A nervous Abdul grabbed Mo's arm. 'This is it then. Our passage to freedom in Greece,' he said. 'But where's the boat?'

In the semi-darkness, Mo scanned the beach and spotted it partly hidden by a group of men.

It was a RIB, a small grey rigid hulled inflatable rubber boat with an outboard motor on the back.

It appeared to be animated, with a life of its own. The men were desperately trying to launch it as it was buffeted by the waves.

Eventually two of the group waded out into the water holding ropes at the front of the dinghy to keep it head on into the waves.

Mo was surprised to see how small it was as it bucked on the swell. He estimated it was big enough for only twenty people, but the waiting migrants numbered double that amount.

'We aren't all going to get in that,' he said to Abdul.

'No, it looks very small. Perhaps there is another one coming later,' Abdul suggested optimistically.

As the line of migrants reached the RIB, they were ordered in. Some were told to sit on the inflated sides, others to kneel or sit in the centre.

Having been told previously by their smugglers that only one small rucksack could be taken, there were several vicious arguments from some migrants who had ignored the restriction and were taking suitcases.

The Gang masters didn't take any messing, and roughly handled those who had ignored the rules.

It was a stark choice, ditch the cases or stay behind. But as the refugees had already paid for their passage, some men were frantically unpacking their cases to salvage a few valuables.

Migrants wearing life jackets were told to discard them, as there wouldn't be enough room for all those wanting to leave.

The only person with a life jacket on, turned out to be the sailor who was going to steer the boat.

He too was involved in a melee with the other Gang members when he said, the volume of people were too many.

'I will be overloaded,' he protested.

At first, he refused to take any more. But a revolver, pressed to his ear, persuaded him otherwise.

As the boat filled up, people waiting to board started to panic. Concerned that they were going to be left behind, they rushed to climb onboard. Frantic adults trampling over screaming children in their rush to secure a place.

Pandemonium broke out as families were separated and wives and children were screaming for their fathers to ignore the suitcases and get on the boat.

Mo and Abdul were pushed out of the way in the scramble and feared that they would be left behind, but fortunately they were the last to be crammed in next to the man who was going to be steering the boat.

When everyone was on board, as the sailor attempted to start the outboard motor, gang members pushed the boat off from the Turkish shore.

Mo and Abdul had to stand up to allow him the full length of the pull of the starter rope. But despite frantically tugging on the pull cord the outboard refused to start.

'Excuse me Sir,' Abdul said to the sweating sailor, 'but have you tried the choke? I have started lots of American generators at Camp Bastion and they usually need the choke out to start them.'

The man devoid of any other thoughts, reached to the back of the engine, found the lever and pulled the choke out.

Finally, after more cursing, the outboard engine coughed into life and they started making headway through the choppy waves.

So, the boat designed to carry twenty, now set sail with fifty people on board. Providentially, the boys were unaware of the failure rate of these nocturnal boat trips. For, having bypassed all the dangers of their long overland journeys whilst hoping to start a better life, many thousands had drowned during this waterborne phase.

As they left, Mo could see through the gloom, the beach littered with discarded life jackets and cases.

Within minutes, the gang of smugglers descended on the castoff cases like vultures, taking any valuables that had been left by the desperate migrants.

Glad at last to be on the sea leg of their journey, the migrants relief at leaving the Turkish shore however, was short lived, for, soon after leaving the beach, the inflatable started taking on water.

The sailor shouted at the frightened occupants to bail the rising sea water out as fast as they could.

The occupants, with nothing other than their hands to scoop out the water, frantically complied. Their combined efforts at keeping the boat afloat seemed to be working.

'Mo, we are in the middle of the sea. I can't see land anymore.' Abdul observed, after a while. 'I'm scared and I feel sick.'

'We will be alright my friend. Just keep scooping the water out and we will soon be there,' Mo tried to reassure him.

But Mo was himself fearful of being plunged into the sea, as neither he or Abdul could swim. Without life jackets, his life expectancy would be very short.

But despite Mo's attempt to appease a frightened Abdul, he could see waves were still breaking over the front of the boat and it was settling lower and lower in the water.

Then, suddenly in front of them, Mo could vaguely see land getting closer.

'Are we there yet?' he asked the pilot, hopefully.

'No this is the Dardanelle straight. There is a narrow channel and steep cliff walls that we must navigate through. There will be a strong current here too.

'So what sea is this then?' Mo asked.

'It is the Sea of Marmara and is usually calm, not rough like this. So it does not bode well for when we get out into the open sea of the Aegean.'

Abdul clutched his friends hand. 'How soon will we be there?'

'Shortly, we will going into the Aegean soon,' the pilot explained.

'How will we know?' Mo asked.

'Oh you'll know, without me having to tell you.'

'How?'

'It will get rougher.'

Abdul clutched Mo's hand tighter.

As they sailed out through the straights into the Aegean, the other occupants too became aware of their precarious situation.

With no land either side to shelter them anymore from the wind, the waves were being whipped up into a huge swell, which was throwing the dinghy around. Consequently, more and more waves were breaking over the bow and sides of the dinghy and it was taking on water fast.

Conditions on board were getting worse, some people were sitting in water nearly up to their waist. Panic was spreading through the passengers.

Ignoring the shouts of the smuggler, 'to SIT DOWN'; people were standing up and unsettling the, already, unstable boat.

But by some miracle, the RIB continued its laboured process, when through the spray, Mo suddenly spotted some lights ahead.

'What's that? Is it land?' Mo shouted to the pilot, over the shrieking wind.

'No, it's a ship. It's probably coming to pick us up.' The sailor shouted back.

'Look Abdul. We are saved. A ship is coming towards us.'

'Yes, he might save us, but we'll all be arrested and put in prison.' Abdul whined.

'But at least we will be off this sinking boat,' Mo encouraged.

The RIB occupants cheered and clapped as the large European Border and Coast Guard Agency ship got closer.

The Portuguese Frontex vessel had picked the migrants boat up on their radar and in a frequent, and well executed procedure, had quickly lowered a small flotilla of rescue dinghies.

As a powerful searchlight was switched on to illuminate the RIB, the dinghies headed towards the stricken refugee boat.

# Chapter Nineteen

The Frontex dinghies surrounded the sinking RIB at a safe holding position, ten yards from the hysterical migrants.

Within a few seconds of getting to their holding station, a shower of orange life jackets were thrown onto the refugee's boat.

Eager migrants reached out and grabbed them, making the RIB dangerously unstable and nearly capsizing it.

The strong wind and heavy swell combined with the dark, was making the task difficult; and in the melee, some refugees were pushed overboard, forcing them to swim through the dangerously choppy waters to the Frontex dinghies.

'SIT DOWN,' the pilot ordered, shouting above the shrieking wind and desperate panic of the hysterical occupants. 'Otherwise we will all be overboard'.

Abdul caught two life jackets for the pair of them and they quickly helped each other put them on.

As soon as everyone had fitted themselves into a life preserver, transfers onto the Frontex dinghies were undertaken.

The dinghies then did a speedy shuttle service back and forth to the ship and, just as the last occupants were transferred from the RIB, the refugee's boat finally sank.

As the migrants were brought on board the Frontex ship, they were all given a blanket and offered a hot cup of chocolate. Crew members wandered amongst the frightened survivors, assessing people who might need medical treatment.

As Mo and Abdul cradled their cups to warm themselves, Abdul admitted that he had been frightened and genuinely feared for his life.

'Oh, that was scary.' Abdul said, shaking from a combination of cold and fear. 'Do we have to do anymore sea crossings?' he wondered.

'Yes, a few more I think,' Mo replied, also dreading any more maritime adventures himself.

'That's if we're not arrested, you mean,' Abdul added, pessimistically.

The Frontex mission is to coordinate and organise joint humanitarian exercises and rescue at sea. Its vital presence, on the well-known migrant route, has saved thousands of lives.

Frontex plays a major role in assisting EU Member States to cope with the flood of refugees attempting to get into Europe, irrespective whether they are war zone or economic migrants.

The relieved and jubilant refugees were given snacks and bottles of water whilst the Frontex boat made its way to the port of Skala Sikamineas, on Lesbos – a Greek Island.

On arrival each refugee was processed, names, ages and country of origin were written down and they were given a small slip of paper to recognise their arrival... their arrival in Europe.

Mo waited for Abdul to have his registration completed and immediately rushed over and hugged him.

'We have made it to Europe,' he beamed hugging the other.

'Yes! We are here.'

'Our dream is starting to become a reality,' Mo smiled, and looked around at his new surroundings. 'We must now only speak English so that we are able to communicate well when we get to England, OK?'

'OK.'

Many of the other refugees had sunk down on their knees and broke down into tears for their salvation.

'Where are we exactly? 'Mo asked a uniformed immigration officer.

'You are on the shores of the Greek Island called Lesbos,' the other replied, in broken English.

'What happens next?'

'Well, the Moria refugee camp here on Lesbos is full.'

'Full?'

'Yes. Full because most refugees incarcerated here are awaiting immigration processing. Some have been there for two years.'

'Two years!' Mo said, fearfully; imagining his and Abdul's future locked in a refugee camp.' What about us?'

'You will all be taken to a camp on the mainland of Greece and you will be held there until you have been processed.'

The word 'camp' brought back bad memories of the dreadful experience that they'd had at the hands of the Taliban. But he knew there would be no drone rescue this time to help them escape.

Mo then spotted a huge rubbish tip nearby, the size of half a football pitch with a ten-foot-high pile of deflated RIBs and thousands of damaged orange lifejackets.

'Excuse me again, Sir .What is that?'

'That is a rubbish heap of shattered dreams, left by the thousands who have gone before you. Some weren't as lucky as you. Sadly, in their case, we arrived too late to save all of them.'

# Chapter Twenty

Having survived a sinking dinghy and possible incarceration in a camp in Lesbos, their luck still held. For when they subsequently disembarked in the port of Pireas, on the mainland of Greece, fate gave them a helping hand.

Several rescued migrants, unhappy with the prospect of being incarcerated in a mainland detention camp, fought with the immigration officers and in the ensuing chaos, ran off into the dock complex.

Ignoring warning shots fired over their heads, the escapees continued their escape bid, hotly pursued by the uniformed port officials.

Now unsupervised, Mo saw their opportunity to escape too and grabbed Abdul's hand.

'Come on, lets' run for it.'

'We'll never get out of the port gates,' Abdul observed realistically.

'We've got to try. I don't want to go to the migrant's camp and be stuck there for years. Come on,' he urged.

Together they ran through the labyrinth of port buildings and ended up exhausted in the dead end of a marina.

'I need to sit down, it is so hot,' Abdul said, collapsing in a heap.

'Put your neckerchief over your head to keep the sun off,' Mo directed.

'So where to now?' Abdul panted.

'Well, we're in Greece now and so long as we can dodge the authorities…'

'And get away from the docks,' Abdul interjected.

'Yes of course. When we get away from the docks,' Mo said optimistically. 'We can choose, I suppose.'

'Choose to go where though?' Abdul queried.

'Albania, Macedonia, Bulgaria or across the sea to Italy and then France,' Mo suggested. 'Let's look at the new map they gave us in Lesbos,' he continued, removing it from his rucksack.

Mo felt sad, replacing his Uncle's now ruined newspaper map with the new one, was effectively losing another link with his homeland.

'But, if we go to Albania, Macedonia or Bulgaria, there are a lot of other countries and more borders to get through afterwards, he said studying the map. 'On the other hand, if we go to Italy, there is only one way out and that's through France,' Mo added.

'Yes, that sounds like a better idea. But I don't like the idea of another trip in a small rubber boat.'

'No, neither do I.'

'So what do we do?'

'I don't know,' Abdul said helplessly. 'You're the one with the bright ideas.

The pair were sitting on the dock wearing their neckerchiefs over their heads still wondering what to do, when they heard footsteps approaching.

Mo quickly folded the map.

'Quick,' Mo said, grabbing Abdul. 'We need to go. It's the Police.'

But as they stood and prepared to run, instead of a group of tough policeman, it was a middle-aged man, wearing a floral shirt and shorts, who came around the corner.

Unsure what to do, they stood and watched as the man approached them. 'Geia sas agoria. Endiaféreste gia skáfi?' he asked in Greek.

'Sorry, I don't understand,' Mo replied in English, finally deciding to leave.

'Oh you speak English? I thought you were locals. I said, are you boys interested in boats?'

'Uh...Yes,' Mo replied cautiously, stopping in mid stride.

Abdul looked at his friend in horror.

'Do you want to have a closer look at that Catamaran?' he asked, pointing to a sleek looking boat moored nearby.

'No, we've got to go,' Abdul said hastily and started leaving.

'Yes,' Mo contradicted his travel companion. 'Actually, we are planning to pick up a boat to take us to Italy.' Mo volunteered.

'Oh, you'll be wanting to sail from Igoumenista then. That's the other side of Greece about 475 kilometres from here.

Abdul grimaced at hearing the distance.

'We are planning to walk there,' Mo volunteered.

'Really? Well I've got to deliver this Cat to Igoumenista. If you want an alternative to walking,' the man announced. 'I can give you a lift.'

Mo tossed the options over in his mind. 'If they walked, they would have to find their own way. Then there was a danger that they could be caught and end up in a refugee camp near Athens. However, If they went by boat, the chances of being caught were almost nil and, it would be so much easier than navigating through Greece.'

Although unhappy by the distance that they would have to walk, Abdul, looked at Mo and shook his head, suspicious of the man's motives.

'Well, to be honest, it's such an easy boat to sail that I'm intending to sail the boat myself anyway. But I wouldn't mind a bit of company, if you both want to come along?' the man added.

# Chapter Twenty-one

'Having weighed up the alternatives, Mo made up his mind. 'Yes please. It will save us a long walk,' Mo said, looking at a shocked Abdul.

Abdul looked at him in horror and dragged Mo aside.

'What if he's going to kidnap us?' he whispered in Pashto.

'Kidnap us! Why would he do that? Mo replied in English, to reinforce their earlier agreement about not using their native tongue.

'Because...because..'

'No, I reckon he's alright,' Mo assured him confidently. 'He's going to save us a long tiring journey. Do you realise, that if we walk there. It's nearly 500 kilometres and we could end up being caught?'

Abdul nevertheless was shaking his head in disbelief, trying to get Mo to see sense.

'A boat with a strange man alone,' Abdul warned. 'Whatever are you thinking of?'

But Mo ignored his protestations and confirmed to the man that they would indeed like to accept his offer. 'Yes please,' he said.

"Oh great. If we're going to be ship mates it might be a good idea if we knew each other's name,' the man suggested. 'I'm Geoff and you are?'

'I'm Mohammed and this is Abdul,' Mo advised the man.

'Now we know who we are, that's a good start. The trip will take us a couple of days, depending on the weather, unless you need to get there any sooner?'

'No, that's fine. We're in no rush,' Mo replied. 'It will take us much longer than that if we walked.'

'Certainly would. Excuse me, but I seem to recognise your headwear. It's a Scout neckerchief isn't it?

'Yes, that's right,' Mo confirmed.

'Oh, well there's a coincidence, I used to be in the Sea Scouts for many years, both as a Scout and then as a Leader.'

'Oh great,' Abdul said relieved. 'We are Scouts from Afghanistan.'

'Yes I thought that was where you were from. Pleased to meet you both,' the man said, extending his left hand and shaking theirs. 'I must say your English is very good.'

'Yes, we have had many soldiers in our country from England and USA,' Mo informed him. So we quickly learnt.'

'I have even worked for the Americans,' Abdul admitted.

By then they had arrived at the twin hulled, thirteen metre Helia 44 catamaran.

'Anyway, here she is then,' he announced.

The boys stared in awe at the large boat rocking gently at its moorings, the rigging 'tinged' a rhythmic tune against the tall aluminium mast.

Set against the azure blue sea, its white construction emphasised the boat's sleek lines.

The mainsail was neatly folded away which made it look like a butterfly at rest.

All the ropes were neatly coiled on the deck forming several perfect circles.

Along the side of the boat blue fenders dangled from short ropes. The torpedo shaped devices were distributed evenly in meticulous precision along the side of the boat, protecting it from damage against the floating pontoon.

She looks gorgeous, doesn't she?' Geoff said proudly.

'Just like me then,' a woman's voice announced from inside the boat.

'Hi darling, he chuckled. 'That, of course, goes without saying. I hope you're decent. I have two young gentlemen with me who would like to help me sail the boat.'

'Thank goodness for that. It will mean I don't get shouted at for mixing my port and starboard up,' she replied, emerging from the large central cabin that spanned the twin hulls.

'This is Mohammed, and this is Abdul,' the man advised her.

'Hello guys,' she smiled. 'I'm Angie.'

'Hello,' Abdul said, open mouthed, gazing at the scantily clad woman. The boys were unused to seeing a woman exposing herself so much. Angie's skimpy shorts made her suntanned legs look even longer than they were. Her halter top revealed even more of her curvaceous and voluptuous bronze body.

'I expect you guys could do with a drink? It's a bit warm isn't it? she continued.

'Yes please,' the boys chorused.

'What would you like a beer or a G and T?' the man asked, smiling.

The boys looked at each other, horror struck.

'No, I'm only joking. I appreciate that alcohol is forbidden in your religion. Angie could you make us three glasses of squash please?'

'Of course. Be with you shortly, she replied, disappearing down into the boat.

'What do you think of the boat lads?'

'Wow, it is beautiful,' Mo said gushingly, his eyes absorbing every exquisite detail of the vessel.

'Climb aboard,' he invited. 'Just to be strictly correct. We tend to call boats a 'she', rather than an 'it'. But you're right. She is beautiful. I wish I could afford to own her.'

'But you're going to sail it. Are you stealing it?' Abdul asked, naively, following Mo as he climbed onto the deck.

'No. I am delivering it for a customer, who will sail it from the west coast port of Igoumenista.

'When do we leave?' Mo asked, excited at the prospect of this new adventure.

'Right away, unless you guys need to get anything?'

'No, we're good to go,' Mo confirmed.

'In fact, the sooner the better,' Abdul said, looking nervously towards the port buildings.

'I understand,' the man said, knowingly. 'Pleased to have you on board. We'll get out of the harbour on the engines, and then see if conditions are right for hoisting some sail.'

'OK.'

'I'll show you how to slip the moorings, he said starting the twin Volvo engines and then we'll be on our way.'

Just as they were casting off, they heard people on the pontoon approaching them.

'Quick lads get down below,' Geoff instructed.

The boys duly complied and entered the spacious cabin as two uniformed immigration people arrived on the dock side.

'Have you see two boys?' the officer called.

'No,' Geoff lied, untying the moorings and manoeuvring away from the pontoon.

'If you see them, let us know,' they called as the boat got further away from the Policemen. 'They are immigrants on their way to the detention camp.'

'Ok, will do,' he responded.

# Chapter Twenty-two

When they were clear of the harbour walls, Geoff called the boys back out.

'So, you are illegal?' he said as a matter of fact.

'Yes,' Mo admitted, expecting Geoff to turn the boat around.

'Only in their eyes,' he declared. 'We've got some sailing to do.'

'Thank you. You are a most kind person,' Abdul declared.

'When we're out a bit further, I will show you how to steer under sail. Are you guys up for that?'

'Yes please,' Mo said enthusiastically.

'I will watch,' Abdul said, already starting to feel queasy in the gentle swell.

As promised, Geoff showed Mo what to do with the sails when they were off shore and soon they were skimming along on sail power only.

Abdul looked tense as the 'Cat' pitched over to catch the wind.

'Don't worry if she leans over a bit,' Geoff advised. 'She won't capsize.'

Despite having programmed the route into the boats navigation system, Geoff also showed Mo the technique of steering the Cat.

'We'll make a sailor out of you yet, young Mohammed,' Geoff said, smiling as Mo mastered his task.

Mo was a hard worker and fast learner and soon proved himself to be an able seaman.

Unfortunately, Abdul suffered from seasickness and spent most of his time laying on a bunk below.

During the trip Geoff and Angie asked about the boys plans and quizzed them about their reasons for embarking on the odyssey.

'I gather you guys are escaping from something, somewhere.'

'We are from Afghanistan,' Mo advised. 'There is so much fighting and killing. All we want is to grow up in peace.'

'We are both orphans,' Abdul added.

'Oh how terrible,' Angie said, tearfully.

'So you see, there is no reason to stay. We are hoping for a new and peaceful life,' Mo explained.

'Yes, I can see why you'd want to leave there. Where do you hope to get to finally?

'To Italy, France and then England,' Mo informed them.

'Well, best of luck with that.' Angie said genuinely.

'You've still got a few miles to go then,' Geoff advised. And a challenge or two to get from France across the channel to England.'

'Is it difficult? Mo queried. 'It looks so close on the map.'

'Yes, it is close in distance, I don't want to put you guys off, but some people have been waiting in France to cross into England for a long time.'

'Oh. Perhaps we could sail to England instead of Igoumenista?' Mo suggested hopefully.

'Unfortunately, I must get this Cat to port by the day after tomorrow otherwise I'd take you all the way, at least to Italy, myself.

'Thanks.'

'As it is, there are a lot of ferries going back and forth between Greece and Italy, and so long as you've got money for the fare, you should have no problems.'

'Yes, we have money. Hopefully it will be enough,' Mo confirmed.

'Just be aware that sometimes the officials do special checks to make sure migrants aren't using the ferries,' Geoff warned.

'Oh!' Mo said. 'That might be a problem then?'

'Don't you worry about it. I'm sure we can bluff our way through.'

'Can I ask why you agreed to take us,' Abdul asked suspiciously.

'I could see that you were migrants and I've heard some terrible stories about the camps that they are running here. If you make the effort to find a better life for yourselves, I'm all for giving you a fighting chance.'

'Thanks.'

'And as we are all Scouts, *'a friend to all and a brother to everybody no matter where you come from'*, seems to be the right way to go. Clever bloke that founder of the Scouts, Baden Powell,' Geoff summarised.

The wave hopping trip through the clear blue waters of the Ionian Sea was magic. This was the other end of the scale to the traumatic voyage when they left Turkey. This was simply luxurious.

Fortunately the fine weather held and the wind skimmed them along.

'It's like we are millionaires with our own boat,' a smiling Mo shouted over the hissing symphony as the twin hulls kissed the waves. Diadems of light danced around the bows as the sun shone brightly through the spray.

'Yes, that's why I do this job,' Geoff said. 'All the pleasures of ownership without the costs...and getting paid for it too.'

Fortunately, the Mediterranean continued to be kind to them and there was no need for a rescue mission from Frontex, this time.

# Chapter Twenty-three

Over the next day the boys relaxed and relayed the traumas of their journey so far, attracting a lot more sympathy from Angie, who wanted to adopt them both.

Geoff produced a large-scale map of Italy, and, together, they poured over the boy's journey options.

Abdul was dismayed when he saw the size of the task still ahead of them.

'Do we have to travel all the way up there?' he moaned.

'Yes, I'm afraid so,' Geoff confirmed. 'If you think of Italy as a boot, then you will be landing on its heel at Brindisi and you will have to walk the whole of the length of the boot.'

'Pity the leg is so long,' Abdul observed, gloomily.

Geoff and Angie laughed at his black humour.

'I suggest you need to cross the Alps into France at a place called Bardonecchia. There is a road crossing that will take you into France, though, but I would expect it to be heavily patrolled.' Geoff advised.

'Alps! What are Alps?' Abdul asked.

'Umm…big hills that's all,' Angie said, not wishing to further depress him. 'You will be alright, don't worry.'

'We have done well so far,' Mo encouraged. 'We are already half way to our dream.'

'I think if you keep to the east coast it will make your navigation easier. Look! The road runs almost against the coast.' Geoff advised.

'Yes, that sounds like a good idea,' Mo concurred.

'Then you will have to travel to the west when you are at the top of the boot.'

The boy's plight plucked at Geoff and Angie's emotions, they wanted just to 'mother them' rather than push them off into the unknown hazards of their continuing journey. But at least they had helped for a small part of their trip.

When they docked in Igoumenista, and after an emotional farewell from Angie, Geoff escorted the boys through the port to find a tourist boat that would take them to Brindisi on the east coast of Italy. Fortunately they arrived ten minutes prior to sailing time.

'How much is it?' Mo asked the old man at the top of the gang plank taking the fares.

'Fifty euros each,' came the curt reply.

Digging in to their financial reserves, the boys found they had enough money, but the ticket seller was less than friendly.

'Are you immigrants?' he demanded.

'No, they are my nephews. They are here on holiday,' Geoff lied.

'Mmm,' said the Greek sceptically. 'Money,' he demanded.

Mo calculated an exchange rate that he had discussed with Geoff earlier and handed over the fare.

'Dollars!' the ticket seller observed.

'Is that a problem?' Geoff asked.

'No. I suppose not,' the Greek conceded and grudgingly gave them the tickets.

Then it was the moment to say goodbye. Mo turned to Geoff and looked at the man who had given them some confidence and comfort in their long journey.

'Thank you, Geoff, for helping and feeding us,' Mo said with tears in his eyes.

'It was my pleasure,' Geoff said, hugging them in turn and watched as the boys boarded the ferry.

'Goodbye guys, best of luck,' he said and wondered how far they'd get. 'Would these two end up in an awful refugee camp for years, wishing that they'd never left home?'

Unbeknown to the boys, the European governments were actively trying to control the flow of thousands of migrants through their countries, and were putting political and physical obstacles in their way.

# Chapter Twenty-four

The ferry from Greece pulled into the port of Brindisi in continuing hot weather.

People in the port were wearing holiday clothes, shorts, short sleeved shirts, blouses and everyone was wearing a hat to protect them from the blazing sun.

The boys put their neckerchiefs round their heads, hoping that they might attract another Scouting contact as they had done in Greece.

'I'm glad that boat trip's over,' Abdul said. 'No more sea crossings now are there?' he asked, hopefully.

'Not unless we get another trip by someone like Geoff. No.'

'Thank goodness, Abdul said happily.

'That is, not until we get to Calais, ready to get to England,' Mo added. 'And we haven't got enough money to spend on anymore big things either,' Mo informed him.

As they disembarked and much to the boy's concern on the dock side there was a policeman, his uniform identified him as a Polizia di Stato. The policeman was talking to the ferry skipper and they both kept looking at the boys, while the skipper gesticulated.

'What shall we do?' Abdul asked fearfully.

'Just act normally,' Mo advised. 'We haven't done anything wrong.'

But as the boys walked past the policeman, they could see that he had a dog with him. Unable to stop himself, Mo stroked the large Alsatian.

'Ti piacciono i cani?' the policeman asked.

'Sorry, I do not understand Italian,' Mo confessed.

'I said, do youa likea dogs?' the policeman repeated.

'Yes, I used to have one myself,' Mo added, still stroking the dog.

'He seems a to like a you,' the policeman added. 'Where are you boys a from?'

And before Mo could say anything. Abdul said, 'Afghanistan.'

'Are a you here on a holiday?'

Abdul said 'No,' as Mo said 'yes.'

'I see! If you're here a on holiday, where are you a staying?'

'We...ummm...not sure. Someone was going to meet us here,' Mo lied.

'Do you have any paperwork?' the policeman persisted.

'No,' Abdul confessed.

'I believe that you are a migrants, here illegally. I am a going to have to arrest a you. You will come a with me. If you try to run a, I will set the dog on a you. Is that understood?' he said sternly.

'Yes Sir,' they chorused.

The dream was over. They had been caught.

Silently they climbed into the back of the policeman's car. Mo could see the Skipper of the ferry smirking as the policeman shut the rear passenger door. With his dog caged in the boot, the policeman drove out of the docks.

'Where were you a heading?' the policeman asked, looking at them in his rear-view mirror.

'We were going north to Bardonecchia,' Mo said sullenly.

'I expect you were a heading into France from there were you?'

'Yes.'

They had been driving for about an hour when the Policeman pulled off the road into a forested area.

'I think a the dog needs to stretch his legs,' the policeman said, opening the boot and getting the dog out. 'I expect you could a do with a rest yourself,' he continued, opening the passenger doors.

'Here! The dog wants to play,' he said, throwing Mo a ball.

Mo spent several minutes throwing the ball for the dog while wondering what was going on.

Finally, the policeman put the dog back in the boot and closed the tailgate. The boys went to get back in to patrol car, but the policeman closed the doors.

'Ok boys. Here is a the score. The ferry owners don't a like migrants hanging around the a terminals, because it puts off a the tourists. Tourists are a their bread and butter. You understand?'

'Yes Sir."

'So, I have brought you a here. And you are now a out of my area of responsibility. You are a free to go. But a keep away from the a tourist areas. Got it?'

'Yes,' the pair said in unison.

The boys looked at each other and were concerned to see the policeman drawing his pistol.

'Quick, let's run.' Mo said, grabbing Abdul.

'Don't a come back,' the Policeman laughed as he discharged his gun into the air twice.

# Chapter Twenty-five

The boys had run through the forest, fearful for their lives, expecting any minute for the policeman and his dog to be hot on their heels. Although they could hear the dog barking, fortunately, neither appeared.

After running for twenty minutes along a forestry track, they eventually  emerged out of the woods, back on to the main road.

'What was that all about?' Abdul gasped.

'I don't think he was going to hurt us,' Mo added, breathlessly. 'I think he was playing games.'

'You're probably right.' Abdul puffed, leaning against a tree.

'Anyway, we won't be going back that way. And, at least, he's saved us a bit of the walk.' Mo observed.

'How far do you think he drove us?'

'I think it might be between thirty or forty miles and I noticed from the compass in his rear view mirror that we were travelling north too.'

'Is that the way we wanted to go?'

'Yes'

'Oh good. So how far now do we have to walk through Italy?' Abdul asked, not really wanting to know the answer.

'I think originally it was about six hundred and twenty-five miles. But thanks to the policeman, we only have to walk five hundred and ninety,' Mo informed him.

'Only five hundred and ninety! You must be joking! Oh, my poor feet,' Abdul moaned.

'I think it will take us about 25 days if we walk 8 hours a day.' Mo suggested.

'Twenty-five days!'

'Yes. Come on. We've got to keep going,' he urged, ignoring his friend's dour face.

As Geoff had suggested, they chose a route along the east coast of the Italian peninsular, for easier navigation, keeping the coast in sight for as much as possible.

Bearing in mind the policeman's warning, they didn't hang around when they reached tourist spots or big cities.

Despite the seemingly endless caravan of refugees trudging through their communities, Mo and Abdul were welcomed with 'open arms' during their Italian pilgrimage.

Several humanitarian organisations had set themselves up to help the migrants with food handouts.

In addition, the locals generosity also addressed their basic needs for changes of clothes and replacement shoes.

Mo took the opportunity to replace his worn-out trainers that he'd been wearing since he'd left Afghanistan.

Initially, fearful of the reception they would receive, especially after the episode with the Policeman; they were overwhelmed by the friendliness of many local villagers, who also gave them food and encouragement and wished them good luck; *'Buona fortuna'*, in following their dream.

'Perhaps they are being kind to ensure that we don't stay and are encouraging us to continue our journey.' Abdul observed, cynically.

Occasionally, some villagers even stepped in to rescue them from verbal abuse from drunken yobs, who disapproved of the refugee's journey.

As they headed further north, they travelled through many beautiful east coast holiday resorts with immaculate beaches and all forms of water activities. The resorts catered for and were focussed on the enjoyment of thousands of happy holiday makers filling the area.

Abdul kept stopping and staring at the many bikini clad young ladies.

'Come on Abdul. Stop drooling over those...those girls. We've got a long way to go still,' Mo encouraged, trying to drag his friend away from the distractions.

'Oh, do we have to. It's so beautiful here. Shall we stay in Italy, rather than go to England?' Abdul suggested hopefully.

'No. Come on,' Mo said, grabbing his friend's hand.

# Chapter Twenty-six

Endless numbers of white tourist coaches, passed them, taking their customers to visit the large number of well-preserved ancient buildings.

The boys struggled through several groups as they haemorrhaged out of their air-conditioned transport, blocking the pavement as if they owned it.

Each coach had a guide, who, pied piper-like, led a crocodile of people through the busy streets, holding an umbrella or small placard above their heads to ensure that their customers followed their lead.

Many of the tourists from Cruise liners wore badges to indicate what tour they were on, in case they got mixed up with other groups visiting the same property.

'This place is full of old buildings,' Abdul observed, as they fought their way through some ancient villages. 'Why would anyone want to go and see them? When you've seen one pile of old bricks, you've seen them all.'

'It's all to do with history,' Mo informed him.

'History? That's the past, it's gone. The future is more important,' Abdul countered.

'Some people like to imagine what it was like living all those years ago,' Mo added. 'After all, that's where we all came from, our forefathers.'

'Yeah, right,' Abdul said dismissively.

Although footsore, the continuing fine warm weather made walking comfortable for the pair, unlike the very high temperatures that they suffered walking through the deserts.

They slept many nights on empty beaches, under the stars, and a few nights in migrant hostels where they met fellow travellers and shared stories of their respective journeys.

They had decided earlier, during their own journey, that they wouldn't join up with anyone else, fearing possible problems.

As they travelled further north, the boys saw signs for the 'Giro d'Italia' and wondered what it was, until they saw more and more groups of people dressed in brightly coloured lycra on racing bikes.

'It must be a bike race around Italy,' Mo observed.

The pair were impressed with the cyclist's bright multicoloured tops emblazoned with sponsors names; although the names, Sky, Astana, Team Dimension, meant nothing to Mo and Abdul.

Each rider wore a helmet, stylish sunglasses, thigh length cycling shorts and fingerless gloves. All the high-tech bikes had water bottles caged on the frame.

But the pair had the opportunity to try their own cycling prowess when they discovered that one of the migrant hostels loaned bikes out to hikers and ramblers.

Although the boys hadn't ridden before, having seen the fun that the cyclists were having, Mo was keen to give it a go.

'Shall we see if we can borrow a bike?' Mo asked a foot weary Abdul.' We can get there twice as fast on one of those.'

'Anything that will help us get there quicker,' Abdul agreed.

The bikes that the boys subsequently borrowed, was a world, and several thousand dollars, away from the flashy bikes that they'd seen on route though.

The only loan rule was that they had to leave the bikes, after use, at a sister hostel. Most migrants complied with this honesty pledge.

A very kind hostel warden showed them the bits of the bike, explained about the rules of the road and the basic riding techniques. They were given helmets and the warden emphasised the importance of wearing them.

Kitted up with their helmets, the boys pushed the bikes out of the hostel and thanked the warden.

Mounting the bikes, they started off their riding experience by sitting on the saddle and just scooting the bikes along with their feet.

'This is great fun,' Mo said, moving along the pavement in a reasonably straight line.

'I'm having trouble handling it,' Abdul uttered, wobbling all over the place.

But, once they'd gained some balance and courage, they felt brave enough to try riding properly.

'Put your feet on the pedals,' Mo encouraged his friend.

'I'll try, Abdul said bravely. 'Hey, it's easier to ride, if you go faster,' he discovered.

Led by Mo, they increased their speed, until their legs wouldn't go any faster.

'What did the warden say about the gears?' Mo shouted.

'You've got to push that lever forward, I think,' Abdul announced.

'Yes, got it,' Mo confirmed, the cadence of his pedalling immediately changing. So he started pedalling faster and faster, flicking through the gears.

He felt that he was flying, until lycra clad riders passed them by going fast, which goaded the boys to increase their pace, too.

Unfortunately, they hadn't quite got the hang of using the brakes, and when approaching a sharp bend, Mo pulled on the front brake too harshly and found himself airborne.

In preventing his face from hitting the tarmac, he put his injured arm out to protect himself and had a sharp reminder of the fragility of the limb.

# Chapter Twenty-seven

'You Ok Mo?' an anguished Abdul asked, dropping his bike and going to the prostrate figure.

'Ouch, that really hurt,' Mo replied sitting up and holding his arm.

'Do you think it's broken?' the other enquired anxiously.

'No, I can still move it,' he said slowly standing. 'I think it's only jarred.'

'Just as well that you had a helmet on, otherwise it would have knocked some sense in to you.'

'Thanks for that,' Mo said, picking the bike up. 'Ouch. I don't think I'm going to be able to ride it to the hostel though.'

'I'll push it for you then,' Abdul suggested. 'Perhaps they will have a look at your arm to make sure that it is alright too.

'Yeah, I'm sure it will be fine though,' Mo said optimistically. Not wishing to have to delay their journey with an enforced stop.

Fortunately, the hostel staff agreed with the boy's diagnosis, so they decided to continue their pilgrimage on foot after all.

Each of the regions they travelled through offered so many different glimpses of the diversity that is Italy. Again they found the majority of Italians were charitable and the boys were never hungry or without shelter.

The pair travelled through busy tourist spots and circumnavigated historic buildings, including Monforte Castle and many Romanesque churches.

For some reason they were drawn to the sandy Adriatic Coast with its traditional wooden fishing piers too.

They marvelled at the majestic Apennine Mountains with its rich wildlife and trails to its rugged interior of ancient hilltop towns. Unlike home it seemed that there was lush foliage everywhere and endless acres of regimentally ordered vineyards.

Interspersed with the scenic beauty of the country the boys were amazed at the sheer spectrum of leisure activities including all manner of water sports, mountain-bike and horseback-riding trails.

Eventually they arrived in Rimini, four hundred and twenty miles from their Italian landfall in Brindisi and the state of their feet was starting to cause them some concern.

'Come on,' Mo directed. 'Let's keep going.'

'Oh do we have to?' Abdul moaned, holding his aching foot.

'Yes we do.'

'I just wanted to stay here a bit longer and rest my feet...and look at...'

'I know. At those girls.'

'Well, yes them too. What's wrong with that?'

'Nothing, but we've still got a long way to go.'

'Let's just have a rest in the marina before we start again.' Abdul persisted.

'It's only like all the other seaside places that we've walked through,' Mo pointed out.

'Anyway, I could do with cooling my feet off in the sea.' Abdul said rubbing his foot.

'Oh OK. It will be your last opportunity to paddle because we are now going inland to Turin and then to the French Border. So you can say goodbye to the sea,' Mo informed his companion.

# Chapter Twenty-eight

As they walked towards the marina, they passed a man delivering fish for a nearby restaurant, who stopped and acknowledged them.

'Ciao.'

'Ciao,' Mo responded, having picked up a few Italian phrases during the current phase of their journey.

'Excuse me guys, but I couldn't help overhearing your conversation. By the look of you, you're refugees. Yes?

'Yes,' Mo confirmed hesitantly, surprised that the driver was English.

'Where are you heading?' he asked.

'North to France.' Mo advised him.

'Well I'm not going that far, but I am going north to Asti to deliver some fish. So if it's any help and you want a lift. I'm sure I can cram you in the lorry.'

'Yes please,' the boys chorused.

Forgetting his wish for a last dip in the sea, Abdul followed Mo in clambering into the front seat of the refrigerated lorry.

'My name is Luigi,' he advised them, starting up the large delivery lorry.

'I'm Mohammed and this is Abdul. We're from Afghanistan,' Mo told him.

'How long have you been travelling?' Luigi asked.

'It seems like years,' Abdul said.

'I see you are wearing neckerchiefs around your necks,' the driver observed. 'Are you Scouts?'

'Yes,' Mo replied. 'These are very special ones. Our Scout Leader is a soldier and he got them for us.'

'Then you might be interested to know that there is an International Scout Camp at Parco Naturale di Stupinigi this week. I delivered some supplies to them a few days ago.'

'Where's that ?'

'It's near to Turin. At an 18th century hunting lodge and royal residence. The place has luxury apartments & grand gardens,' he explained. 'It's a beautiful place. The Scout camp is in the grounds.'

'Oh, yes that sounds like a good idea,' Mo said, enthusiastically.

'Unfortunately, I can't take you there. I finish in Asti. But it's not too far away. I'm sure if you can get there, you'll be made welcome,' the driver encouraged.

'Yes, we'll see if we can get in. It would be nice to see Scouts from other countries,' the boys agreed.

'On our way there, we travel by the famous motor racing circuit at Imola,' the driver informed them. 'That is where the great Formula one racing driver, Ayrton Senna, was killed in 1994.'

'I heard he was a brilliant driver,' Mo said.

'Yes he was,' Luigi confirmed. 'And to look at some of the drivers on these roads, you would think half of them are racing drivers too.' Luigi said, planting his hand on his horn and gesticulating at a car that cut in front of him.

Where are we going next?' Abdul asked, white knuckled at the manic driving of the other road users.

'From here we go to Bologna, Modena, Parma, and then Asti. It won't take too long now.'

'Excuse me for asking, but if you are Italian, why do you speak like an English person?' Mo asked.

'I was brought up in England, went to school there and come back to lovely Italy from time to time. This job helps me pay for my stay here. I could ask you the same about your English,' Luigi said.

'Lots of soldiers in our country,' Abdul explained. 'We've picked it up from them.'

To break the journey, Luigi stopped several times at roadside cafes en-route and the boys scraped together enough money to buy some snacks and a drink.

Eventually, they arrived safely in Asti and thanked Luigi for helping to cut out another two hundred and fifty miles off their journey.

*'In bocca al lupo,'* my friends. It literally means, go into the wolf's mouth or Good Luck in English,' he said waving them off.

'I'm glad that's over,' Abdul admitted. 'I thought we were going to crash several times.'

# Chapter Twenty-nine

'What do you reckon about going to that International Scout camp then?' Mo asked his travel companion.

'Where did he say it was?'

'I think he said it was just outside Turin at a place called Parco Naturale di Stupinigi.'

'Let's give it a try,' Abdul agreed.

'I wonder if they can help us to go further on our journey,' Mo said, hopefully.

'How far is it to the camp site?' Abdul asked cautiously.

'About thirty miles, that's all.'

'Oh that will take us all day,' Abdul moaned

'No it won't. We'll be there in no time,' Mo said, encouragingly.

'Look there's a Scout badge on that road sign. I wonder if it's the signs to the  Scout camp?' Abdul pondered.

The pair followed a series of signs over a few miles, until it got to the main road. We can't walk along there, we'll have to find some minor roads.

'Does that mean it will be longer?' Abdul questioned.

'Probably. But we're going in the right direction.' Mo tried to sound encouraging but despite the trip in the lorry he was himself starting to feel exhausted.

'Come on Mo, let's just stop here for a bit. My feet are really sore. I could do with a rest.' Abdul complained.

Reluctantly Mo agreed and they sat down on the grass verge.

'Thank you,' Abdul said, removing his trainers and massaging his feet.

After a short break, the pair made their way painfully slowly along the minor roads. Several hours later they came to a collection of large stately buildings. The Parco Naturale di Stupinigi. The magnificent buildings were set within a massive roundabout surrounded by a large manicured lawn.

The layout reminded Mo of the hub of a gigantic wheel with the mansions situated in the centre and a roundel of buildings around the perimeter road, like tyres on a bicycle.

'Wow, look at that lot.' Abdul said, forgetting his aching feet and admiring the beautiful architecture. 'Do you think the Scout Camp is in one of those buildings?'

'No. It will be somewhere on the estate.' Mo said, looking for direction signs.

'Oh there's one over there,' Abdul observed, pointing at a similar logo to the ones they had been following.

Finally they came across a large encampment of tents and marquees, a huge banner spanning the track confirmed that it was indeed an International Scout Camp.

'Yes, at last. That must be it,' Abdul said, relieved that their long trek was hopefully over.

'There are lots of cars and minibuses with Scout badges on the sides. This must be it,' Mo confirmed.

The boys walked up to a security barrier blocking the track. It was manned by three people in black tee shirts.

The word 'Security' and a camp logo emblazoned on their shirts seemed to indicate their jobs.

'Hi, is this the International Scout campsite?' Mo asked unnecessarily.

'Dhur! Yes, obviously,' came the terse response.

'Do you think we could come in and have a look around please?' Mo continued.

'Sorry we can't let you in. You need a special pass.'

'But we are Scouts. We are from Afghanistan,' Mo informed them.

'Afghanistan eh? How do we know you are Scouts?' the tall security man said, looking at their dishevelled state.

'We have our neckerchiefs,' Abdul said meekly, holding it up. And...err we know the scout promise.'

The security trio looked at them suspiciously and at each other wondering what to do. Then after a few minutes one of them said, 'I'll call our Camp Leader and see if he will let you on to the site for a short time.'

'OK. Thanks.'

The security man picked up his radio and called. *'David from Security.*

After a few minutes, he got a crackly response.

*'Yeah go ahead, over.'*

*'We have some guys here claiming to be Scouts from Afghanistan, can we let them on the site for a quick visit.'*

*'Are you sure they're Scouts?'*

*'Yes, they seem genuine.'*

*'OK, I'll pop down and see them.'*

The boys waited anxiously for the organisers arrival, all forms of negative thoughts going through their minds.

# Chapter Thirty

After ten minutes, David duly arrived in a land rover. Like the security team, he was wearing shorts, but his tee shirt was red and had the word 'Organiser' in white lettering over the top of the badge.

The organiser listened, as Mo explained about their pilgrimage and their ongoing plans to get to France.

Satisfied that they were genuine, he introduced himself.

'As you can see from my name badge, I am David. What are your names?'

'Mohammed'

'Abdul'

'Pleased to meet you both. Welcome to the camp.'

A left handshake with them both 'sealed the deal'.

'Climb in,' he invited, opening the backdoor.

The boys duly climbed into the back of the land rover and David pulled away.

'Afghanistan eh? We don't have anyone from your country here. So that will be another feather in our international friendship cap. Most of the countries represented here are European,' he informed them.

'You can have a look around the site, by all means. Join in where you want. We can also give you some food and put you up overnight. How's that?'

'Great, thanks', Mo said feeling able to relax at last.

'Then tomorrow or when you're ready to leave, we can help you to get close to the border by transporting you to Bardonecchia. But we can't condone illegal movement of migrants by taking you into France, irrespective of the Scout bond. Sorry.'

'That's OK. It sounds great, thank you.' Mo said, overwhelmed already by his generosity.

As they drove further on to the site, Abdul was in awe. 'Look, there's hundreds of little green tents and so many people here.'

'Yes, we have about four thousand young people on the camp,' David informed them.

'What are the larger white tents?'

'You mean the marquees? They are for the team of adults who are running everything on the camp.'

'Is that a stage?' Mo asked, surprised to see a huge great platform in the middle of the field.

'Yes, they will be performing on there tonight. You must come and see the show, it's really good.'

'Wow,' Abdul said, overwhelmed by the sheer scale of it all.

'Right. I will take you to the Admin tent and get you a wrist-band so that you can have some food and you won't be challenged by security.'

'Thanks.'

Mo and Abdul got out of the vehicle and followed David into one of the marquees passing a big wooden sign bearing the word 'ADMIN' on it .

Quickly he signed them in with one of the Admin team.

'This is Mohammed, and this is Abdul,' he said introducing them. Put their Scout group down as Afghanistan.'

'Here's your coloured wrist band. You must wear it all the times that you're on camp, ok?'

'Yes,' they said, clipping the bands on.

'I'll take you to your tent where you can leave your stuff, is that OK?'

'Yes.'

'Incidentally if you want a shower, they are over there, in the large portable green trailers.'

'Ok.'

'Feel free to wander around and have a go on anything. There are instructors who will fit you with the appropriate safety gear.'

'What a lot of activities,' Abdul added, as he continued in his wide-eyed assessment of the camp.

'There are some water activities off site too,' David informed them.

'I think we'll give those a miss,' Mo said quickly, as recollections of the sinking dinghy flooded back in to his memory.

'No thanks,' Abdul concurred.

'We had a disaster when our boat sank on our way to Greece,' Mo explained.

'I can understand that might have put you off. But you would be perfectly safe here with life jackets and instructors monitoring you all the time.'

'We'll have a look around here instead,' Mo decided.

'Right. I've got a few things to get organised. Hopefully I will bump into you later, if not, have a safe onward journey and enjoy yourselves while you're here.'

And with a final left handshake, David disappeared into the crowd.

Mo and Abdul made straight for the food tent and they consumed several plates of pasta before indulging in a bowl or two of ice cream.

They ignored the showers and went straight to the activity centre where they joined the others using a zip line that cut across the site. They took part in archery and air rifle shooting, where they topped the result sheets. They soon got the technique for trampolining too.

During the evening, they joined the vast crowd of Scouts watching the acts on stage and added their voice to some of the songs that the Sergeant had taught them. They made several friends as they followed the activities on stage.

The boys went to bed very happy and despite the late-night chatter of other excited campers, they slept soundly.

# Chapter Thirty-one

In the morning they joined the queue for breakfast.

"Did you have a good time yesterday? David said, spotting them in the queue.

'Brilliant. I wish we could stay, but we need to carry on,' Mo said positively.

'Oh! do we have to?' Abdul said. 'Can't we stay just one more day?'

'No. We need to get on with our journey, otherwise we will be tempted to give up.' Mo insisted.

''I should put a few rolls and pieces of fruit in your rucksack for your journey, if I was you,' David encouraged. 'When you're ready to leave, pop over to the Admin tent and come and see me and I'll arrange some transport for you.'

'Thanks.'

After several helpings of cereals and croissants, the boys made their way to the Admin tent and tracked David down.

'We're ready to go now, 'Mo confirmed, much to Abdul's disgust.

'It was a pleasure to meet you both. Best of luck with the rest of your mammoth journey. I hope you get there without too many challenges along the way,' David said, shaking their hands.' Oh, by the way, would you like a special international camp neckerchief?'

'Yes please.'

'And you'll need a special woggle too,' David said, giving each one a scarf with a special badge on the back.

'Thank you, so much,' Mo said, proudly putting the neckerchief on. Completely overwhelmed and amazed at his kindness and generosity, Mo filled up.

After collecting their things from their tent, the boys were taken down to the carpark and, as promised, a minibus took them to Bardonecchia.

During the relatively short drive, the driver, knowing of their plans, gave them a pessimistic perspective of their planned alpine trip.

'You know that people are trying this crossing at all times of the year. Winter snows don't deter them from continuing to attempt the hazardous crossing.

Many of them are ill equipped for the harsh conditions. Some had never seen snow before and didn't understand the consequences of being so ill prepared, until it was too late. They suffered badly from frostbite.'

'I don't think we'll have that trouble with this heat,' Mo said optimistically.

'No. I suppose you'll have quite the opposite, but it does get cold the higher you go. Have you got enough water?'

'Yes thanks. David gave us several bottles each.'

'Well, good luck my friends,' the driver said. 'Keep an eye out for the French Border guards. They make regular patrols along the road to prevent any unauthorised entry.'

'What happens if we're caught?' Abdul asked, apprehensively.

'Refugees who get caught are rounded up and quickly returned to their starting point back here.'

'Oh, is that all that happens?' Mo queried.

'Yes. But the incident doesn't appear to put them off though. The same people make other attempts on a later occasion.'

'We hope we don't have that problem,' Mo said unconvincingly.

'Hope you make it,' he added, driving off.

# Chapter Thirty-two

Now, after their long journey through Italy, they had arrived at last on the border, at the place where Geoff, their friend from the Catamaran, had recommended to cross into France.

Here the border lay on a pass high in the mountains. A steep meandering road which led to the Col de L'Echelle and involved a 16-kilometre trek.

Although it had been only a short break at the Scout camp, the pair felt rested. The mountains ahead of them looked daunting but they felt ready to attempt crossing the Alps to get to France.

Finally, they left the village and started the ascent of the foothills, proudly wearing their special commemorative neckerchief with the international scout badge on it.

'So where do we go from here,' Abdul asked, already starting to puff from the increasing incline.

'Once we are in France, we will go west to Grenoble and then north west to Calais.' Mo explained, panting.

'How long will that take us?' Abdul asked, not really wanting to know the answer.

'It's about another 1,000 km and If we have to walk it all the way...at about five kilometres per hour... about

30 days. Including rest stops. We could do it quicker if we walked longer each day though,' Mo added.

'My legs are getting shorter with all this walking. Soon I shall have worn my legs away and I won't have any left,' Abdul moaned.

Mo laughed at his mental image of Abdul waddling along with just a pair of feet sticking out from his waist.

'Do you reckon that driver, was just trying to scare us about people suffering from frostbite and losing limbs and fingers? Abdul asked, concerned.

'Yes, of course he was,' Mo confirmed.

'Just imagine doing it in the winter though, when there is snow on the ground,' Abdul continued, shuddering at the thought.

'Just ignore what he said,' Mo said, dismissively.

'He reckoned that there were so many trying the crossing, that the local authorities had converted a little room at the station into a dormitory, for rescued refugees... and they even staffed it with a volunteer medic too,' Abdul added.

'Just forget it. At least we have some fine weather to do our climb, and we can appreciate how lovely the scenery is too,' Mo counselled.

As they plodded up the steep tarmacked road leading away from the village, they kept their ears open for any vehicles.

Geoff's warning about the Border Police patrolling the road kept them on edge, consequently, their progress was slowed as they kept leaping off the road and hiding in the bushes at the sound of any approaching engine.

Fortunately none of the vehicles was a Border guard vehicle.

After a few nervous and tiring hours, they arrived at a marker stone on the side of the road.

Walking a few paces ahead of Abdul, Mo looked back towards his friend.

'I think we have just entered France,' he said, excitedly. 'Here look. 'F' for France on this side and there is a definite change in the texture of the road surface too.'

'And 'I' for Italy on this side,' Abdul observed, touching the cold granite pillar.

'We've made it to France.' The boys squealed in delight and hugged each other. 'We've made it to France,' Mo repeated, absorbing the enormity of their achievement. 'That's another goal achieved,' he blurted.

As they continued their pilgrimage along the narrow meandering mountain road, the pair marvelled at their surroundings, 'It is so lovely, everything is so green.'

'Not like our home at all is it?' Abdul added.' And I thought Italy was lovely. It just gets better and better.'

Eventually the road levelled off and a few kilometres further on they came to a sign which indicated that they were at the 'Col de L'Echelle 1762 m'.

'This must be the top of the pass,' Abdul said, breathlessly leaning against the sign.

'It's obviously a popular spot. Look, there's even a big car park over there.' Mo observed, cautiously looking for any official looking vehicles.

'Look at the rugged mountain tops. I'm glad we don't have to go up there,' Abdul declared.

'Who said we don't?' Mo challenged.

'Oh no. We don't have to, do we?' Abdul demanded, helplessly. 'I don't think I could. You'd better leave me here,' he continued, slumping to his knees.

'No, you're right...fooled you,' Mo giggled, gently pushing Abdul over.

'You! I'll get you for that,' Abdul said, chasing after him.

The euphoria of their achievement wore off after a short bout of chasing each other.

It was while they were catching their breath, after their game of chase, when a car drew silently alongside them.

# Chapter Thirty-three

Mo suddenly realised that the car was there, and in a panic, was just about to grab Abdul and run, when he realised that it was not a Border force car.

The car was a white Mercedes E class saloon driven by an Asian looking woman. The driver had short black hair, she was wearing shorts and wore a tee shirt with a picture of a military jet across the front..

'Excuse me, do you speak English?' she asked.

Mo nodded, wondering what she wanted, fearful that she was a border official after all'

'We were parked in the car park and I noticed that you appeared to be on foot,' she said, removing her stylish sunglasses. The woman had an American accent.

'Yes, we walked up from Bardonecchia in Italy,' he replied.

'My, that's a bit of a haul. Do you want a lift?' she asked

Immediately the boys were suspicious of her offer, said nothing, but just stared at her.

'I said, do you want a lift?' she repeated, after a pregnant pause, while Mo and Abdul waited for each other to answer.

'Well...errr,' Abdul stuttered.

'Well do you, or don't you?' the lady repeated. 'Don't worry. I'm not an official, just a tourist, like you?' she reassured them.

'Um...that would be very kind of you.' Mo said, finding his tongue.

'Where you heading?'

'We are going to Grenoble. But you can drop us anywhere nearby,' Mo replied.

'Well, this is your lucky day. My hotel is in Grenoble and I am on my way back there now. We've had enough of sightseeing for today. But it is lovely here, is it not?' she added, looking at the snow-covered peaks high above.

'Yes, it is. Really beautiful. Nice and green, not like home.' Abdul declared.

'You're obviously not from around here. So where is home for you?' she asked.

'We are from Afghanistan.' Abdul explained, and got a dig in the ribs from Mo as a result. 'What?' he mouthed to his companion.

'She might be a Policeperson,' he whispered, as they opened the back-passenger door and clambered in.

'This is my son, Tyrone,' indicating a tall, heavily built African American young man sitting beside her. 'We are celebrating his 18th birthday,' the woman volunteered, 'with a tour of France and Italy.

The boy nodded in greeting. 'Hi guys,' he said.

'My name is Kim,' the woman informed them. 'And you are?'

'I'm Mohammed and this is Abdul,' Mo replied.

'The reason that I stopped was because I guessed, from your neckerchiefs that you were Scouts,' Kim said.'

'Yes, that's right,' Mo confirmed.

'Tyrone used to be in the Boy Scouts of America,' she continued.

'Yeah, I had some good times,' Tyrone confirmed.

'I guess you are refugees?' the woman observed.

'Y...yes,' Abdul said cagily, waiting for another dig from Mo.

'How old are you?' she enquired.

'Fourteen, maybe fifteen, we think,' Mo informed her. 'We don't really celebrate birthdays.'

'You are so young to be making such a journey. You have come a very long way,' she observed. 'I too was a refugee once. I am originally from Vietnam, so I know how you must feel leaving your home and your families.'

'We don't have any families,' Mo revealed. 'We are both orphans.'

'Oh, that's dreadful. You poor things. No wonder you are seeking a different life.'

'A better life, we hope,' Mo suggested.

As they pulled away from the car park, a French border patrol vehicle drove by, in the direction of their escape route from Italy.

'That was close,' Mo observed, swivelling around and watching the vehicle disappear down the road.

'Do you think they were looking for you?' the woman asked, looking in the rear-view mirror.

'No, I don't think so. We haven't seen anyone on the road since we left the village several hours ago.'

'Are they stopping suspects?'

'Yes...and taking them back to Italy too.'

During the long ride to Grenoble the boys dozed off in the back seat, relieved that they didn't have to walk anymore that day.

# Chapter Thirty-four

The boys awoke as the car engine was switched off. They were parked underneath a building, which they soon realised was an underground carpark of a hotel.

'Thank you very much for the lift,' Mo said gratefully. 'You have saved us a lot of walking.'

'Where are you aiming for? What is the end of your pilgrimage?' Kim asked.

'England,' the boys chorused. 'We are going to go to Calais to get a ferry to England.'

'Well I can't take you there, but I can get you a bit nearer. I have to take the car back to the airport tomorrow,' she advised them.

'Where's that? 'Mo asked.

'Charles de Gaulle airport. It is just north of Paris. Closer to Calais than we are here. Do you want another lift?'

'Oh yes please.' they said, not believing their luck.

'That will take another large 'chunk' out of your journey,' she confirmed. 'I will meet you here, in the car park tomorrow morning. If you are not here, I will assume something has happened and we will leave without you. OK?'

'OK. What time should we be here?'

'Shall we say…Zero seven thirty hours?'

'We don't have a watch. But we will make sure that we are here at that time,' Mo confirmed.

'Look. I assume you haven't got a lot of money?' Kim suggested.

'No unfortunately not. The trip from Greece to Italy cost us most of our money,' Mo volunteered.

'Why don't you go and have a MacDonald's meal with Tyrone? I will pay.'

The boy's eyes lit up. 'Wow, thank you,' they chorused.

'I believe there is a Mac just around the corner. That will give me the chance to pack our suitcases without Tyrone moping around me.'

'Mum! I'm not that bad,' her son replied, defensively.

The woman dug in to her purse and gave Tyrone a fifty euro note. 'Here, that should be enough for three meals,' she said.

The boys shouldered their rucksacks and followed the eighteen-year-old to the fast food place a few streets away.

'This should be great,' Mo said excitedly. 'I've never been to a McDonalds before.'

'No neither have I,' Abdul concurred, his mouth already salivating on the prospect.

'You guys don't know what you've been missing. I have one or two twice a week,' Tyrone informed them. 'Do you want to eat in or out?' he asked.

'We have seen enough of the outside world. Can we eat inside?' Mo asked, drooling, his gastric juices stirring at the thought of the meal.

'Yes of course.'

Tyrone took charge of putting the order in to the electronic machine and requested a large burger with fries and a coke for each of them.

Within a few moments their meal was ready and the boys took them to a table near the front window.

'Transport and a meal. How lucky are we?' Mo thought.

'So, what made you leave home?' Tyrone asked.

'War. We have both lost our parents to suicide bombers. There is nothing there for us. Mo explained, unemotionally.

'Jeez!' Tyrone exclaimed. 'No wonder you want to get out of that shit. I don't know what I'd do if I lost Mom.'

'We were afraid that soon it would be our time to be killed,' Mo said, dramatically.

'So, we left and hope to start a new and safer life in England.' Abdul said, through a mouthful of burger.

'I want to find a soldier that helped dig me out the ruins of my house after it was blown up,' Mo added.

'Don't forget his dog,' Abdul reminded him.

'Oh yes. She is a lovely dog, called Jersey, who found me in the debris. I was in hospital for several weeks and the soldier came to visit me every day. He said he would like to adopt me. That's why I want to go to England to find him.' Mo added.

'That's a great story,' Tyrone admitted.

# Chapter Thirty-five

Just as they were tucking in to their burger meal, a noisy demonstration of nationalist protesters, carrying French flags and racist banners, paraded along the road in front of the restaurant.

A small splinter group of aggressive young men broke away from the main protest and walked along in front of the line of shops and businesses.

When they saw Tyrone and the two Afghan boys inside, they started banging on the window and hurling racist abuse at them.

'Just ignore them,' Tyrone advised. 'They are idiots. Right wing thugs, that's all. They call themselves Nationalists.'

However, as he finished speaking, a large rock hit the window and it dissolved in a cascade of glass shards. Fortunately, none of the boys was hit.

'Don't worry guys, I'll protect you,' Tyrone said, standing. His six foot six and eighteen stone frame dwarfing Mo and Abdul.

'Shall we move to the back of the restaurant?' Abdul suggested.

'Good idea,' Tyrone agreed.

As they moved to the back of the restaurant, the Manager came in to see what was going on. Outside, the troublemakers were emboldened by the smashed window and were getting more and more aggressive and vocal.

'Quick, phone the Police,' he instructed his staff, as he surveyed the damaged window.

Fortunately, a Police vehicle that had been monitoring the protest march, quickly dispensed a squad of police, fully kitted out in riot gear. This was enough to cause the troublemakers to leave. As they did so a Policemen came into the restaurant to assess the damage.

'We need to leave,' Mo whispered.

'Why?' Tyrone asked.

'Our papers are not correct.' If they want to see them. We will be sent back to Greece.'

As the Policeman was talking to the Manager, the group grabbed their burgers and drinks and slipped out of the front door, running off into the darkness away from the departing protesters.

A member of staff told the Policeman that the boy's presence had been the catalyst for the incident, and he raced outside and shouted for them to stop.

Ignoring the Policeman's orders, the boys ran as fast as they could, hoping that they wouldn't run into the group of protesters again.

After running for ten minutes, Tyrone ground to a halt.

'Sorry guys, I can't run any more,' he panted, breathlessly.

'I think we've got clear enough of the Police,' Mo gasped.

'Let's hope we don't run into those idiot thugs,' Abdul said, nervously looking around.

They stopped near a park and breathlessly assessed their options.

'Why are we running? We didn't do anything wrong,' Abdul queried.

'We could be sent back to Greece,' Mo repeated. 'We haven't got the right papers, remember.'

'If you guys are OK to be left alone, I think we need to split up,' Tyrone said. I can see that we are near the hotel, I think that's the back entrance.'

'Well...' Abdul started to say, but Mo cut him off. 'Yes, we'll be fine,' Mo said bravely.

'Right, I'll leave you and hopefully see you in the morning.'

'Ok. we'll hide in the bushes and see you then.'

'Best of luck.' Tyrone said, quickly melting into the darkness.

Mo and Abdul found a large hedge and climbed inside making sure nobody could see them.

They ate their burgers in silence. Their fear dried mouths didn't help their digestion, especially when a group of noisy teenagers, from the Nationalist protest, came and sat on a nearby bench, drinking.

As the night progressed and the alcohol kicked in, the protesters got louder and louder. Several of them came and urinated into the hedge, fortunately they were far enough away to miss the boys.

# Chapter Thirty-six

Eventually the noisy teenagers left the park in the early hours, and after their tense and sleepless night in the hedge, the boys crept out of their hide and made their way back to the hotel.

Fortunately the hotel had a digital clock on the front of the building, and they were relieved to see they were ahead of time.

'Well at least, we're in time, that's a relief,' Mo said.

'Yes but look there,' Abdul said, pointing at a Policeman standing by his car and two others near the entrance of the underground car park..

'What do we do?' Abdul asked, standing behind Mo, as if to hide.

'I don't know. Kim said they would leave with or without us,' Mo reminded him.

'We have half an hour to get to the car, but how?' Abdul puzzled.

'Perhaps we should forget the lift and carry on walking,' Mo suggested.

'No way,' Abdul protested. 'I've had enough of walking.'

'The trouble is, the Police might now be looking for us too,' Mo suggested.

'Do you think so?'

'Well we ran away from the Policeman last night didn't we?'

'Yes. But I still think our best bet is to get a lift, somehow,' Abdul said hopefully.

'Well I suppose we could wait here and perhaps the Police might go before Kim leaves.' Mo suggested

But they were to be disappointed. The Policemen showed no intention of leaving their post.

Through the maze of concrete pillars, the boys could see the back entrance of the hotel and saw Kim and Tyrone carrying suitcases to the car.

After a second visit to the hotel back door they climbed into the car before starting the engine. The vehicle remained stationary for a few more minutes.

'They're obviously waiting for us,' Mo suggested.

Finally, the Mercedes moved off and drove out of the car park on to the road.

'What do we do, what do we do?' said Abdul panicking. 'That's it, she's gone.'

'Look, I reckon that the road comes around here. She has to come this way,' Mo said, hoping he assessed the situation correctly. 'It's a one-way street. Get ready to run.'

Sure enough, the Mercedes glided into view in the middle of a line of traffic. Mo and Abdul stood up and ran to the kerbside. Kim spotted them and suddenly pulled over, much to the annoyance of the car behind, who leant on his horn.

The boys quickly got in and the woman pulled back into the traffic.

'We couldn't get to the carpark. There was a Police Patrol outside.' Mo explained.

'Yes, I know. There was a big Nationalist dignitary staying at the hotel and there were lots of protesters surrounding it. Are you both ok? Tyrone told me about your disturbed meal.'

'Yes. We are fine thank you. 'Mo informed her.

'Although we didn't sleep much because of it,' Abdul chipped in.

'We've brought you some breakfast though. Croissants and fruit,' Tyrone said, offering them the paper plates that he retrieved from the floor in-between his feet.

'Wow, thank you,' Mo said, taking the plates.

Mo and Abdul quickly demolished the food.

'That was the best breakfast we've had,' Mo revealed.

'That's because we don't normally have anything, that's why,' Abdul clarified; which attracted a dig in the ribs from Mo for his apparent ingratitude.

# Chapter Thirty-seven

How long will it take us to get to the airport?' Abdul wondered.

'Five to six hours I expect, depending on traffic, of course. It is about 600 kilometres.'

During the long journey, the boys found out that Tyrone was at a college in California and in the college football team as a 'line backer'.

'We play football, but never heard of that position,' Mo confessed.

'No, because you and the Brits play soccer, not football. We are talking about a different, very hard, sport. Not like that soft soccer stuff, with all that diving and pretending to be hurt.' Tyrone said, haughtily.

'What's a line-backer?' Abdul asked.

'Line-backers are members of the defensive team, and line up behind the defensive linemen, and therefore "back up the line",' Tyrone informed them.

'Anyway, football... soccer, is worldwide,' Mo argued. 'Manchester United is my team and when I get to England, I'm going to see them play.'

'Time out boys. Nobody will win that argument,' the woman said calmly. 'Both sports have their merits and their place in the world. Like everything else.'

'Where are you flying to?' Mo asked.

'California, in the US of A.' Kim informed him.

'What do you do?' Abdul wondered.

'I'm in the United States Air force,' the woman replied.

'Yeah, Mom is a pilot. She flies...'Tyrone started to reveal.

'Hush Tyrone. Remember what I said.'

'Oh Mom. These guys are hardly going to tell anyone.'

Mo and Abdul were now intrigued.

'No. We won't tell,' Abdul said, eagerly.

'Well Mom is better at computer games than I am,' the boy said, smiling. Showing a clear respect of her skills.

'I have never played a computer game,' Mo volunteered.

'Never! You got to be kidding me,' Tyrone exclaimed.

'Not everybody in the world has the same opportunities that you take for granted Tyrone,' his Mother observed.

'Yeah Ok, I get it,' Tyrone continued. 'Well you have this lever, it's called a joystick...right?'

'Joystick?' Mo repeated.

'Yeah and you can control things with it... It's a bit like a steering wheel on a car and you can guide things around using it.'

'Oh, I see,' Abdul said, not really grasping the explanation. 'What sort of things?'

'Really big things. Only Mom can guide things a long way away...'

'Hush, Tyrone,' the woman said firmly.

'Have you heard of a drone?'

'Yes, there are lots flying in Afghanistan,' Mo confirmed.

'Tyrone, that is enough now.'

Mo and Abdul were fascinated. A woman being allowed to be a pilot! And was he suggesting flying a drone too?

'I have to tell you of a strange coincidence then. Just before we left Afghanistan, we...we were kidnapped by the Taliban...'Mo revealed.

'Wow, scary shit,' Tyrone interrupted.

'And we escaped during an air raid. We think it was done by a drone firing missiles. We were asleep and woken up by massive explosions. Then there was a big firefight.'

'Holy cow,' Tyrone continued.

'Perhaps that could have been you flying that drone,' Abdul added, looking at the back of the woman's head.

'If it was you. You saved our lives,' Mo concluded, gratefully.

'Now, that really would be scary shit,' Tyrone repeated.

'Tyrone, there is no need for using that language,' she scolded.

'Sorry Mom, but heh. That's a hell of a coincidence isn't it?'

'The chances that it could have been me are slim,' she said, downplaying the incident. 'There are a lot of pilots working all around the clock.'

However, she felt sure that it was her handiwork, as she remembered the details of her briefing before the mission.

Suddenly she felt a surge of happiness. Here was living proof of a positive outcome to her remote and sanitised warfare.

'But you might have been our liberator that allowed us to escape the camp. I don't know what to say,' Mo persisted, filling up.

'Look it might or might not have been me. Who can tell? What is important is that you take the opportunity given to you with your freedom. Now you have the chance to make your dreams come true,' Kim counselled.

'Yes we intend to,' Mo said, smiling at Abdul.

'I was lucky to escape the restrictions in Vietnam and to become an American Citizen. I followed my dream and had the opportunity to fly. When you get to England, or wherever you go, just seize any breaks that life throws at you,' she continued.

'Thank you. I..., I mean, we will,' Mo said feeling good about his decision to make the marathon trip.

'Just be the person that you can be. Anyway, lecture over. We're nearly there now,' she concluded.

The refugees smiled at each other. This was what they wanted to hear. A new life with lots of opportunities.

The woman dropped them off north of the airport away from the crowds and they exchanged a hug with her and Tyrone.

'Are you going to fly the plane home? Abdul asked, innocently.

'No. I'm going to be just a regular passenger like everybody else,' she smiled.

'Don't forget what I said. You can be what you want to be,' she reminded them, climbing back into the car.

'Hope you enjoy watching your Manchester United soccer team,' Tyrone added. 'Best of luck.'

'Thanks,' Mo said, feeling sad, that they were saying goodbye, yet again, to someone whom they had grown to like.

Mo and Abdul waved to the departing car and felt a million dollars. Not only had they had a boost to their morale, but they'd also cut a large distance out of their pilgrimage.

'Only 280 kilometres to go now,' Mo said, starting the final leg of their journey.

# PART THREE

## The Jungle

# Chapter Thirty-eight

Despite their aching feet, their excitement at nearing their goal of Calais, buoyed their spirits and imperceptibly increased their pace.

As they walked along the side of the D943, they were conscious of the constant roar of the traffic on the parallel A26, busy with vehicles heading to and from the vibrant port. The cacophony of noise, seemed to beckon them in. An incantation of journeys end.

Soon their long walk through the countryside, past the agriculturally rich fields, filled with ripening crops ended. The small quaint villages which had punctuated their journey were replaced by the city's main habitation. Rows of red roofed houses and large industrial units now became their backdrop.

Before they got too far into Calais town however, they were shepherded away from following the signs for the port by the Police, and were told to follow a series of signs indicating the migrant camp.

Self-consciously, they followed a crocodile line of others who seemed to know where they were going. Uncomfortable that their solo journey was now joining with strangers, all of whom were making the same pilgrimage.

As they got closer to the camp there were more and more groups of refugees aimlessly hanging around street corners. They stared at the boys as they passed.

Mo and Abdul were starting to feel uncomfortable about the situation. This wasn't the mecca that they were expecting to find.

'I don't like this,' Abdul whispered. 'Can we go back to Italy?'

'No. We're nearly there now. Be patient,' Mo said, trying to control his own fears.

Eventually, the tired pair came to a large muddy encampment of huts and tents. There were more groups of people just hanging around here too. Litter carpeted the muddy entrance.

Naively they had expected only a few fellow migrants, and the awful truth of seeing large numbers here, confirmed their worst nightmare, that Calais was a roadblock on their dreams.

Bewildered, they wandered around in a confused state. There didn't appear to be any signs or instructions to let them know what to do.

Frightened by the intimidating squalor, the boys didn't want to engage with any of the men eyeing them suspiciously either.

Suddenly a man sauntered up to the pair.

'You new here?' he said coldly.

'Y…Yes,' Mo volunteered, hesitantly.

'You have something for me,' the tall, hoody wearing Eritrean said.

'No. We haven't,' Mo said clutching his rucksack closer to himself.

'Wrong answer. I said, you HAVE something for me,' the African said menacingly, reaching to grab Mo's neckerchief.

Just then a tabard wearing young lady came over and stood between them and the tall thug. 'Come this way boys,' she instructed. 'You need to be processed.'

As the boys followed the woman to a shabby looking hut containing a table and three chairs, the African did a cut-throat gesture to them.

'I don't like it here,' Abdul said fearfully.

'Don't worry about him, he's just a bully,' the woman said, comfortingly. 'You will get a lot of that around here I'm afraid. But just ignore it,' she advised. 'My name is Nicole. I am one of the administrators for the camp.

Would you mind giving me your names, ages and your homeland please?'

'Why do you want to know? Are you going to send us back?' Abdul wondered.

'No. It's so that we can keep an eye on you while you're here,' she reassured him.

'Ok,' Mo said quietly. 'Thank you. Sorry, I'm a bit confused. We have come a long way and we are very tired. This is not at all what I thought it was going to be like.'

'Don't worry. We will make sure that you don't come to any harm,' she promised, more in hope than in reality. 'If you are the right age, you might be entitled to some special arrangements too,' she continued.

The boys duly gave her the relevant information required to be 'processed'.

'Now. How long ago did you have something to eat or drink?'

'I don't know, we haven't got a watch. Probably six hours ago on the outskirts of Calais. Someone kindly gave us a bread roll and a drink.'

'Right. Here is a small box of food for now,' she said, handing over a small sealed box '

'Thank you.'

'You will find that there are several other areas, scattered around the camp, where you can get more food later. You will need to show them this bracelet,' she said crimping a plastic tag on both of their wrists.'

Although they were ravenously hungry, the pair resisted the temptation to tear the box open and consume the contents there and then.

'You must be exhausted after your long journey. Do you have any medical needs; blisters, cuts etc?' she asked.

'No, But I think I have worn my trainers out,' Abdul said, looking at the bottom of his footwear.'

'Ok, we'll see what we can do to replace them.'

'Thanks.'

'Now because of your age, and although you have done a man-sized journey, you are still children, minors, in the eyes of the law. We will therefore house you in one of the shipping containers that have been converted into accommodation.'

'Thank you.'

'I'm afraid you will have to share it with other children though.

'That's OK,' Mo said, looking at Abdul for confirmation.

'Here is a blanket each for you,' she said, handing them some shabby looking woollen blankets. 'You've probably realised that it is a lot cooler up here in Europe than from where you've come from. So, keep warm.'

'How long can we stay here?' Mo asked, tentatively.

'I think that I know what your intentions are,' she said smiling. 'Let's just say until you need them. Is that OK?'

'Yes, thank you for your kindness,' Mo said, gratefully.

The woman led them through groups of young men, who stopped chatting and watched as the three passed by.

She took them to a long line of white painted, shipping containers that had been converted for habitation, and re-checked her paperwork.

'This is the one. Number 88,' Nicole advised them. 'You will find bunk beds inside. Now, unfortunately, because we are overcrowded, I'm afraid you will have to share one bunk for both of you. Yours is nine lower.'

'Ok, thank you,' Abdul said, tentatively looking inside the container.

There was no-one inside. Against the far wall there was a line of ten wooden double tier bunks.

Bags and suitcases of different sizes and contents were scattered all around the floor and on the deserted beds.

At one end of the container there was a small grimy washbasin. A small wet patch on the floor underneath it, indicated its poor maintenance.

Abdul stepped hastily back out of the container, for despite his own body odour, there was a pungent smell of unwashed bodies pervading it, that made him hold his nose.

Picking up on Abdul's reaction, Nicole said, 'Sorry about the smell. You'll soon get used to it. If you want anything, come to the hut and see me or one of my colleagues.'

'Thanks,' Mo managed to say, still in shock. The realism of what they'd entered was devastating. He felt fear gnawing at his confidence, frightened by the menacing looking groups hanging around.

'Right, I will leave you now,' Nicole said. 'Hope you soon acclimatise.'

'Thank you,' Mo said, reluctantly stepping into the container. 'I suppose that empty bunk is ours,' he observed, putting his blanket on the thin stained mattress.

'I could do with a sleep. That was a long walk today after Kim dropped us off,' Abdul observed.

'Still, it could have been even further had she not given us a lift,' Mo pointed out.

They devoured the food from the boxes that Nicole had given them and celebrated their arrival with a bottle of water.

'There are some very kind people in the world after all,' Mo yawned.

'I hope your feet don't smell too much,' Abdul said, laying down on the bunk.'

Because of the narrowness of the bunk, the boys 'topped and tailed', sleeping with each other's feet in their faces.

They were so exhausted that they didn't hear all the other occupants of the hut progressively arriving during the evening.

In the morning, they introduced themselves.to the 'melting pot' of other hut occupants

Their cohabitees included teenagers from Eritrea, Iraq, Iran, Morocco, all of whom had made long journeys with the same goal of seeking a better life in England.

The others told the boys that when the weather was clear, it was possible to see the British coast only 33 kilometres away. The apparent close proximity gave them further encouragement that their dreams were within reach.

However, the boys were soon to learn that the relatively short distance between France and England would provide them with their biggest challenge yet.

# Chapter Thirty-nine

It took Mo and Abdul a day or two to understand what was happening in the camp, and how and with whom they needed to talk, for arranging the next leg of their journey.

The fact that there were a lot of people hanging around, did not give Mo any confidence that this was going to be a quick or easy task.

As in all the other countries, that they had travelled through, smugglers had set up lucrative businesses on the dreams of refugees wishing to seek a better life. Calais was no different.

'I never knew so many people wanted to go to England,' Mo said, as they wandered through the squalid, crowded camp.

'We must be at the back of the queue with all of these people. We are going to be here forever,' Abdul moaned, pessimistically. 'Perhaps we should forget England and stay in France or go back to Italy.'

'No, I want to go to England to find Sergeant Tom,' Mo said, firmly.

'What if he doesn't want to see you?'

'He will. He will,' Mo argued, suddenly realising that that might well be a possibility which he hadn't even considered.

As the boys were preparing to return to their filthy container, they were approached by a well-dressed, shifty looking Asian man in his mid-thirties.

'Do you want to go to England?' he asked, his eyes continually sweeping the crowds to ensure that his rival gang weren't watching him, poaching the boys from their 'patch'.

'Yes, but we don't know what to do,' Mo confessed.

'It's easy. I will find you a lorry to smuggle you out of here.'

'OK, but then what do we have to do?'

'When it stops, you climb in the back and you're straight to England. No problem,' the fixer said, making it sound so simple.

'When can we go?' Abdul queried, easily swayed.

'Now if you want.'

'Now?' Mo queried, suspiciously, wondering if it was so simple then why there were so many people still waiting. Perhaps this man was a better smuggler than the others.

'Yes, now,' the man repeated. 'But first you pay me 100 euros,' the man said, holding out his hand.

'How do we know you will get us a lorry and won't just run off with the money?'

'If you want to get to England, you need to trust me. 100 Euros,' he repeated.

'We only have dollars,' Mo explained, apprehensively.

'Dollars are OK too,' the man confirmed.

'We don't have the money here, I will need to get it,' Mo informed the man.

'Meet me back here in half an hour, I will look to see which lorries are coming through.'

Although the boys did have the money on them, as they carried all their belonging around with them all of the time, they didn't want to display the location of the sewn-in bank. They went back to their container, made sure nobody was in and, surreptitiously, extracted the money from their, now sorry, looking coats.

'We've nearly spent it all. Hopefully this will be enough to get us there,' Mo said, stuffing the money into his pocket.

They returned to the same spot with their precious belongings and, after an anxious wait, the man duly arrived.

'Right. There is a line of lorries coming through. I know they will have their back doors unlocked.

'What if there are lots who want to jump on the lorry?' Abdul asked.

'The other fixers and I have agreed who has what lorry, so don't worry. Now, you give me the money and we will go.'

Mo duly handed over the money and the man counted it quickly.

'We go to the road now,' he directed, leading them through the crowds.

The boys followed him out onto the road where a line of lorries was queuing to go through the dock gates. They walked past several and suddenly the man grabbed the handle of one of the artic's back doors and yanked it open.

'Quick inside,' he commanded. 'Hide in-between the load.'

Mo and Abdul duly followed his orders and clambered up on to the lorry, going as far forward as the wooden packing cases would allow.

The lorry moved on a short distance and the back doors opened several more times as the man allowed others onto the lorry.

The boys smiled at each other in the semi-darkness. They were on their way. In a few hours they would have achieved their dream. They would be in England!

The doors clanked shut and the inside became pitch black.

Suddenly the lorry slowed and there were voices, it moved off again only to stop a short distance later and this time the engine was switched off.

More voices and the boys heard the side curtains move and something was shoved in under the curtain near where were hiding.

'Yes, there's some in here,' the voice announced.

Shortly after, the side curtain of the lorry was pulled completely back, flooding the inside of the lorry with floodlights from the large warehouse that they were now in.

'OK, everyone out,' the English voice commanded.

Mo and Abdul stayed perfectly still. They could hear the other late arrivals standing up and getting off the lorry and hoped that they'd be overlooked, but a uniformed man wearing a hi vis jacket appeared over the top of the packing crates and ushered them off too.

'Come on you two, off you get.'

The boys did as they were ordered, fearful of what would happen next. Was this the end of their dream? Would they be sent to prison and then back home?

But they were fortunate. For after being given a talking to about attempting any further trips in a lorry, they were ushered out of the warehouse and back through the port's security gates and back out onto the road.

'We are not being arrested.' Abdul said joyfully. 'They are letting us go'.

'Yes, but that 100 dollars got us nowhere,' Mo pointed out.

'And I ripped off the strap of my rucksack getting out of the lorry, Abdul complained. I'll have to see if Nicole has got something that I can mend it with.'

Mo struck up a conversation with one of the other stowaways as they walked out of the port. 'Do you know what it is like in England?'

'The English, some of them like us, and will help… they will give you money food and shelter – but others will attack you.'

'Oh. Just like here then,' Mo observed.

'Except there are more troublemakers concentrated here,' the other commented.

'How did they know we were there, on the lorry?' Mo asked.

'They use a probe to detect movement or the carbon dioxide that we breathe out.'

'That's what I heard coming under the curtain then,' Mo told him.

'They choose lorries at random. I guess we were unlucky today.'

'I suppose they will be looking out for us next time?' Abdul asked.

'No. Don't worry about that, this is my fifth attempt. One day I'll make it,' the stowaway said, optimistically.

# Chapter Forty

Mo and Abdul had been attempting to get out of the melting pot of violence and intimidation in Calais for almost a month.

The lack of success on this seemingly impenetrable escape route had demoralised them both. But Abdul was becoming depressed about their inertia and more and more morose.

For even when they were fortunate to get inside a lorry, fate decided that it was the one to be searched and they were found and ejected.

'Why is it always us?' Mo moaned. 'It's bad enough waiting for our turn, but even when we get on a lorry, they always find us.'

'At least we don't have to pay anymore, I guess we are lucky he isn't charging us every time we try.'

They had tried various hiding places on the succession of lorries. If the probes didn't detect them, the sniffer dogs did.

'I'm fed up too with the filthy conditions and the gang violence. I'm beginning to feel the same hopelessness as the people who have been here almost two years,' Abdul confessed.

They had heard about large-scale deportations that were occurring from the camp and surrounding areas, which made their attempts to get out of the Jungle even more urgent.

'Come on Abdul, let's give it one more try and then we'll decide what to do if we don't make it this time,' Mo said, picking up his rucksack.

'We won't make it,' Abdul said morosely. 'Why bother? Let's go back to Italy.'

'No, come on. I think it has to be our turn to get lucky.'

'If we must,' Abdul said lethargically, picking up his rucksack. 'But it'll end as it normally does. You mark my words.'

It was night time and the boys had discovered it was a good time to creep around the port, despite the floodlights that covered most, but not all, of the area.

The boys had been watching a steady stream of lorries and coaches going through the port, but for some reason, the line of traffic had been stationary for some time.

They watched as other migrants crept quickly down from their hiding places, secreting themselves under the chassis of the lorries and coaches.

'What do they do when they're under there? Abdul asked.

'I guess they just hang on tightly, or tie themselves to the stuff underneath,' Mo explained.

'I'm going for that coach,' Abdul said, after watching a big 54-seater in the queue. 'Are you coming?

'No, I'm scared that my arm isn't strong enough to hold on. Let's wait for another lorry that we can get into,' Mo pleaded.

'I'm fed up waiting. I can't take any more of this hanging around. I've had it Mo. If you're not coming, I'm going to go for it alone,' Abdul insisted.

Mo watched in panic as Abdul, his long-term companion, cautiously left their hiding place and ran crouching to the coach and disappeared under the side of the stationary vehicle.

'I must go with him, I must go,' Mo said to himself, standing up. But in spite of trying to overcome his fear, he was unable to move. 'If only my arm was strong enough, I would do it,' he tried to convince himself.

Shortly after, the coach started moving towards the ferry terminal.

'Goodbye my friend,' Mo said tearfully. 'Best of luck!' He felt devastated that he had failed to take the opportunity.

He watched as the coach rounded a mini roundabout, the driver had difficulty in manoeuvring the long vehicle around the small tarmac hump, consequently the back half of the coach cut across the obstacle.

This manoeuvre caused the bodywork to scrape on the tarmac and the chassis clearance was minimised. The reduction in space between road and vehicle trapped the stowaway and caused him to lose his grip on the framework.

Exhilaration of finally starting his journey to England changed to fear and panic as he was jettisoned from underneath the coach.

Frantically, he tried to grab hold of the frame again, but by now the coach was moving too fast.

His manic scramble to avoid the huge back wheels came too late.

His scream was short lived. It echoed around the ferry terminal and sent an arrow to Mo's heart.

The coach driver, unaware of the tragedy, assumed that the bump was from clipping the roundabout and drove on, leaving the crushed body lying in the middle of the darkened road.

Mo was horrified. 'Abdul, he screamed. Abdul.'

He dashed from his hiding place, but as he got closer, it was obvious that the person was beyond help.

Another refugee pulled the hysterical and traumatised Mo back into hiding.

'Come on brother. There is nothing you can do for him now. Don't let the Police see you.'

Mo didn't argue. Shock had robbed him of coherent thought. He allowed himself to be led away from his vantage point.

Soon the port police and security guards were on the scene, but it was obvious, from the catastrophic injuries, that it was a fatal accident.

Mo was beside himself with grief. 'He was my friend. He helped me escape the Taliban. He saved me from many dangers during our long journey. He is gone,' Mo wept. 'Our dream of reaching England and a peaceful life is over. No, this cannot be happening. It can't, it can't,' he wailed.

Mo was devastated. Their plans for a new life living together, away from the constant fear of war just seemed impossible.

'It was my fault that he is dead. He didn't want to go. I should have listened to him. I have killed my friend,' he thought. 'Perhaps he should return to Afghanistan after all; His dream of meeting up with the soldier again had turned into a nightmare. And even if he found him, would Sergeant Tom want to know him anyway? His all-consuming desire to get to England had caused the death of his friend.' He was mortified.

# Chapter Forty-one

But the Police had seen and heard Mo and quickly tracked him down before he could go very far. The fellow migrant, who had initially rescued the traumatised Mo, left him as the Police closed in.

The Police took the distraught Mo to their office near to the docks. Eventually, after half an hour and being given several cups of coffee, Mo became calm enough to answer some questions about Abdul.

Do you speak good enough English to discuss what has happened, or do we need an interpreter?' the Policeman asked, gently.

'No interpreter. I can speak good English,' Mo replied.

'Can I ask what you were doing on the embankment?'

'We were waiting to get in the back of a lorry, Mo volunteered.'

'But you were seen in a distressed state on the embankment, crying. Why was that?'

'My friend had gone to...to hide under a coach...but I was too frightened to go with him. I then saw him killed by the coach.'

'I'm so sorry for your loss. But we need to confirm his identity,' the Policeman continued. 'Do you recognise this?' the policeman asked, showing Mo the rucksack that they had recovered from the scene.

'Yes, that is my friend's rucksack. There look, is the repair that he did on the strap. Can I see him?'

'No. I don't think that is wise. He has catastrophic head injuries. However, we did recover these trainers from his...from his body. Do you recognise these?'

'Yes...but a lot of people were given new trainers like that too.'

'Thank you for your help. That is all we wanted to speak to you about. We will make suitable funeral arrangements. We know where to contact you. Number 88 isn't it?'

'Yes.'

'I'm sorry about your friend, and I don't wish to lecture you at this sad moment. But you can see how dangerous it is stowing away on vehicles. I should rethink your plans and perhaps seek asylum somewhere other than England.'

'Thank you,' Mo nodded numbly, not absorbing the advice.


Mo took Abdul's rucksack back to their hut, retrieved his neckerchief from inside it and subconsciously picked up his own rucksack. Then, lost in his misery, he immediately left the camp.

He didn't know where he was going or what he was going to do, he just needed to get away from the depression that was sucking at his soul. He still yearned to see the Sergeant. He remembered his strong arms around him when he had comforted him in hospital. He really needed that cuddle now.


Chris pulled the car and caravan off the Autoroute into the Aire, service area.

'That's was a good trip up from Brittany,' he said, pulling the unit to a halt.

'And we're well ahead of the ferry time too,' his wife Janet added.

'We'll stop here for an hour or so, rather than joining the queue near the ferry port, and being a sitting target for the migrants hanging around there,' her husband suggested.

'If you take the dog for a wee, I'll put the kettle on for a cuppa,' Janet proposed.

'Yes OK. I could do with stretching my legs myself,' Chris added, getting stiffly out of the car.

'In the meantime, I'll put the chairs out,' his wife added.

Mo was lost in his despair and had been walking in the dark for what seemed hours, when he arrived at a single arm security barrier across the road. Ahead of him he was vaguely aware of the sounds of a busy road.

He ducked under the barrier, unaware that he had gone up the service road supporting the Autoroute Aire.

Deep in shock, he slunk away to a darkened corner of the service area, his heart heavy with grief. Subconsciously, he sat on a nearby wooden bench.

With his head in hands, another wave of helplessness overwhelmed him, as he contemplated his future, alone.

He thought about what Abdul and he had planned to do when they got to England. How they would become rich business men and own lots of cars and live in a castle.

'Why couldn't something nice happen, for a change,' he thought. 'Was this an omen that he should go home? Then again, perhaps he owed it to his friend to give it one more try? But how?'

That was when he spotted the caravan.

Summoning up all his courage, he decided to act.

Mo tentatively approached the man, now drinking a cup of tea outside his caravan. 'Excuse me Sir. Are you English?'

'What's it to do with you?' came the blunt reply.

'You are English. Oh Good. I need to get to England. I will pay you, he lied. Can I come with you in your caravan?'

'No, of course not. Now clear off before I call the Police.'

'Please. I am desperate to get to England.'

'No. And I won't tell you again,' the man said standing up. 'Now go away.'

'I am from Afghanistan. My family are dead.' Mo explained. 'I have a friend in the army in England,' Mo added, all in a rush. 'He was going to adopt me, but he was posted before we could make arrangements for me to go with him.' Mo lied.

'Well that's your hard luck. Now clear off.'

Hearing the conversation outside, the caravanner's wife stuck her head out through the open caravan door.

'What is it Chris?' she asked and then spotted Mo. 'What does he want? Tell him, whatever he's selling, we don't want any.'

'He wants to come back to England with us. He's come up with a cock and bull story about going to be adopted by an army family. But they left before all the paperwork was finalised,' the man said, coldly.

'Oh, how awful, if it's true,' the woman said, sympathetically.

'It's all lies. Don't be fooled by his sob story. They're all at it, these illegals.'

At that moment, their dog came to the caravan door and seeing the boy, leapt out and ran to him, jumping up and down, pawing his leg and barking excitedly, his wagging tail, displaying his joy.

'Hello little dog,' the boy said, stroking the small terrier. 'What's your name? I had a dog once.' Mo recalled, a tear brimming. 'He was killed with my family.'

'Oh, I'm so sorry to hear that. The dog's called Ajax, and he obviously likes you,' the woman said, smiling.

Suddenly there was a loud bang and the sky lit up, as a large firework was launched from a field next to the autoroute.

The noise rekindled the awful nightmare sound of the explosion that had killed his family and Mo instinctively dropped to the ground.

As he threw himself to the floor, the dog, also frightened by the noise of the firework, took off. It ran into the busy road; miraculously avoiding being hit by several cars, who swerved to avoid the petrified animal.

'Ajax,' the owners chorused in panic.

Mo jumped up and stared at the fleeing dog.

'You, stupid idiot. You've killed our dog,' the man berated Mo.

'Oh my god, I can't bear to look,' the woman said, turning her back on the busy road. Instinctively putting her fingers in her ears, not wanting to hear the inevitable collision, leading to the death of her much-loved dog.

# Chapter Forty-two

Fortunately, the dog made it over to the concrete central reservation of the autoroute and cowered down, clearly petrified.

Having not heard a collision, the woman hesitantly turned around again and, in the gap between the cars charging down the autoroute, saw that the dog was still alive.

'Oh my god! How are we going to get him back?' The woman sobbed, nervously putting her hands over her face.

'If we call him, he'll be killed. He won't be so lucky the next time,' Chris announced unhelpfully.

'I'll get him,' Mo said, feeling embarrassed by his over-reaction to the firework.

'No. Don't you dare try. I'll call the police,' the man said, reaching into his pocket for his mobile phone. 'They'll stop the traffic or something.'

But Mo had already made his mind up and ran to the side of the busy Autoroute.

Dazzled by the oncoming headlights, he nervously waited for a gap in the busy traffic. He estimated that after the articulated lorry and car had passed, there would be a gap, sufficiently long enough, for him to make it across the three lanes to the dog.

Behind, he could hear the couple shouting for him to stop. But as soon as the lorry and car had passed, gathering all his courage, and with his heart in his mouth, he made a frantic dash across the road.

As the headlights of the approaching cars lit Mo's running figure, drivers showed their displeasure at his heroics and blasted their horns.

A ripple of brake lights ran back along the autoroute as drivers reacted to his suicidal dash. Tyre squeal added to the cacophony of road noise.

Finally, after what seemed like an eternity, Mo reached the concrete wall and picked up the shaking dog.

'It's OK Ajax, don't be frightened. I've got you,' Mo reassured the hound.

The youngster felt very vulnerable standing in the middle of the autoroute as cars zoomed past him in both directions at 100 kilometres an hour.

But, holding the dog tightly to his chest, he waited until the traffic had thinned again and accompanied by another cacophony of horns, he dashed back to the waiting caravanners.

Breathing heavily from his exertions and realising that playing 'Russian roulette' with the traffic had paid off, he handed the dog to the grateful woman.

'You bloody fool,' the husband berated. 'You could have got yourself killed.'

'Chris, that's no way to thank him for saving Ajax,' the woman scolded.

'Oh well...if I must... I suppose, thanks, is in order,' he said, reluctantly.

'So long as he's OK, that's all that matters,' Mo panted. 'I miss my dog, so I know how much you must love him.'

'Can we give you some money to help you on your travels?' the woman asked.

'That would be very kind of you. But a lift to the next service area would help me,' Mo proposed, hopefully.

'No. Sorry. You're not going to con us into getting in to my car, Mister,' the man said, firmly. 'Besides, there's no room in there and it's illegal for people to travel in the caravan.'

'Chris! He's too young to be wandering around by himself at this time of night. Besides which, he's just risked his own life to save Ajax. The least we can do is to give him a lift,' the woman remonstrated.

'Well...Oh, if you put it like that. I suppose it won't hurt,' the man replied, grudgingly. 'As long as it's just to the next service area, that's all.

So much for a restful stop,' the caravanner muttered. 'Come on then. Let's get going. 'But you'll have to go in the caravan after all. I just hope we don't get stopped.'

'Thank you. Thank you very much,' Mo smiled gratefully. At last something was going right for him.

# Chapter Forty-three

After securing the tea things back in the caravan, the trio set off along the A26 back towards Calais.

Unfortunately for the caravanner, there were no other rest areas open. And they soon found themselves in the outskirts of Calais. Here gangs of young men watched them menacingly, as they passed by.

'We daren't stop here,' the wife said, nervously looking around at the unruly mob, and double checking that her car door was locked.

'We've got to,' her husband directed. 'We have to get rid of that boy in the caravan before we get to the docks.

Do you realise we could get imprisoned if they catch us smuggling him in to England? What the hell! I'm going to pull over.'

But as he slowed, he quickly regretted his actions, for they were immediately surrounded by a large group of men, who blocked the road.

In his caravan mirrors he could see that they were attempting to break into the caravan door.

'Oh my God,' the woman panicked. 'Get us out of here.'

'I can't. I'm not going to run them over. I'll get slung in jail,' the driver said, revving his engine in the hope the mob would part.

Then he caught sight of the caravan door opening and Mo standing in the doorway with a large carving knife.

'That boy has got a knife...he's threatening the yobs.'

'Where did he get that from? He didn't have it earlier,' his wife screamed.

'I don't know, he must have found it in the cutlery drawer.'

The group by the door stood back in surprise and the men at the front of the car, who were blocking the road, saw an opportunity to get into the caravan and ran towards the open door.

With the road ahead now clear, the driver immediately floored the accelerator and the car and caravan shot off down the road, chased by the mob.

Out of the corner of his eye, as he shot around a corner, away from the baying crowd, he saw a body from inside the caravan fall out.

'Well I think that's got rid of our problem hitchhiker too,' he announced.

'What do you mean?' his wife demanded.

'The kid who rescued the dog. I think he just fell out of the 'van.'

'Oh my god! We need to go back and see if he's alright,' the woman said, looking back along the road.

'What! And get involved with that mob again? You've got to be joking. No, I'm not going to stop until we get in to the port now.'

As they got closer to the floodlit port, there were more and more groups of men hanging around. But the appearance of Police patrols helped ease their discomfort, as they followed the slow convoy into the ferry terminal.

# Chapter Forty-four

Finally, they arrived in the terminal and pulled up in the designated queue to await their sailing.

'I'll just make sure everything is OK in the caravan and lock the door again,' the man said, getting out of the car. 'Thankfully that lad saw the mob off, but obviously the door is now unlocked.'

'I do hope he's OK,' the woman said quietly, joining her husband at the caravan door.

The man opened it and looked inside.

'Oh bugger, the cutlery drawer has spilled all its contents,' he observed.

'And I bet all the clothes have fallen off the clothes rail too, with you driving like a lunatic,' she berated.

'I had to. It was the only way to get rid of that mob,' he said, defensively.

'If you say so!' Janet said, dismissively.

'Would you have preferred that I let them ransack the caravan then?'

'Look, even the seat, where we put the bedding, has sprung up,' she pointed out.'

'Well this won't take a few minutes to sort,' Chris said, stepping in to the caravan.

Together they picked up all the fallen cutlery, flattened the seat and made a cup of tea while they waited.

After a short time, the ferry arrived, and they were quickly shepherded aboard.

As they followed a line of other cars and caravans up a short ramp into the bowels of the ferry, Janet reminded him. 'Don't forget, the dog is not allowed to join us in the ship's lounge.'

'Yes, I know. You remind me every time we come across on the ferry,' he said irritably. 'But he can stay with the car and caravan,' he mimicked.

'Alright Mr Grumpy, 'I was only saying. I'll put him in the caravan, he'll have more room to roam around. 'Don't forget to put his bed down, he can sleep off the trip,' Janet instructed.

Finally, they were directed into a parking place by a hi-vis jacket wearing crewman, and Chris switched off the engine.

'They don't give you a lot of room do they?' Janet said, struggling to open the door in the narrow space between the adjoining vehicle.' Come on Ajax,' the woman whispered, lifting the dog out of the car. 'We'll give you a change of scenery.'

Carefully, she opened the caravan door and stepped in, closing the door behind her. She put the dog down on a seat, but he immediately jumped off and started barking at the opposite one.

'Now what's all that noise about,' Janet said to the dog. 'Be a good boy. You've done this trip lots of times.' But the dog continued to bark at the seat.

Behind her, the man entered with the dogs bed, that he'd retrieved from the car. 'Here you are Ajax, now you've got your bed you can stop that barking. Has he got some water?' the man asked.

'No, but I'll put his drinking bowl down now,' Janet said, topping the bowl up from a small bottle of water. 'We won't be long.' 'Be a good boy,' she said as they stepped out of the 'van'.

'I'll lock the door,' Chris said, turning his key in the lock.

'Just remember what deck we're on,' the woman instructed as they left the now crowded car deck.

'You can remember as well as I can,' the man reminded her sternly.

'I usually have to, because you're hopeless,' the woman countered.

They made their way through the big steel flood doors and followed a stream of people clanging their way up the metal stairway to the large lounge areas.

The crossing was relatively calm, and they dozed for an hour in the lounge chairs during the trip.

Just before they arrived in Dover, the ship's tannoy invited them *'to re-join your vehicles'*.

The couple joined a crocodile of people heading back to their cars.

As they returned down the metal staircase, the man stopped and examined the signwriting on a metal door leading off the landing. 'Is this our deck?' he asked his wife.

'No, it's the next one down. See, I told you, you're hopeless,' she chided.

Finally, after squeezing between tightly packed cars and vans, they found their unit. The man unlocked the car, as his wife went to the caravan, unlocked it and stepped in.

The dog was sitting on the floor at the far end of the caravan and wagged its tail when it saw her but didn't move.

'Hello darling. See that wasn't too long was it? Come to Mummy then,' she instructed. 'It's time to get back in the car. We're nearly home.'

But Ajax stayed put.

'Come on you daft thing.'

Still the dog refused to move.

'Oh, are you so tired that you want me to take you?' the woman purred and picked up the dog and it's bed.

As they left the caravan, the dog barked again, looking back over the woman's shoulder, as if trying to draw her attention to something.

'Come on, you noisy animal,' she fussed and took the dog to the car. Janet put his bed on the back seat and Ajax settled back down on it.

'I wish I could sleep like him,' the man said, driving the unit towards the ferry exit doors.

# Chapter Forty-five

After a short time in the queue waiting to leave the ferry, they disembarked and joined the line of vehicles exiting the port.

But much to Chris's frustration they were randomly selected to go into the immigration area for a search.

'Oh damn, another delay,' he moaned. 'All I want to do is get home and go to bed.'

Chris wound down his window as a uniformed immigration officer stood by the side of his door.

'Hello Sir. We just want to check your vehicle and caravan to make sure that you don't have any uninvited guests on board.'

'Ok,' he agreed, reluctantly.

Chris and Janet exchanged a quick glance and breathed a sigh of relief. The thought of being caught with the boy on board would have ruined, what had been, a great holiday.

'If you'd like to go that way,' the officer said, pointing to a painted line on the ground that went around the far side of a large building.

'Ok,' Chris confirmed and steered car and 'van' to where they were shown.

They were beckoned into a parking area under a large floodlit canopy, where other uniformed people were waiting.

'Please switch off the engine and unlock the caravan for me.' he was instructed. 'Then if you and your wife wouldn't mind popping into the waiting room, while we conduct a search.

'Ok,' Chris said, doing as instructed and stepping out of the car. The immigration officer followed as he walked around the back of the unit and unlocked the caravan.

The official took a small instrument from his shoulder bag and switched it on. He opened the door and placed the device on the caravan floor, quickly closing it again.

'What's that for?' Chris queried.

'It's a $CO_2$ monitor. It measures the levels of carbon dioxide present in the air. We use it for detecting people hidden away. We usually use it with a probe for sticking into lorry's loads. But it works just as well without.'

Through the window of the caravan's door Chris could see various lights flashing on the instrument and after a few minutes, the Officer opened the door again and studied the display.

'Oh, that's interesting. There appears to be an elevated level of $CO_2$ in here, consistent with someone being present. Have you been in here recently?'

'No. Well yes. Obviously. Prior to the caravan going in to the hold. But we weren't allowed down there while the ship was sailing. Please feel free to search it. We have nothing to hide, I assure you.'

The immigration official stepped into the caravan.

'Oh. I wonder,' Chris pondered. 'It might be because we had a gang of immigrants who tried to climb in the caravan while we were in Calais. But one of them got in and left in a hurry, when I went around a corner to escape the mob.'

'Calais you say? No,' the official replied. 'Over that period of time, the carbon dioxide would have dispersed through the caravan's' ventilation.'

'What about a build up from being in the hold?' Chris suggested.

'No, very unlikely. Perhaps you might have an uninvited guest in here after all. I think I'll search the caravan.'

'As I say, I have nothing to hide....Oh, of course! Silly me,' the owner said suddenly.

'What's that?'

'I forgot. We left the dog in here while we were onboard. We only took him out as we were disembarking. Could that be the cause?'

'Hmm, yes might be. But I'll just have a quick look around anyway.'

At that moment, there was a shout from one of the border force man's colleagues who had been searching a nearby lorry.

'Barry! Looks like we've got a large group of illegals here. We could do with your help,' the other officer called.

'Ok. I'd better give them a hand,' the immigration official said. 'Well, it looks like you're an honest bloke. I trust you aren't smuggling.'

'No definitely not. I can assure you. However, I shall be glad to get home, that's for sure,' the caravanner admitted tiredly.

'Where's home?' the immigration man asked, scooping up his meter.

'Cheltenham. I hope to get home before the morning rush hour starts.'

'How long will that take you?'

'At this time of night, probably about three and a half hours.'

'Have a safe journey.'

'Cheers.'

The caravaner collected his wife from the waiting room.

'That was a close thing, if that man we picked up...'

'Boy,' she corrected him.

'Boy, man. Whatever! If that boy had still been in there we would have been in trouble. As usual, I was right,' the man crowed and got a disparaging look from his wife in return.

# Chapter Forty-six

Relieved to be on their way at last, the couple left Dover and headed for home. The journey was uneventful but as they came off the A417 by the Air Balloon roundabout near Gloucester, Chris could see his route into Cheltenham was closed.

'Damn!'

'What's the matter?

'The road's closed, look, he said pointing to the 'Road Closed' signs. We'll have to go the long way around and I'm bursting for a pee. I was hoping to wait until we got home.'

'Well you can't stop here.' Janet said firmly.

'Obviously, I wasn't,' he replied tetchily.

'There are some laybys down near Gloucester that you can pull in to,' she suggested.

Unfortunately, all the laybys were full of 'foreign' lorries waiting to load up the following morning.

'Bleedin' foreigners.' Chris yawned.

'Are you sure you can't wait until we're home?'

'No I can't, my bladder is about to burst.'

'Well what about the place along the Golden Valley bypass. You might be lucky there.'

'I bleedin' hope so.' he added.

'The dog could probably do with a wee as well,' she suggested.

As they drove along the A40 towards Cheltenham he was pleased to see an empty layby ahead.

'I think you're going to be lucky. There look, no-one's in that one,' his wife pointed.

Chris pulled off the road into the vacant layby, switched off the ignition and lights.

'I'll just be a minute,' he said, grovelling in his pocket to get his caravan keys out.

''What are you getting those out for?' she demanded.

'To have a pee in the caravan, obviously,' he retorted, irritably.

'Can't you go in the hedge?' she demanded. 'I've already cleaned out the toilet.'

'Oh, if I must,' he grumped, opening the car door. 'God, my legs are stiff.'

'What can you expect after that long drive?' she said, unsympathetically.

Chris hobbled his way to the front of the car and duly relieved himself in the bushes.

Meanwhile, his wife was keeping a lookout to make sure that he wasn't caught in the act, when she thought she saw movement reflected in the caravan mirror mounted on her passenger door.

'What the...?'

She looked again but saw nothing out of the ordinary.

'I must be seeing things. It's been a long old day,' she thought.

However, when her husband arrived back to collect the dog for Ajax's convenience break, she mentioned it to him.

'I thought I saw something move at the back of the caravan.'

'At this time of night! Really! It's probably only a fox or a badger,' he said, dismissively.

'No, I'm sure... I think,' she insisted.

'If you're so sure, you'd better come with me then and check,' he said, reluctantly.

The couple made their way cautiously to the back of the caravan. The dog led the way, straining on its leash and barking.

'Sssh Ajax. There's nothing to bark at,' the woman instructed.

'He's probably smelt a fox or something,' the man suggested. 'I'd imagine there's a lot out here.'

'Sssh Ajax.'

The dog continued to yap.

The man put his key in the caravan lock.

'It's already undone,' he said surprised, turning the key.

'I thought you'd locked the door at Dover?' his wife said accusingly.

'I did, I'm sure of it,' he replied adamantly.

'Well, if it's not locked now. You must have imagined it,' she suggested.

'Perhaps. I'm fairly knackered for sure,' he replied tiredly.


But in the bushes nearby, Mo watched as the couple disappeared into the caravan.

It had seemed like an impossible dream. But he was in England...at last.

# PART FOUR

# Mission accomplished

# Chapter Forty-seven

Mo had looked out of the side window of the caravan and realised that they were pulling off the road. 'This was his opportunity, to leave before they found him,' he thought.

He had quickly grabbed some cereal bars out of the overhead food locker and a duvet from beneath the storage area under the seat, where he had been hiding. With his rucksack over his shoulder, he had leapt out of the stationary caravan, hoping to escape before he was detected.

He had cuddled the dog in the caravan during the channel crossing and had only just got back into his hiding place, as the woman returned and opened the caravan door.

Ajax had nearly given him away by his reluctance to leave the caravan.

And then, he had waited with bated breath as the border security officer was doing his checks.

At the mention of Carbon Dioxide , 'his heart was in his mouth,' and thought that the game was up. That his nemesis, the CO2 monitor, would give him away yet again.

So he was very surprised and much relieved that they didn't do a full search and find him.

It had been hot and stuffy hiding in the seat locker under the duvets for several hours, and now at last he was free to stretch his aching limbs.

Now he was out of the caravan, he listened to the two-people arguing about seeing something in the mirror. He hoped they wouldn't let Ajax off the leash, otherwise the dog would go straight to him.

Following their abortive search inside the caravan for the mystery movement that Janet had seen out of the corner of her eye, the couple re-emerged and locked the door.

'See I told you that you were imagining things,' he berated. 'Come on let's get home. I've had enough now.'

'Stop that noise Ajax. Come on, back in the car.' Janet encouraged the yapping canine.

But the dog continued to bark at Mo in his hiding place as they got back into the car.

Mo heard the car start up and felt a moment of panic as they drove off and disappeared down the road.

Despite all the problems that he had endured to get to England, escape from the Taliban, long desert treks, maniacal drivers, sinking dinghies, violent gangs, he was now overwhelmed with fear.

For now he was completely alone. He was in a foreign country in the dead of night and his body trembled with an unexpected mixture of emotions. He didn't know whether to laugh or cry.

He knew he should feel happy but instead, he felt deflated. His euphoria was suffocated by the fatigue of his long pilgrimage....and the sadness he felt for the loss of his friend Abdul.

His eyes brimmed. Tears ran down his cheeks.

He reminded himself that this was the culmination of his impossible dream. The dream which had filled his waking hours for so long since the Sergeant had ended his posting.

Mo was confronted with another problem though. For, yes, he was in England. But he had no idea where about in England he was, or where to find Sergeant Tom.

Shaking himself out of his thoughtful inertia, however, he decided his first priority was to get away from the road and find somewhere to hide.

The other refugees in Calais had told Mo, that if he made it to England, he had to keep a low profile, because if he was found, he would be deported.

So, that it was imperative that he remained undetected, until he found Sergeant Tom.

His single, all-consuming, goal of getting to England had now been achieved. But what next? He hadn't thought beyond getting here and had no idea of how he was going to track down the Sergeant.

A car coming along the road reminded him of his vulnerable position. He shook himself out of his lethargy and self-pity, slithering away from the road.

Dragging the duvet and rucksack behind him, he crawled down a short embankment, under a barbed wire fence and on to a rough track. He was now desperate to find somewhere to hide and possibly sleep before it got light.

Unsure which direction to take, he walked on a parallel track in the same direction that the caravan had gone.

After a few hundred yards, he came to a large concrete tunnel that ran underneath the main road. The track zigzagged out of sight.

The subway was about fifteen feet high and considerably wider. Graffiti on the walls indicated its use by 'street artists' or vandals.

He checked out the tracks either side of the tunnel , both seemed to be well used. So he decided that it was not suitable for his use and remaining undiscovered. And although an ideal shelter if it rained, it would also be cold and windy too.'

Leaving the hard-surfaced track, he continued to walk back along the same parallel footpath that he had previously followed, this time inspecting the thick hedge that bordered the field and highway above.

Soon he discovered a large hole in the hedge and checked it out. Slowly he crept in, hoping that it wasn't already occupied by either animal or man.

He was relieved to find it empty. Through the filtered moonlight of the early morning, he could just about establish that the void was about two feet high and about six feet round. He decided that it would make a cosy den to sleep in.

'In there, he would be out of sight of anyone walking along the path too,' he thought.

He pushed the duvet into the farthest corner of the den and lay down, exhausted by the events of the last twenty-four hours.

As he dozed off, his last thoughts were of his friend Abdul. If only he'd made it, he wouldn't feel so scared now.

He took a long deep breath of the cool, fresh English air and smiled. Something had gone right for him after all. Within minutes he was fast asleep. He smiled in his sleep as he dreamed his special dream of meeting Sergeant Tom again.

# Chapter Forty-eight

He could hear the plane getting closer; the scream of its high-pitched jet engine getting louder and louder.

He knew that the noise was always a precursor for mayhem.

He covered his ears, and rolled into a foetal position, in anticipation of the explosion and the excruciating noise and devastation that would follow.

But before the explosion occurred, Mo awoke. He was trembling. It was daylight.

As his sleep-fogged mind cleared, he remembered that he was not in Afghanistan any more.

He pinched himself to make sure that he was awake. 'Yes, he was!

'It wasn't a dream. He was in England. Yes, he had made it, at last.'

He crawled towards the entrance of his 'hole in the hedge' and cautiously looked out.

A few hundred yards away, across the other side of a grass covered field, he could see a red helicopter airborne and pitching away.

The frightening sound of his nightmare jet engine was instead, the roar of a turboshaft engine on a helicopter.

So, was the helicopter looking for him? Had he been seen getting out of the caravan?

Nearby were large buildings which he recognised as hangars. Then he realised his hide was next to an airfield.

He crept back into his hide and wrapped the duvet around himself. The few hours he'd slept was not enough to recharge his tired body, after all he'd endured, he still felt exhausted.

He thought about the last manic 24 hours. His friend's death, the dog rescue, the caravan trip, the near miss with the immigration people. It had all contributed to his mental exhaustion.

Yes he was tired, but also exhilarated with his success, so far.

He made a mental list of what he was going to do.

A rumble in his stomach reminded him that firstly, he needed food and a drink.

His next task would then be to try and find Sergeant Tom, although he had no idea of how to go about it.

He dug out a cereal bar from his jacket pocket, that he had stolen from the caravan, and ate it in a few bites, thinking that he would need to ration himself before eating the others.

Then he heard someone walking along the path, approaching the hole in the hedge. He quietly moved to the back of the hide and froze, wondering if he'd been seen.

Suddenly, a Springer Spaniel put its nose inside his hidey hole and looked at him. It froze as it saw Mo, then started barking.

Its sudden appearance made Mo jump.

'Was this the end?' he wondered. 'Had they sent out the police with tracker dogs to find him. Was he now about to be caught?'

Initially, he thought that it was Jersey and his search was over already, but disappointed, he soon realised it wasn't her.

However, he resisted his instinct to hold out his hand to the dog and calm it down with some gentle words.

But instead remained still. His heart in his mouth as he heard the dog's owner call it.

'Millie come away from there,' the man called. 'It would serve you right if a fox came out and bit you. Now come here.'

The dog reluctantly backed out of the hole and still barking, followed its master along the path.

Mo was relieved, it wasn't a police tracker dog after all, but decided he needed to find a better hiding place, away from the footpath.

He was now faced with another dilemma, should he leave his hide in the daylight or wait until night time?'

'It should be OK,' he thought. 'Anyone will think I'm a local having a walk. My clothes aren't any different to the English people that I saw in Calais,' he convinced himself.

He listened to see if anyone else was around and then, cautiously poked his head out of the hole in the hedge.

Satisfied that he was alone, he climbed out of his hide and stood up, stretching his arms. The air felt cool and fresh.

The morning sun was casting shadows of the thick green hedge into the field in front of him. Fluffy powderpuff clouds floated on the clear blue sky, somehow it looked so different to what he was used to at home.

Behind him the rush hour traffic was creating a cacophony of noise on the main road.

The helicopter that had disturbed his sleep had disappeared and clearly hadn't been looking for him after all.

# Chapter Forty-nine

Leaving his duvet and precious rucksack behind in the den, he walked along the footpath which continued around the edge of the airfield.

As he made his way along the path he was taken in by the breath-taking scenery.

The thick hedges that bordered the path, were bedecked with beautiful autumn flowers, set against a backdrop of lush green leaves.

'There are so many different types of plants here. Each showing off their lovely colours of pink and red and white. It is so beautiful,' he thought. 'This certainly is a world away from my home and that dreadful 'Jungle' camp.'

A tapestry of ripe blackberries, mixed with red unripe ones, attracted his hungry attention.

He spent some time breakfasting on the ripe fruit, the squashed berries staining his fingers and leaving black traces around his lips.

Mo was startled as a small single propeller plane took off from the runaway, and passed directly overhead, quickly gaining altitude.

Across to his right, the path skirted alongside a rusty single stranded wire fence, badly in need of repair. It appeared to be the perimeter fence of the airport.

As there was no one else around, he decided to venture further along the grassy path to try to establish his bearings.

Parts of the track was slightly overgrown, with knee-high grass punctuated by 'halos' of downy thistles.

At the top of the thistle stalks, the ripe seeds were waiting for nature's gentle breath to scatter them on their gossamer parachutes.

The path turned right, and soon he could see that it hugged the steep sided banks of a small, meandering stream. Thick weeds and nettles clothed it's banks, but nevertheless, there was a good flow of water running over the shallow bed.

Looking at the large trees that lined the small stream, Mo decided they might provide him a shelter off the ground, as well as an ideal hiding place. More importantly he'd be away from the noisy main road.

Further still, the path went through a tunnel of foliage created by the canopy of more trees either side of the track.

Small muddy puddles lay across the width of the path, which he carefully stepped over, not wishing to 'mess up' his donated trainers, courtesy of the camp in Calais.

As he emerged from underneath the canopy of trees, he could see that the stream meandered back towards the path.

He made his way to a low point on the bank of the stream, where there were fewer weeds.

Bare earth indicated regular visitors here, and he wondered if it was the place where the wild animals came.

'I wonder if this water is clean enough to drink?' he thought. 'If it's good enough for the animals, it ought to be good enough for me. I'm pretty thirsty.'

He reckoned that the last drink he'd had, was over twenty-four hours ago in France. 'No wonder he felt dry.'

Holding on to a willow tree branch, to stop himself falling in, he knelt and scooped a handful of water with his hand. It was cold but clear. He smelt it. It didn't smell of anything. He took a small sip and held it in his mouth, while he decided whether to risk it or not.

'What the hell, if I don't drink, I'll die anyway,' he decided.

He took several more scoops and slurped them up, feeling the cold-water trickle down his throat and into his blackberry filled belly.

He splashed water on to his face, the chilly liquid momentarily taking his breath away. He wiped his wet face in the sleeve of his coat, as he walked back to the path.

Shortly after, on the airfield side, he spotted a rubbish dump of discarded building materials.

The pile included, wooden planks and broken corrugated asbestos sheets. This got him thinking about building a weather resistant shelter, somewhere.

Nearby, a willow tree, took his attention. The end of one of its large branches lay on the ground, as if it had collapsed.

'That tree might provide a new home for me,' he thought. 'it will be easy to get up and down. I'll see what's up there.'

Stepping over several small branches, he climbed on to the large branch and was able to easily walk up it. Small side branches provided a handrail as he clambered up to the top. Hopefully, he gazed inside. 'The hollow bole was massive, and would be big enough for his needs,' he concluded..

'That will do nicely,' he thought. Satisfied with his find, he slowly walked down the branch and slithered his way back to the path.

Looking back up at the tree, he confirmed his choice. 'Nobody will be able to see me up there, through those branches and leaves. Good find.'

# Chapter Fifty

He ventured further still, until the path took a dog-leg and crossed the stream, over a small wooden foot bridge.

In front of him was a large fenced off field, with acres of ripe yellow maize. His stomach rumbled as he thought about his last real meal.

He decided to come back later and harvest some, but first wanted to explore the path along its full length.

He was now on the other side of the stream, which was fenced off with relatively new chain link fencing. This area had obviously been recently widened. Mother nature had recovered from the building work and carpeted it thickly with various weeds and water borne plants.

Ahead of him, on the left-hand side of the path, there was a solitary house with a huge crop field for a back garden.

The path stopped at the junction with a busy road, and opposite he could see signs for a golf course.

'Perhaps a future source of food from the clubhouse kitchens,' he thought.

Finally, he decided that he'd ventured far enough for the time being.

The volume of traffic on the road indicated that it was probably rush hour, and still unsure about showing himself in public, he withdrew along the path to where he'd seen the maize.

Checking both ways that no-one was coming, he climbed over the wooden fence and leapt in to the crop field.

The plants were tightly sown together, and he carefully made his way around the edges of the crop, trying not to damage the tall stalks.

Retrieving his penknife, that the Sergeant had given him, from his trouser pocket, he cut off several cobs over a large area and stuffed them into his pockets. Hoping that by selecting them this way, his harvesting would go unnoticed by the farmer.

Satisfied with his new food supply, he returned to leave the field, but could see someone coming along the track.

Silently, he crept back into the maize, and hid until they had passed by. Allowing them a few minutes to clear the area, and checking that no-one else was coming, he quickly clambered back over the fence.

'I wonder if I can eat these raw?' he pondered, biting into a cob. 'Oh. they're very hard,' he said, looking at the intact cob. 'What if I cooked them first, they'd be any softer. Mmm, but how do I cook them?' he mused.

Mo touched his pocket and was reassured by the shape of the 'Bear Grylls' flint fire starter. 'Yes, he had the means,' he concluded.

'So, making a fire was not going to be a problem. However, having something to boil the cobs in might be,' he reasoned.

Undaunted, he went back to the dump of building materials and found that an avalanche of discarded soil had knocked a hole in the chain link fence.

Carefully he scrambled through the gap, and after a few minutes rummaging in the discarded rubbish, he came across an old battered kettle.

'Yes, that will do fine,' he said, clutching his prize.

'There's lots of dry wood here too,' he thought. 'That will make a good, smokeless fire.'

He scooped a large armful of wood up, and together with his battered kettle, made his way back through the hole in the fence.

He washed out the kettle, as well as he could in the stream and filled it with water. Relieved to see that, despite its battered condition, it didn't leak.

'Now, where to light my fire?' he wondered. 'I know, I'll go back into the maize field, out of sight from people on the path.'

# Chapter Fifty-one

Armed with his kettle of water and pieces of firewood, Mo made his way back to the maize field. Carefully choosing his way, to avoid damaging as few plants as possible and leaving a tell-tale route through the crop.

Now, crouched down in the middle of the field, he cleared away nearby plants to ensure they didn't accidentally catch fire too, and prepared the base of his campfire.

He remembered the technique that Sergeant Tom had shown them, using his red handled penknife for 'feathering' branches, to make fine shavings for kindling. The Soldier had demonstrated that the small feathered pieces of timber catch fire easily from the spark, generated by the flint.

To his delight, after a few strikes of the flint, the spark ignited the shavings he had made. So, within a few moments his fire was burning well, and he was able to progressively put the larger bits of wood on.

When it was well alight, Mo took the maize out of his pocket and put several kernels into the lidless kettle. Carefully he put his food source on to the fire.

As he gazed at the flickering flames, Mo was suddenly overwhelmed by self-doubt about the wisdom of his pilgrimage.

'Had he done the right thing, leaving his home to come to a land he knew virtually nothing about? To find a man that he thought liked him enough to adopt him? Had he just been blind to the enormity of the task?

After all, he didn't know how or where to find the soldier, and if he did find him, what reaction would he receive?

On the other hand, Sergeant Tom must have liked him because he gave him the penknife and flint. He didn't give presents to anyone else,' he reasoned. 'Perhaps he just felt sorry for me, because I had lost my family and he didn't really like me at all.'

'Then there would be the constant threat of the immigration people, who would return him back home, if they found him. I have no papers to allow me to be here anyway. What have I done?

It really was a hopeless quest. Should he just hand himself in?

Then he thought about losing his friend Abdul. That really was the worst thing.' A tear of self-pity trickled down his cheek. 'Perhaps he owed it to him to continue.' His fatigue was playing games with his mind.

The maize in the kettle had been boiling for ten long and hungry minutes, and his rumbling stomach told him that was long enough.

Pulling his sleeve down, to protect his hand from the hot kettle handle, he lifted it carefully off the fire.

Impatiently, he grabbed hold of the end of a hot cob and plucked it out, waving it around in the air to cool it off.

Cautiously, he bit into the yellow corn and was pleased that it was now relatively soft.

Hungrily he devoured the small cob, stripping it back to the core and pulled another out of the kettle, scalding his lips as he attacked it with vigour.

Finally, he ate the last one, but still felt hungry and toyed with the idea of cooking more from the vast supply surrounding him. But instead, he finished the meal off with some more blackberries, that he had put in his pocket earlier.

Feeling quite full, he lay down by the fire and closed his tired eyes.

'Now he had eaten, perhaps life wasn't so bad after all, 'he thought.

He reviewed his long tiring journey and marvelled at the good fortune that had befallen him, the catamaran boat trip, the lorry journey to Asti, the Scout Camp, the car ride to Grenoble and then Paris and the McDonalds meal too. Perhaps it hadn't been so bad. So perhaps he would stay in England and find the Sergeant after all.'

Suddenly, he heard the sound of a large truck coming towards him, its engine noise increasing in volume.

As the road was a few hundred yards away, the only place that he could think that the vehicle was coming from, was the airfield or maybe the farmer in his tractor.

Whatever it was, it came to a halt, then several doors slammed. He could hear voices approaching and they seemed to be coming to his location.

Quickly he roused himself and poured water from the kettle over the fire creating a cloud of steam and heard a voice say, 'Yeah, there look. It's over there.'

Then he could hear people running towards him.

All of a panic, he picked up his things and ran farther into the middle of the maize field trying not to damage the plants or leave a trail. His heart was in his mouth as he stumbled through the tall plants.

After a hundred yards he stopped running and knelt. As he was kneeling down, he caught a brief glimpse of the visitors and recognised them as firemen. They made their way directly to the site of his fire.

'Looks like somebody's had a fire here,' one of the uniformed men said, examining Mo's steaming camp fire.

'Probably got a homeless person on our patch,' one of the other firemen added. 'Or kids. Can't be too far away. Hiding probably.'

They used a small portable extinguisher to douse the smouldering embers to ensure it was completely out.

'Well, so long as whoever it is, doesn't interfere with the flights or cause problems for the airport, then that's not our problem.'

'Unless they set fire to the field that is,' one of the others added.

'I'll let control know and if they want to let the police and the farmer know that's down to them.

Come on guys, let's get back to that game of snooker.'

With that, they left the maize field leaving a very relieved Mo.

Mo heard the fire tender driving off and decided he needed to move from the field and get on and build his house in the tree as soon as possible.

# Chapter Fifty-two

Mo was feeling very vulnerable. He had been in England for less than a day and had already experienced two situations when he could have been discovered.

These 'near misses' had unsettled him and potentially he could be on his way home before he'd even started his search for the Sergeant. That would have ended his dream, and all of his efforts would have been for nothing.

So, with this threat hanging over him, he set to with urgent intent to build himself a tree house in the willow tree that he'd surveyed earlier.

The advantages were obvious, he thought. It was away from passers-by, curious dogs, their owners prying eyes and the noisy road.

It would also provide him with a high-level observation platform to spot any unwelcome visits by the authorities. Fortunately, the top of the tree was well hidden by the leaf covered branches.

At one stage, Mo was tempted to use an empty abandoned shed near the rubbish tip, which would need no work at all to make it ready for use.

However, the risk of discovery by someone working on the airfield was too great, he decided.

So, Mo busied himself going back and forth between the tip and the willow tree, constantly vigilant about people walking along the path.

Raiding the discarded pile of 'thrown out' material on the airfield, he constructed a den in the bole of the willow tree using planks of wood. He built a roof over the top for shelter, using some canvas and a corrugated iron sheet, although the current weather was dry and mild.

Satsfied with his efforts, Mo went back towards his hide, where he'd slept the previous night to retrieve his stolen duvet and rucksack.

Half way into his journey, in the distance, he spotted someone who appeared to be sitting on a chair in the middle of the path.

He froze. Were they after him? Was this some sort of trap?

# Chapter Fifty-three

Unsure whether to turn back or not, he carried on nonchalantly, to avoid raising suspicions.

As he drew closer, he could see that it was an old woman sitting in an electric wheelchair. She was cursing and swearing.

'Bloody wheelchair...stupid thing,' she said, thumping the arm rest.

Noticing Mo, she stopped her cursing and demanded, 'What are you looking at?'

'Umm,' Mo muttered, frightened by the vitriolic woman.

Still staring at him, she appeared to be turning something over in her mind and then suddenly said, 'Oh, you must be the repairman that the salesman told me would automatically come to repair it, if I paid him an extra premium.'

Mo looked at her blankly, gauging whether to run away from this bizarre conversation.

'Well? Come on then,' the woman demanded.

'Sorry, I don't know what you mean,' he puzzled.

'Well this chair isn't going to sort itself out. Get on with it.'

'You think I have come to...Oh! I a..' At last, Mo grasped what she was on about.

'I paid good money for breakdown cover on this chair. Now get on with it. I haven't got all day.'

Bemused by the situation, and always taught to be respectful to his elders, Mo thought he ought to do something to help the confused old lady.

He knelt and studied the wheelchair, not really expecting to be able to help at all. Then he spotted the problem.

'The wheels are tangled in the grass,' Mo explained. 'If you get out, I will be able to untangle them for you.'

'Get out...get out! I haven't been able to get out of my chair for fifteen years,' she replied indignantly.

'Oh, so do you sleep in it?' Mo asked, innocently.

'No, of course I don't. Are you stupid or something?'

'Oh, Ok,' he said, and not wishing to antagonise her or spend any more time with the lady than was necessary, he started trying to untangle the grass from around the wheels.

He soon discovered that the stems were so tightly wrapped around the drive wheels, that he couldn't undo them with his hands. 'She had obviously just continued on until the grass had wound her to a stop,' he concluded.

The only option open to him, he decided, was to cut the tangled grass off the wheels with his knife, so he took it out of his pocket and opened the blade ready to chop through the tough stalks.

At which stage the old lady became agitated and flew out of the wheelchair without a hint of infirmity.

'Don't you threaten me! You put that knife away! I shall call the police,' she said nervously, backing away from him.

'It's OK. Don't worry. I am only using my knife to cut the grass off,' he explained, sawing away. 'I thought you couldn't move?' he added quietly.

'Ohhh...I didn't realise I could,' she lied, her ruse of complete infirmity now exposed.

After a few minutes of sawing through the tangled mess, he succeeded.

'There. That looks like the last bit,' he said discarding a large tangle of knotted grass. 'I think you are free now,' he advised her.

Not expecting any gratitude from the old lady, Mo stood up, closed his pen-knife and walked away from the wheelchair, intending to continue his trip to retrieve his property.

Meanwhile, the old lady was watching him suspiciously and as soon as he was a few yards away, she rushed back to her 'chariot'.

Immediately, she grabbed the joy stick on the wheelchair and intended to reverse it away from him... but nothing happened. She made several attempts, but the wheelchair motor did not even start.

'Well so much for your repair,' she shouted, having regained her confidence now that the knife was out of sight.

'I think you must have run down the battery trying to get out of the grass. I expect it is now flat,' Mo observed.

'Don't be so stupid. My battery is square. It is NOT flat,' she shouted belligerently. 'What sort of wheelchair mechanic are you? Why, you don't even know that batteries are square?'

'I'm not a qualified mechanic...'Mo started too say.

'That's obvious. Well if you can't repair it, you'll just have to push me back to the house,' she commanded.

'I...I...'Mo was wrong-footed and lost for words.

'Come on. I'll be late for my afternoon tea, if you don't hurry.'

Mo didn't know what to do. He was being asked to go somewhere where people would see him, which he'd been desperately trying to avoid all day.

But what could he do? He couldn't leave the old lady abandoned on the track. She might die. There was no-one else in sight, so he just had to risk being seen. That was all there was to it. After all, he remembered, he was a Scout and should help people.

Reluctantly, he grabbed hold of the push handles, turned the wheelchair around and started pushing her back along the track. It was hard going over the long grasses and progress was slow.

He pushed her past his den and the hidden duvet and rucksack.

As they arrived at the large tunnel under the main road, that Mo had seen in the early hours, the path sloped down dramatically. He was concerned that she might fall out and so decided it would be safer to wheel the chair backwards down the slope.

However, he soon regretted his decision because the combined weight of woman and chair was too much for his weakened arm to restrain. Consequently, the handle bar, rammed, with some force, painfully into his side.

'Ouch,' Mo said, rubbing himself, thinking the blow had been heavy enough to damage his kidneys.

'Did that hurt you?'

'Yes,' he groaned.

'Well, you shouldn't have been so clumsy,' she said, unsympathetically. 'Now if you wouldn't mind, we go under the bridge here and up on to a path the other side,' she ordered.

Mo was more concerned with his painful side than pushing a cantankerous old woman in a broken-down wheelchair.

'Well, what are we waiting for?' she questioned.

He was already getting more apprehensive about going this far into civilisation and was toying with the idea of leaving her there anyway.

'Come on,' she goaded. 'I shall miss my afternoon tea.'

Mo was still unsure, 'What if he was spotted? Then again why would anyone ask him who he was? He was with the old lady anyway, and she had accepted him without question.'

'I won't tell you again, let's go,' she ordered.

Mo decided he didn't have a choice and the old lady might be a good cover for him. So he resumed his efforts and quickly regretted it as he attempted to push the wheelchair up the sloping path the other side.

Having not eaten much for a few days, he was feeling quite weak anyway.

'If you get out, I will be able to get the wheelchair to the top,' he suggested.

'Get out? Get out!' I wouldn't need the wheelchair if I could get out,' she ranted.

So Mo struggled up the path and by the time he got to level ground he was exhausted, he stopped.

'Well what are we stopping for now?' she demanded.

'I need to catch my breath for a minute,' he panted.

'Come on, I shall miss my tea,' the old lady repeated.

Reluctantly he started pushing again, but at least now the track was a proper gravelled path.

Meanwhile, the woman continued to mutter under her breath and suddenly turned around and looked at him.

'You're not a proper wheelchair mechanic, are you?' she stated.

'Well...no...not really...' he admitted awkwardly.

'Mmm, you look foreign to me and your accent...are you from the camp?'

'Camp! What camp?'

'There is only one camp around here. It's the army camp of course.'

''Yes...yes that's right. I'm from the camp,' he said excitedly, thinking on his feet. 'An army camp nearby, what luck. Perhaps he wasn't too far away from Sergeant Tom after all,' he thought.

Suddenly, pushing the old woman didn't feel so much of a chore. Excitement was building in his stomach.

'Yes, I used to be an English teacher abroad. Those were the best days of my life,' she said, drifting off, visiting her memories of yesteryear.

'You smell of smoke,' she randomly observed.

'Oh do I?' Mo said , realising that the smoke from his campfire had obviously permeated his clothes.

'Not much further,' she encouraged.

Mo pushed her along a path into a recreation park. On one side of the park, a football pitch had been marked out. On the other side, vegetables were being grown on several patches of divided land.

'A future food source for me,' he thought.

The tiring push continued past a child's play area, complete with swings, a roundabout and a slide.

'What he would have done to have had those toys at home, when he was a kid,' he thought.

He had to manoeuvre the wheelchair through a gate, designed to prevent cars and motorbikes getting into the park. Unfortunately, he scraped the side of the wheelchair and was berated for his 'clumsiness'.

'Why don't you look what you're doing. I get through there without scraping it. I don't know. Young people. Huh!' she ranted.

'He wondered if all English people were as grumpy as this lady.'

She directed him through a carpark and to the main entrance of the park. Just before the exit, there was a single storey building, next to which was a tall mast with a CCTV camera on top.

On spotting it, Mo bowed his head to hide his face.

As they got out to the entrance, the old lady pointed to the right.

'This is my house here,' she said, indicating a large nursing home.

He pushed her down the drive towards 'her house' and was halfway down the tarmacked road when a nurse came out to meet them.

'Hello Jennifer. Been on one of your adventures again, have you?' And you've found someone to bring you back again, I see,' she said, smiling at Mo. 'Battery again I expect?'

Mo nodded.

'Julie, he's not a mechanic you know. He doesn't even know what a battery looks like. He thinks it's flat.' Jennifer added.

'Well thank you for bringing her back young man. You must be exhausted pushing the wheelchair. Would you like a drink?'

'A drink?'

'Water, a cup of Tea, squash?'

'Squash, please.' Mo loved the taste of the Sergeant's squash that he used to bring to Scouts.

'We'll just take Jennifer inside, and I'll take you into the kitchen. Sarah, our chef, will get you a drink.'

Mo followed the nurse and Jennifer into the building. He had not expected to be treated so well. Perhaps his luck was in after all.

# Chapter Fifty-four

Mo left the nursing home satiated, with a stomach full of sandwiches and cake, washed down by several glasses of squash.

For, after Julie had explained about Mo's gallant efforts in rescuing Jennifer, Sarah had served Mo with a generous quantity of food and drink, in the well-equipped modern kitchen.

'I can see that you're a growing lad with a big appetite,' Sarah said, watching the hungry young man quickly devouring whatever she put in front of him.

'By the way, what's your name?'

'Mohammed,' he said, barely pausing to answer.

'Pleased to meet you, Mohammed. Would you like some more?'

'Yes, please.'

After restocking his plate several times, finally, the offer for more, ended.

'Thank you once again for rescuing Jennifer.' Sarah said, walking Mo to the door.

'Thank you for the food and drink,' Mo said, smiling.

Mo left the Nursing home and intended to resume his interrupted journey to collect his duvet and rucksack.

Now full and, feeling quite relaxed about his contact with the English people, for no-one had tried to stop or question him, quite the opposite. The people in the Nursing home had been very kind and chatty.

As he made his way back through the recreation park, he had time to look around without the distraction of Jennifer's ranting.

He spotted a map board and found that he was in a village called Churchdown. This revelation meant nothing to him, because there was no reference to where that was in England.

He stopped nearby and enviously watched a group of children having fun on a large concrete skateboard ramp. The youngsters, of varying ages, were pulling stunts on their trick scooters; something that Mo hadn't seen before.

As he moved on, he noticed there was a deserted basketball court and beyond that the undulating humps of a BMX bike track.

Next to the building, that said 'Parish Council Offices', he spotted a toilet sign and investigated it.

The door was unlocked, and he made full use of the facilities, including washing himself.

Afterwards, he took some time looking at the row of allotments nearby and the various produce growing there. He also noted a tap on a wall, which he assumed was for a water supply.

Feeling more comfortable in his surroundings, he left the park and wandered back to the hole in the hedge, to finally reclaim his duvet and rucksack.

Making sure that no-one was watching, he knelt and put his hand in to the 'hole in the hedge' to retrieve them.

His effort was rewarded with a sharp painful injury to the back of his hand, accompanied by a frightening hiss from something inside.

Ouch, that hurt,' he said in total shock, quickly withdrawing his hand and examining it.

He was surprised to see three long red scratch marks on it. 'What did that?' he wondered.

The euphoria of a full belly and a 'wash and brush up' was destroyed in an instant. His heart was pounding.

'What's in there? What have I disturbed?' His imagination ran wild, Perhaps a wild animal, fox or badger...perhaps a vagrant...or another migrant like himself.

Perhaps he ought to run. Unsure what to do, he debated his options;- whether to forget his things and leave it to whatever was guarding it, or to brave it out and quickly retrieve it using a stick.

Then he heard a quiet mewing coming from inside and decided to investigate further.

With his heart in his mouth, he cautiously crept forward on all fours. Craning his neck, to see the current resident. He was tensed up like a coiled spring and ready to exit quickly, if it was anything dangerous.

Slowly he moved forward, an inch at a time, until he could see the perpetrator. Immediately he relaxed, for lying on his duvet, was a short coat white cat with three newly born kittens.

The cat had obviously gone into the hide to have her kittens and was guarding them, when the strange hand, that she thought was going to steal them, had appeared.

Each kitten had different markings. One was tabby with white feet, the other two were white, like their mother. Looking closer, he could see that one had a ginger 'bonnet' markings on its head, while the other two sported black markings.

Mo smiled at the scene. 'Hello kitty,' he said softly. 'So, it was you was it? It's OK, I'm not going to take your babies.'

Reassured by his calm voice, the mother seemed to relax and started licking her brood.

'Now what am I going to do?' he wondered. 'I will need that duvet for tonight. But I can't throw you off. And if I leave you here that nosey dog or a fox might come and kill your kittens.'

He stroked the cat, who purred at his touch, while he decided what to do. Finally, he made his mind up.

'Ok. You're all coming back to my tree house with me,' he said finally.

Checking again that no-one was around, he backed out of the hole in the hedge, put his rucksack on and dragged the duvet with him. The cat didn't move from the duvet as he pulled it out.

'Ok Mum we are going to go for a short trip,' he said, scooping up the duvet and kittens. But the cat wasn't keen on staying in the bundle, so she jumped out and watched Mo tenderly cradle her brood.

'You going to follow then?' he asked, looking at the cat. Slowly he started walking with the precious cargo. The mother cat followed on behind him, like an obedient dog.

When he arrived at the tree house, he put the duvet, containing the kittens, down on the ground and took off his rucksack and coat. He lifted the kittens one by one from the duvet and put them into his rucksack.

He climbed the branch, carrying the duvet over his shoulder, then laid it in the bole of the tree.

He took the kittens out of his rucksack, one at a time and laid them on the duvet, shortly after mother cat climbed up and laid herself by her brood.

Mo looked at his new companions.

'Welcome to your new home. So what shall we call you all?' he asked, looking at the three bundles of fur snuggling into their mother.

'I think ginger cap, you will be Abdul,' his voice catching in his throat as he said his friends name. 'I will call black cap after my Uncle Hassim and you my Tabby friend will be Tom, after my Sergeant Tom.

Tomorrow we will have to make some special arrangements for a toilet tray and food. But now I am very tired, so we can all go to sleep together.'

Content that he was safe with his new friends, Mo lay down by the side of them and although it was still daylight, his busy schedule had tired him out, and within a few minutes he was fast asleep.

His first day in England, a success.

# Chapter Fifty-five

It was night time when Mo awoke. The moon and stars gave the scenery a ghostly appearance. It was quiet. There was no sound of traffic either.

His sandwich and cake tea were now long forgotten, and he felt hungry again. He tried to go back to sleep, but the emptiness in his stomach prayed on his mind, so eventually he decided to go looking for something to eat.

He slid down from his tree house and followed his route back through the recreation park, and with his newly gained self-confidence, he emerged on to the road, near the nursing home. There was no-one around. He had the empty road to himself.

Instead of turning right towards the Nursing home, where he returned Jennifer and her broken down wheelchair, he walked straight across the road and over a mini roundabout.

As he wandered along the road, he saw that virtually all the houses had at least one, but mostly two cars, parked in front of them.

He concluded that it was obviously a wealthy community.

On the pavement, in front of each house, there were small and large green plastic containers.

'I wonder what these are?' he pondered.

His curiosity got the better of him and as there was no-one around, he opened the lid of one of the small green containers and was surprised to see food inside.

A chicken carcass lay on top of a pile of cooked vegetables and the sight and the delicious smell made him salivate.

He picked up the carcass and could see that there was still a lot of meat on the bones. Hungrily, he started tearing the meat off it.

'If this is a rubbish bin, why would anyone throw good food away,' he wondered, savouring each delicious mouthful.

'I expect the cat would like some,' he decided, slipping a few pieces into his jacket pocket.

After a few minutes, and satisfied that he'd stripped as much of the white meat off the bones as possible, he put the now meatless carcass back into the container.

Hoping for a similar feast, he moved on to another small green bin at the next house, but the contents smelt foul. So he moved on to another and was rewarded by finding some apples and oranges in it. Although they were near the end of being edible, they were very soft, and deliciously sweet and juicy.

'Great,' he thought, 'looks like these containers will provide me with a guaranteed supply of food. People must be so rich that they can afford to throw good food away. What a waste.'

He looked in several large green bins, but found only general rubbish, nothing edible.

'So, I guess they must be rich people to pay for someone to take their rubbish away,' he concluded.

As he wandered further into the estate, he noted that in front of some people's doors there were empty bottles and wondered what they were for.

He didn't have long to wait to find out, for he heard a vehicle coming along the road, stopping and starting every few minutes.

As it got closer, he hid in a large carpark nearby, and watched as the vehicle arrived opposite to his hiding place.

He watched as a man got out of his small truck, then went around to the back of it and took two bottles containing a white liquid from inside. He then carried the bottles around to the house, where the empty bottles were and swapped them.

The man put the empty bottles in the back of his truck, and then drove off for a short distance and repeated the same action over again.

Mo was fascinated by this early morning ritual. Obviously, it was a delivery of something, but what?

He cautiously left his hiding place, and walked up to a house that had two bottles of the white liquid. He picked one up and sniffed it. It didn't smell of anything particularly.

The bottle was sealed with a round silver top, and as he picked it up, his thumb pushed through the top of the bottle. A small fountain of white liquid splashed out over his hand. He licked his fingers and discovered that it was milk.

'They have a man deliver their milk to their door, rather than get it from the shops. Is there no end to their richness?' he wondered.

'I doubt that they will miss this bottle, as they are obviously so rich. I will take this one back for me and the cats,' he decided.

On his way back to the treehouse, he started looking in the large green bins for something that he could pour the milk into for the cat, and found a chipped cup and saucer that someone was throwing away.

'That will do nicely' he decided, taking them.

After his nocturnal exploration around the housing estate, he made his way back and scrambled up the branch, carefully carrying his 'booty' just as it was starting to get light.

'It's only me,' he whispered to the cat.

But she was already alert to his arrival, and lay back when she recognised him. The kittens were all snuggled up into their mother, so he carefully joined them on the duvet.

'I've got something for you Mum,' he said, digging into his pocket and retrieving the chicken pieces.

Mo fed her the meat, and carefully poured some milk into the recycled saucer.

'There you are, a nice drink for you and your babies,' he told her.

Suspicious at first, she sniffed the white liquid and then, satisfied it was milk, lapped it up hungrily and cleared the saucer. She licked her whiskers, and lay back down again.

After watching her consume it, Mo stroked the cat for a short while, then snuggled down too and was quickly asleep again.

# Chapter Fifty-six

Having kittens sleeping and living in the same area as himself, did present its smelly problems when they needed to do their business, although Mother cat was good at tending to them. And she was quite content to leave her sightless and deaf brood in Mo's care while she did her own business around the base of the tree.

Despite supervising the kittens, the day seemed to drag and the chicken that he'd shared with the cat in the early hours was long forgotten by his grumbling stomach.

So he decided to go and find some more food from somewhere. Although it was daylight, with his new won confidence, of just blending in to the community, he slithered back down from the tree and ventured out.

In his excitement of looking after the cat and her three tiny kittens, Mo had forgotten that the old lady had mentioned an army camp nearby.

After all, his single purpose for coming to England was to track down Sergeant Tom.

But, his first priority was to find something for himself and the cat to eat and then he would try and find the camp...and hopefully Sergeant Tom.

He retraced his steps through the recreation field and on to the road to where he found the chicken carcass in the small green bin, hoping that it would have been topped up with more food. But he was disappointed to find that it had disappeared, in fact there were no plastic bins out anywhere.

Worse still, all the bottles of milk had disappeared too, and there were only a few empty ones out instead.

'Oh, now what do I do?' he wondered. 'I hoped that was going to be my ready supply of meals. I'll have to go elsewhere and see what I can find,' he thought. 'I don't really want to risk having another fire to cook more corn cobs.'

He wandered further along several roads and was surprised to see that people were leaving clothes outside their houses in plastic bags. 'These were rich people indeed,' he concluded, 'if they could give away their clothes.'

Deeper into the estate, he came across a lady struggling with two heavy bags of shopping.

He stopped and looked at her for a few minutes, wondering whether to say anything. Now emboldened by his visit to the nursing home, he decided to offer his assistance. 'Can I help?' he asked. 'Those bags look really heavy.'

The woman looked at him suspiciously.

'I'm quite strong,' he reiterated.

The woman looked at the bags and at him again and reasoned that if he was going to do anything to her, they were in the middle of the village and she could scream anyway. Feeling quite fatigued, she decided to take up his offer.

'Yes please, I haven't got that far to go, but the bags are a lot heavier than I thought. Either that or I'm getting old. My husband Roger normally takes me, but the car is in for a service.'

'Oh,' Mo said, without a clue about what sort of religious service would be performed on a car.

'Yes please, young man,' the lady said. 'I'm only going to the Church hall, it's just up the road here.'

'Ok, 'he said, moving to pick up the bags.

'Don't strain yourself, I can carry one of them,' she added.

'No, it's OK. I can carry both,' he insisted, immediately regretting his macho stance, for as he lifted the bags, he found that they were, really heavy.

'That's very kind of you. You're like a knight in shining armour.'

'Sorry, I don't understand.'

'No, don't worry it's just an old saying.'

'Ok.'

'I'm going to be doing some cooking for a large group of people and I've got all the food in these bags. That's why they're so heavy,' she explained.

Food! Mo had a large quantity of food in his hands, possibly enough for his and the cats needs for some time and he was tempted with the idea of running off with the bags. But quickly dismissed the idea, he didn't want to attract unwelcome attention to himself.

'Yes, I'm doing bread and soup today. Soup is my speciality,' she continued. 'If you're not in a rush, I'll let you taste some.'

'Mo's eyes lit up. 'Yes please,' he replied without hesitation. 'I am not rushing off anywhere,' he confirmed.

When they got to the Church hall there was a group of ladies arriving who greeted the 'Soup maker'.

'Hi Julie, I see you've got yourself some help today.'

'Yes, this young man came to my rescue. I'd forgotten how heavy those bags are with all my catering stuff in.'

Julie led Mo through the hall to a large kitchen.

'Thank you for helping me. Please put the bags down. Grab yourself a stool while I start preparing things.'

'I will help you,' he offered.

'No, thanks. I have a routine that I'm used to. If you want to be helpful, would you mind doing some washing up for me?'

'Sure, what do I have to do?'

As she finished with the various implements, Julie showed Mo how to do the washing and wiping up.

In the meantime, she had put the contents for the soup into large stainless-steel saucepans and was heating them up.

'Those ladies who we saw earlier, are they your soup eaters?'

'No, they are people who get together to do knitting for people in refugee camps in Syria.'

'They are paid?'

'No. They do it voluntarily. They donate their time and the wool, and don't charge.' Julie informed him. 'When I'm not doing this, I usually join them.'

'That is so kind that people do this to help others,' Mo said, reviewing his initial thoughts about the rich pampered people of the area.

'We call it knit and natter,' Julie laughed.

'Knit and natter,' Mo repeated. 'That truly is strange.'

'Natter is like people talking together,' Julie explained. 'Right, I think the first batch of soup is almost ready.' She said, peering into a steaming saucepan. 'Would you like to taste some?

'Yes please,' Mo confirmed excitedly.

'The first one is chicken. Be careful. There are some big pieces of meat in it,' she advised, ladling the soup into a dish.'

Mo had been salivating as soon as the soup had gone on the stove and now at last, he had the opportunity to fill his empty stomach.

'Would you like some bread with it? she asked.

'Yes please,' Mo replied, surreptitiously removing and pocketing some of the chicken for the cat.

By the time she had cut a few slices of bread, Julie was surprised to see that half the contents of his bowl had already disappeared.

'My, you do have a healthy appetite. When you've finished that, do you want some more?'

'Yes please,' he confirmed, briefly pausing in between shovelling spoonsful of the delicious soup into his mouth.

'It truly is lovely. Thank you,' he beamed.

'By the way, I forgot to ask your name?' she said.

'Mohammed,' he said, not stopping eating for a second.

'Mohammed! Are you from the camp?'

'Yes,' he lied, and seeing his opportunity to find out where the camp was, he said, 'I forget the name of the road.'

'The one in Innsworth Lane you mean?'

'Innsworth Lane, he repeated. 'Yes, I get lost around here. Is that down this road here?' he gesticulated vaguely.

Julie then explained where it was in relation to their present location at the Church Hall.

'Yes, I remember now,' he lied.

After his third bowl of soup, and insisting on washing up, Mo said he would leave before her diners arrived.

'Thank you, Mohammed. I hope you don't get lost following my instructions.'

'No, I'm sure I'll be OK. Thank you once again for the soup. It was very nice.'

# Chapter Fifty-seven

However, following Julie's directions, Mo did take a wrong turn and eventually arrived at a large carpark with a brick building set back off the road.

To his great delight, he spotted a noticeboard at the front of the carpark with a badge that he recognised. It was a scout badge.

The door of the building was closed, but there was a car in the carpark and a grey-haired man was on his hands and knees painting white lines for parking spaces.

Mo stood watching him for a few minutes, then finally worked up courage to go and speak to him.

'Excuse me Sir.'

No response.

Mo walked closer to the man and repeated louder. 'Excuse me Sir.'

The man looked up.

'Oh, sorry. I was miles away. Yes, young man, how can I help?' the bearded, bespectacled man asked kindly.

'Umm...do Scouts meet here?' Mo asked, suddenly feeling self-conscious at getting the man's attention.

'Yes. They meet on a Tuesday, which is tonight of course.'

'Umm...what time?'

'Quarter to eight. Why do you ask? Were you thinking about coming along?'

'Yes. I am a Scout from Afghanistan and I'd like to meet other Scouts.'

'Well, I'm sure they'd be delighted to meet you too. I will try to remember to tell the Scout Leader that you might come along. If not, I'm sure that he will be pleased to meet you,' the old man said.

'Thank you, Sir.'

'Not Sir. I haven't been knighted. My name is Paul and I'm the President of the Scout Group,' the white-haired pensioner informed him. 'And they haven't even painted my house white yet.'

Mo looked at him puzzled.

'Sorry. You probably don't know what I'm on about. Do you?' the old man said apologetically. 'I think it should be a president's privilege to live in a white house. After all the President of the United States lives in the White House,' he joked.

Mo stared at him blankly.

'Just my little joke,' the man said, embarrassed that his humour had fallen flat.

'Oh, I see,' Mo said politely, thinking that the old man was a bit strange. 'Is there a Scout Leader by the name of Tom here?'

'Yes,' the pensioner confirmed.

'Thank you. Thank you very much. I will come back tonight.' Mo left with a spring in his step.

Could his search be at an end so soon?

Overjoyed that he might make contact with Sergeant Tom tonight, he almost flew back to the tree house.

He decided that if Sergeant Tom was going to be at Scouts, he didn't need to look for the camp after all.

But after feeding the cat with the food from the soup lady, he fell asleep.

# Chapter Fifty-eight

Mo dreamt about meeting Sergeant Tom and how he would welcome him with open arms. Then reluctantly he woke up, and as he didn't have a watch, he wondered if he'd missed the Scout's meeting.

He judged that it was early evening, based on the low volume of traffic noise from the nearby road.

Unsure about the time though, he decided that he would go up to the Scout building and see if anyone was around anyway.

He was excited by the prospect that Sergeant Tom was going to be there.

Wanting to show that he really was a Scout, he dug out his very crumpled Afghan neckerchief that the Sergeant had given them all. He put it around his neck and tightened it up with the turks head woggle that he'd made.

He was beside himself with excitement, as he said goodbye to the cat, quickly making his way through the recreational field.

Resisting the temptation to stop and watch the antics of the children in the skate park on their stunt scooters.

As he arrived at the Scout building, there were lots of young girls in brown uniforms arriving with their parents. There was no sign of any Scouts.

Hoping that he hadn't missed the Scout meeting, he decided to wait to see and hung around near the wooden perimeter fence by the noticeboard.

Mo didn't care that he was attracting strange looks from some of the parents. His anticipation at going to see Sergeant Tom again was giving him butterflies.

However, while he was waiting, he was tortured by the delicious smell of food cooking, and then noticed that nearby there were several buildings where the tempting aroma was coming from.

He walked a short distance from where he was holding his vigil and to his delight, he discovered a club, a pub, an Indian and a Chinese restaurant.

Outside each of the buildings he could see large bins and wondered what they contained. Could it be discarded food, perhaps.'

'I'll check later to see what's inside,' he vowed. His stomach rumbled at the thought.

Eventually, after hanging around for what seemed ages, the Brownies meeting finished, and their parents arrived to take them home and shortly after, their Leaders left too.

Mo was starting to panic, had he missed the Scout meeting? But he didn't have to wait long for reassurance for a short time later, cars started arriving again. Mo's excitement mounted as more cars arrived and dropped off young people in green Scout uniform.

As the children waited outside, he attracted a few suspicious looks from several of the Scouts, making him feel slightly uncomfortable.

Then several Leaders arrived and drove into the car park.

As each driver left their vehicle Mo was on tenterhooks was this his long awaited guru.

But, to Mo's disappointment, none of the Leaders was Sergeant Tom.

Trying to counter his disappointment, he convinced himself that the soldier hopefully would arrive later.

Nevertheless he was still excited at the possibility of joining the other Scouts, like he'd done briefly with the International Scouts in Italy. At the same time, he was feeling anxious that they might not welcome him; After all, he only had his neckerchief to prove that he was a Scout.

By now, everyone had disappeared into the building. He was working up courage to go in himself, when the door opened, and a leader walked towards him.

'Hello young man. Were you thinking of joining us tonight?' the uniformed Leader asked. 'Paul said that you were hoping to come back.'

'Yeah,' Mo muttered.

'I see you're wearing a neckerchief. I don't recognise it. Is it from a Scout Group round here?'

Mo cleared his throat. 'No, it is a special one.'

'I can see that. Are you a Scout?'

'Yes I am. From Afghanistan.'

'Would you like to come in to our meeting tonight? We have only just restarted after the summer holidays,' the leader explained.

'Please. Could I?' Mo beamed.

'Before you join us for the evening, can you tell me a bit about yourself?'

Mo felt uneasy and rocked from side to side nervously.

Reading the signs of mistrust, the leader added. 'My name is Dave, I'm an assistant Scout Leader. So, what's yours?'

'Mohammed.'

'Hello Mohammed, pleased to meet you,' he said and extended his left hand.

Immediately Mo extended his left hand too and shook the Scout Leader's hand.

'Welcome to Churchdown. Are you living locally?'

'Yes.'

'You said your 'necker' is from a Scout Group. What was the name of your Scout Leader? Perhaps I know him.'

'Sergeant Tom. Is he here? Do you have a Tom here?' Mo asked excitedly hoping his search was over.

'Yes, we do, but he hasn't mentioned being a Leader anywhere else than here. You say he was a Sergeant, not heard of that rank in Scouting.'

'No, he was in the army and ...' Mo realised he was going to have to divulge more about his circumstances, when the Scouter suddenly looked at his watch.

'Right, the Scout Leader is just about to start the troop meeting. Are you coming in?'

'Please.'

'Come on then. We'll have a further chat later.'

They entered  the single storey brick building, down each side of the hall were continuous low-level varnished storage lockers; the floor was covered in thermoplastic tiles; the roof was supported by open girders where some large flat painted boards were being stored.

At the end of the fifty foot long hall Mo could see some wooden boards recording the names of Queen Scouts and another for a Guides award.

The Scouts were lined up in a 'horseshoe' shape of five patrols. In each patrol there were six scouts. Mo was surprised to see boys and girls in the same patrol. Some of them looked at Mo as he nervously entered with Dave.

Dave spoke to Rich who then introduced Mo to the troop and added him to the Eagles patrol, asking the Patrol Leader to look after him.

'After flag break, we are doing knots and lashings.' Rich informed them.

There was some muttering from the Scouts following this revelation, but Mo was quite happy with this proposal. It was something he'd excelled at with Sergeant Tom.

As the evening progressed, he impressed his patrol by not only doing the variety of knots but was also able to teach two people who had just 'come up' from Cubs as well.

But his excitement of an anticipated meeting with the Sergeant was dashed when he was introduced to a young leader called Tom.

'Oh you're not my Sergeant,' he said crestfallen.

'No, they call me Spatch,' the other informed him.

'That's a strange name,' Mo observed.

'Yeah well that's my nickname. The young leader informed him.

Dave was keeping a watchful eye on the newcomer and spoke to another assistant leader.

'Jacky, it looks like he's getting on Ok with the Eagles,' he observed. 'What do you reckon?'

'He seems to know what he's doing with the knotting too. He's a big lad. He must be nearly fifteen though. I reckon he's got to be Explorer age.'

'Fifteen! Yeah, now you come to mention it. He probably is. He's got some adolescent fur on his top lip too. I didn't get around to asking him his age.'

'He seems to be accepted by the patrol, especially by the Patrol Leader, Angelina. They are about the same age, I would imagine.

'Yes, I think you're right. The other thing is, he smells a bit,' she revealed.

'Really? As you know, I have no sense of smell. Although, the kids don't appear to have a problem with it.'

'Do we know anything about him?'

'Not yet. He was saying his former Scout Leader was a Sergeant in the army, so I could guess he's associated with the military camp down the road.

Mo joined in the games and proved to be a worthy contributor to his patrol. The anxiety and worry of his struggle of getting to England, disappeared in the enjoyment of an evening playing games with the other Scouts.

It wasn't until the end of the evening when all the Scouts were going home that he was reminded of his homeless existence.

The Scout Leader called him into the small kitchen near the front of the hall and quizzed him about the evening.

'Well, Mohammed. How did you enjoy that, tonight?'

'It was great. I had fun. Thank you.'

'I judge from your accent that you aren't from around these parts. Where is home for you?'

'I...umm.' Mo hesitated.

'Don't feel you have to tell me if you don't want to,' Rich reassured him.

'OK. I...'

'Tell you what. Do you want to...are you able to come again next week?'

'Yes please,' Mo beamed.

'Ok. Well for my records, I will need some personal details. Like date of birth, home address, parent's names etc. Do you understand?'

'Yes.' Mo froze. 'How could he tell him about being a stateless orphan and homeless too?

'We will also need some subs.'

'Subs? What is subs?'

'Some people call it a membership fee.'

'Oh!' Mo's lack of money meant that he couldn't come back again. His heart sank.

And worse still, Sergeant Tom wasn't there either.

# Chapter Fifty-nine

Now slightly demoralised by the Scout Leader's need for some personal details, Mo hung around after Scouts had finished to see if he could get at the contents of the large rubbish containers, that he'd spotted earlier.

The smells were so tempting, and not having eaten anything since the three bowls of soup that morning, he was ravenous.

But unfortunately, there were too many people around, so he didn't attempt it, but decided to return later in the night.

However, when he was looking for the bin for the Indian restaurant, he also discovered a large clothes recycling skip, in a nearby public car park and added a change of clothes to his shopping list.

On his way back to the treehouse, and as there was no-one in the recreation field, he cautiously went in to the allotments and looked around several plots. Checking the field again for any late night dog walkers, he grabbed some runner beans and pulled up a few carrots to eat raw to help stave off his hunger pangs. Chewing hungrily on the vegetables, he made his way back to the treehouse. The cat looked at him, expectantly as he climbed back up to the bole.

'Sorry puss. I haven't got anything yet, but I'll get some later,' he said, gently stroking her.

Mo dozed fitfully until he judged it was the early hours. It was a clear moonlit night as he made his way back into the quiet village. Thinking ahead, he took his rucksack with him to bring back any food and clothes that he found.

Despite his rumbling tum, he decided to go first to the clothes recycling container.

Scattered around the base of the container were several plastic bags that somebody hadn't bothered to post into it.

He opened up one of the bags, and found some tops and trousers inside. He held them against himself to make sure that they were his size, decided that they were, so stuffed them into the bottom of the rucksack.

Mo opened up several other bags, but satisfied that there was nothing else that he wanted, he posted the rest of the clothes into the container and kept the plastic carrier bags.

Then he moved quietly to the large portable wheeled bin at the back of the Indian restaurant. Fortunately, the moonlight was bright enough to see inside and Mo was surprised at the variety and quantity of the food waste in it.

He selected various 'delicacies' from the pile of discarded food and, so that it didn't make a mess in his rucksack, he put the food in a plastic bag that he'd recycled from the clothes skip.

Mo ate various tempting food items as he filled the carrier bags and by the time he'd finished his trip round all four premises. he was already feeling full.

Carrying his 'recycled' food supply in his bulging rucksack, he made his way back to the treehouse, enroute he spotted milk on several doorsteps. He hesitated to take any, until he saw three bottles at one house and decided that the householders wouldn't miss one. He walked silently to the doorstep and 'recycled' one.

When he got back to the treehouse, he was greeted with a meow from the cat. Together they checked the spoils of his food trip.

His horde included: - Naan bread, poppadum's, steak, rice, chicken, prawns, omelette, chapatis, bhajis, kebabs, burgers, pasta and chips.

Mo gave the cat some chicken from his large food haul and a saucer of fresh milk.

'There you are Mum, some chicken as promised.'

He hung up the remaining food in the plastic carrier bags on several small branches, hoping that it would still be edible later.

The pair had eaten well and went to sleep with full bellies, as the kittens nuzzled into their mother's soft belly.

# Chapter Sixty

The nightmare was terrifying. He was lying in the sand, under the baking hot sun and being told to shoot the prisoners, his fellow orphans, the ones that had failed their training. He knew them. How could he kill one of his own. They were orphans had they not suffered enough already?

'Shoot or be shot, he was ordered. The instructor was shaking his arm to emphasise his point.

The sound of automatic gunfire was growing louder and louder as the others around him obeyed their orders.

'Kill or be killed,' the voice demanded.

'I can't, I can't shoot my friends,' he shouted, over the sound of gunfire.

Then he awoke, bathed in a cold sweat. But something was still nudging his arm.

The gunfire was real too. Not a dream; Had the Sergeant lied to him? Was there a war going on here, in England, as well?

Perhaps he'd caused a war here by escaping from the Taliban camp and they'd chased him here.

He listened with growing panic at the continuing rapid fire. The sound stirred up bad memories of the many gun battles that raged near to his home.

The volume of noise didn't appear to be getting any closer and then he remembered; he'd been told that there was an army camp nearby.

As his head cleared, he realised that it was probably only soldiers practising on the rifle range, like they had done back home.

But what about his arm being touched? That was real. Then he looked down and realised, to his relief, that it was only the cat nudging him for attention.

'Kitty you made me think I was going mad. I know, I expect you want more food don't you?'

The cat meowed, as if to confirm Mo's assumption.

Eventually the firing ceased, and Mo was able to calm down.

'As it wasn't Sergeant Tom at Scouts last night, I must go and find the army camp and see if he is there,' he thought.

Satisfied that the kittens were safe, Mo climbed down the branch and splashed water from the stream in his face to wake himself up fully.

He set off with great anticipation in the direction of where he thought the gunfire had been coming from, trying desperately to remember the directions that Julie had given him.

But rather than following her exact route, he calculated that he could reach the same location, if his geography was right, by following a footpath there.

He ventured along the treehouse footpath to the golf course, the point where he had reached on his first day recce. He crossed the road and skirted around the greens on a well-used footpath.

Further on he waded across a stream where a fence had been broken down but found his way blocked by houses causing him to retrace his steps.

Feeling self-conscious about his hesitant progress as he blundered along the footpaths, he was pleased that there were few people around on the golf course.

Eventually, after skirting around the edge of the greens, he emerged from the waymarked footpath on to a narrow country lane.

Unsure of which way to travel, he went left in the direction of some military style looking houses.

The lane ended by a small roundabout and to his joy and relief he found a big sign that indicated it was an army base for the Rapid Reaction Force.

Having found it, he wondered what he should do next...hang around and hope to bump in to Sergeant Tom ? Or go to the gate house and ask if they knew where he was?

He was aware that CCTV cameras would pick him up if he hung around, and that would immediately create suspicions of his motives. Worse still, it might even bring his presence to the notice of the authorities and lead to his expulsion.

So, his mind was made up for him. He would go and ask about the Sergeant.

Striding up to the gate house, his heart was in his mouth. 'Was he creating an unnecessary problem for himself by asking? But how else could he find the Sergeant?' he reasoned.

An armed soldier blocked his way. The military man stood next to a sturdy looking barrier and retractable road bollard.

'Yes?' the guard demanded. 'What's your business?'

'I am trying to find Sergeant Tom. He was in Afghanistan,' Mo explained.

'Sergeant Tom who?'

'I don't know his last name,' Mo admitted.

'Well you might have a problem tracking him down then. Have you made your enquiry through the normal channels'?

'No. I don't know how to do that.'

'It's all on the internet.'

'But I don't. Can't...' Mo said, disconsolately.

'Well I can't help you,' the soldier said, turning his attention to an approaching car.

Mo left the soldier and wandered back down the long drive. At the road he decided to walk in the opposite direction that Julie had given him, wondering what to do next.

On his way back to the treehouse he passed another pub, a sign for a supermarket and shop called Coop. He wondered if they would have any food bins that he could raid when his supplies from last night ran out. He made a mental note of them.

But what was he going to do to find Sergeant Tom? He had been given false hopes twice now only to be disappointed. He was beginning to think it was a hopeless task as he didn't even know the Sergeants full name.

# Chapter Sixty-one

Following his disappointing trip to the army camp, Mo had gone back to his tree house, desperately trying to think of a way forward for finding the Sergeant.

However, he took his mind off things by eating some of his food from the carrier bags and feeding the cat and watching the kittens.

Finally, he got bored with that and decided that he needed to go and wash some of his clothes. He thought that the toilets up by the Parish Council offices would be ideal.

So, he changed his top for one that he'd picked up by the recycling clothes container.

It was grey, and had a large motif of '*No bad days on the bike*', displayed boldly on the chest.

After his cycling mishap in Italy, he liked the irony of the logo and thought it was the right one for him. As he put it on, he noticed that there was a small hole in the right shoulder.

'Oh, it doesn't matter,' he convinced himself. 'Nobody will see it. I'm not going to be judged on what I'm wearing.'

Mo put on a pair of trousers that he'd got from the recycle bin too and stuffed his dirty clothes into his rucksack.

'Be a good cat. I'll be back soon,' he said and wandered up to the toilet near the Council offices.

Making sure nobody was around he locked himself in to the toilet and quickly did his small bit of laundry in the wash basin. Halfway through his chore there was a knocking on the door.

'Are you alright in there?' the woman's voice asked.

Not sure whether to reply or not he stopped what he was doing and said nothing.

'Hello. Are you alright. I need to lock the toilets for the night.'

'Umm, yes I won't be a minute,' he said, ringing out his trousers.

'I'll be back in a minute then,' the woman said.

Mo heard her walking away and quickly stuffed the wet washing in his rucksack.

He opened the door, enough to see out, and saw the woman just going back into the office door.

Relieved that she had gone, he quickly left the toilet, leaving the door open as he left, to indicate he was no longer in there.

On his return to the treehouse, he hung his laundry out in the branches above his head and out of sight from anyone walking along the path, hoping that they would dry quickly.

Feeling quite peckish again, Mo dug into the bags of recycled food, that he'd rescued from the food bins, during his night time excursion.

Together with the cat, they feasted on the strange mix of scraps. Feeling quite tired from his previous nocturnal activities, he eventually gave way to his heavy eyelids and, along with the cat dozed fitfully.

In the early evening, as he woke, Mo could hear some pop music being played nearby. Curious as to its source, he left the treehouse and wandered off to see where it was coming from.

It appeared to be coming from the recreation park, so he decided to investigate.

As he got closer, he could see that in the fenced off area there was a small group of teenagers listening to music, talking and drinking.

Mo spent some time observing the group from nearby, desperately wanting to break the days boredom by going in and joining them.

Suddenly, he heard someone coming out of the bushes behind him. Uncomfortable at being found out as a 'peeping tom', Mo pretended to be picking blackberries from a nearby bush.

'Hi mate. I was just having a whazz,' the newcomer slurred, obviously under the influence of alcohol.

'A whazz?' Mo repeated, puzzled.

'You know, having a pee,' the other explained. 'You coming to the party?'

'Well...I...' Mo stuttered.

'Yeah come on bro,' he insisted, throwing his arm around Mo's shoulders.

Mo allowed himself to be steered. The teen led him through a small wooden gate, past several small lakes towards the group. 'What's your name bro?'

'Mo, Mohammed,' Mo said, quietly.

'I'm Colin. You're not from round here are you Mohammed? You one of the kids from the camp?'

'Camp...yes the camp. My father is a soldier there.' Mo lied.

'Great, come and join us. Want a beer?'

'No. no thank you. I do not drink.'

'Come on. Everybody drinks.'

'No thanks, but could I have a coke?' Mo said, recognising several cans of coke amidst a nest of beer tinnies on the large wooden picnic table.

'Yes. I don't think anyone will have any objections. So long as you bring some the next time,' Colin suggested.

Mo picked up a coke and pulled the tab. He thirstily gulped at the sweet liquid and necked it all in one go, belching loudly as he finished.

'Wow. Just as well that wasn't beer,' his new friend observed smilingly. 'Otherwise you'd be flat on your back.'

'I have not had coke for a long time,' Mo said, recalling that the last can he'd had was when in hospital, from Sergeant Tom.

The others in the group watched the newcomer suspiciously, although the girls giggled behind their hands.

One of the girls recognised him. 'Weren't you at Scouts the other night?' she asked.

'Me?'

'Yes. You're Mo aren't you, the girl said. Remember me? I was your PL. Angelina?

'Yes. Of course I do,' Mo confirmed, feeling slightly foolish.

'You were an ace doing the knotting.'

'Oh, that,' he said modestly. 'Yes. I enjoyed it. I had a good Scout Leader,' he enthused. 'Sorry. I didn't recognise you without your Scout uniform on, 'Mo apologised, unnecessarily.

One of the boys had taken an instant dislike to Mo and mimicked him in a silly voice, 'I had a good Scout Leader...well dyb dyb dyb.'

'Just ignore the idiot,' Angelina advised Mo. 'It's just because they threw you out, John Jones isn't it,' she continued.

'Huh! Those Scouts are a waste of time anyway. I didn't want my street cred destroyed by being associated with those losers,' the other shouted.

'Just ignore him, Mohammed,' she suggested. 'He's not the type we want in Scouts anyway.'

'You remembered my name,' Mo said, surprised.

'Yes, well we don't have too many people from the camp come to our meetings,' she observed.

'Hey, I had a top like that,' John Jones interrupted, staring at Mo. 'It had a hole on the shoulder too. I wondered where it had gone. Did you nick it?'

'No...I...' Mo was in a dilemma. He could hardly admit he'd been emptying recycled clothes bags. 'I...fell off my bike and ripped it,' he lied.

'Yeah, a likely story. If I find out it's mine you'd better watch out,' he warned.

'Just ignore him Mohammed,' Angelina counselled. 'He's just full of himself.'

'Please call me Mo,' he said.

'Ok, Mo. John's bark is worse than his bite.'

'Excuse me?' Mo said, puzzled.

'Sorry. It means that he makes a lot of threats but doesn't do anything about it.'

'There are so many strange things in the English language that I don't know,' Mo confessed.

'Where do you come from Mo?' she asked.

'I...I...come from...'Mo didn't know whether to tell her and was going to volunteer the information as a car horn sounded.

"That's my Mum. She's come to pick me up. Will I see you at Scouts next week,' Angelina asked.

'I…I'm not sure. I might, 'Mo said, wishing he could go without having to give Rich all the necessary details. The membership money was an even bigger issue too.

'Hope you can,' Angelina said, going to the carpark, where a car was flashing its lights.

Mo stayed with the group listening to the music and avoided any eye contact with John Jones. When all the drink had gone, they started drifting off to their homes and families, so, he went back to the treehouse and the kittens.

## Chapter Sixty-two

The following night, on one of his nocturnal food missions to replace the now rancid contents of his plastic bag larder, Mo was crossing a pedestrian bridge over the main road when he spotted something that caught his eye..

'Am I imagining it? he wondered. 'That looks like a bike down there. That streetlight is just in the wrong place for me to be sure.

He decided to investigate and carefully climbed over the side rails of the bridge by the overgrown hedgerow.

'If it is a bike, someone must have discarded it from up here,' he concluded. 'It must be at least a fifteen-foot drop.'

Carefully he made his way down the slope towards the bike and stayed well-hidden as a few cars zoomed along the bypass.

'It is a mountain bike. Wow! I wonder if it's still in working order?' he wondered inspecting it briefly. 'It doesn't seem to have suffered any damage. Although, it looks like it's been down here for some time.

As he cautiously tried to lift it, he realised that the bike was imprisoned by the brambles that had grown through the spokes.

After a five-minute struggle, Mo released the bike from the vicious brambles but as he did so, was scratched by the sharp thorns.

He half wheeled; half carried the bike up the steep embankment. Pleased with his find.

Finally, he lifted it over the railings on to the foot bridge when he reached the top.

Now illuminated by the street light, he confirmed his initial assessment, the yellow mountain bike appeared to be in good shape. Even the tyres were still inflated.

Ignoring the bloody scratches on his hands and legs, he sat on the saddle and operated the gear levers and the brakes.

'These all seem to be working Ok,' he thought. 'This will make getting around a lot easier.'

Mo pedalled his find slowly over the footbridge wobbling and 'foot dabbing' as he went. But it didn't take him long before he was riding confidently. The lessons from his Italian cycle ride were still fresh in his aching arm.

Cautiously he cycled along on the well-lit, wide empty pavements. At that time of night there weren't any pedestrians around and very few cars.

As he was now mobile, he decided to visit further afield and targeted the supermarkets that he'd identified earlier.

His intuition paid off as he was rewarded by finding large yellow skips at the back of both the Coop and Tesco's.

On opening their unlocked heavy metal covers, he discovered that instead of scraps, they were stacked full of discarded unopened food.

Although puzzled by the reason for dumping apparently good food, he took a variety of tins and packets, using his rucksack to transport his hoard.

'This will do nicely to make up a store in my camp,' he thought.

With a rucksack full of various foods, he enjoyed a circuitous cycle ride back to the tree house, taking the opportunity of exploring the various gear shift positions and enjoying the wind in his face, as he rode faster.

Now he could show John Jones that he did have a bike to fall off, giving credibility to his story about damaging the cycle top.

His next challenge, when he got back to the tree house, was where to store the bike. It needed to be out of sight from people using the path.

He remembered that there was a broken branch at the back of the tree, at head height, and wondered if he could hang the bike up by the front wheel.

It was difficult in the dark, especially as it was so close to the stream, but eventually he managed it.

He was pleased to see, that when he checked from all angles along the path, that it was out of sight from walkers.

After feeding the cat and pleased with his finds, Mo went to bed happy and slept well.

# Chapter Sixty-three

The following night, after dark, the excitement of having his newly acquired mountain bike was too much for Mo. He simply had to ride it and ride it fast.

He decided to ride it over on the darkened and deserted airfield because he knew that the airport didn't operate at night. So, feeling confident that he wouldn't be disturbed, he carefully weaved the bike through the damaged fencing and on to the airfield perimeter road.

With building excitement, he rode the bike slowly along the perimeter road and turned on to one of the runways.

Despite having no lights on the runway, there was enough starlight to allow his night vision to see where he was going.

Slowly he built up speed, quickly going through the gears, delighted by the feeling of wind in his face. The cadence of his legs increased as he pedalled faster and faster, he was exhilarated by the sensation. He felt free.

However, as he was racing through the middle of the airfield, suddenly the runway lights came on, and, to his shock, behind him he heard the sound of an approaching aeroplane.

Unfortunately, what he didn't know was that tonight, in an exceptional circumstance, the airport had re-opened because of an urgent medical emergency.

A special charted jet was transporting a donor heart from Scotland to Gloucestershire Airport.

A fast response paramedic was standing by for the aircraft to land and would 'blue light' the organ to the Gloucester Royal Hospital for the transplant. The patient was already on the operating table and time was of the essence.

*'Control to hotel alpha echo romeo tango, you are cleared for landing runway zero niner.'*

*'Cleared for landing zero niner, hotel echo alpha romeo tango,* the pilot repeated.

As the plane got closer to the runway, the jet's bright landing lights picked up Mo on the runway.

*'I don't think so control. There is movement on the runway. Do you have a service vehicle on it?'*

*'Negative. No vehicles.'*

As the plane got closer to touch down, the pilot could see what it was.

*'Then it looks like you have part of the tour of Britain taking place on there. You have a cyclist on zero niner,'* the pilot informed an astonished Control.

The controller reached for his binoculars in disbelief and spotted Mo pedalling frantically along the runway.

*'What the...abort landing hotel alpha. I'll get security to chuck the trespasser off. Can you go around, and I'll call you when it's clear.'*

*'Roger that. Remember the urgency.'*

*'Wilco.'*

The pilot pulled out of his landing sequence and flew to a holding pattern around the airport.

The airport fire service was already on station and had been listening to the conversation.

'*Control. Fire one. We're on our way to investigate.*'

'*Roger, Thanks. Give me a sit rep as soon as you can.*'

By this time, Mo, having been frightened by the sound of the incoming jet and illuminated by the planes fast approaching landing lights, had gone into a darkened area of the airfield.

He saw the fire tender entering on to the perimeter road and coming in his direction. With every sinew in his body he pedalled even faster, hoping they couldn't see him.

With his heart bursting from the effort, he quickly headed back for the gap in the fence, and skidded off the bike, as he pulled a sharp turn whilst braking.

He picked himself up and weaved through the hole in the fence. He headed for his tree house. Parking his bike behind the tree, he watched as the fire tender drove slowly around the perimeter road, obviously looking for him.

The fire team spent only a short time looking because of the urgency of the jet's mission and the tight timescale of the hospital operation.

'*Control, no sign of the trespasser. I reckon the cyclist is now long gone.*

'*Ok to call the plane in, do you think??*' the controller asked.

'*Roger We'll clear the runway for his arrival.*'

Mo watched as the plane landed and he could see the activities as the heart was transferred to the fast response ambulance.

Within minutes its blue lights lit up the hedgerows, as it hurtled down the road to Gloucester on its errand of mercy.

'I wonder what that was all about, puss? he said to the cat. Tonight, of all nights that I decide to go over there, and a plane flies in. Just my luck. I hope they won't initiate a bigger search by the police,' he thought. 'Otherwise I'm going to have to move from here. Very quickly.'

Mo slept fitfully all night, fearing a detailed search being conducted. Fortunately the police were unable to respond, and Mo eventually dozed off.

# Chapter Sixty-four

Mo was concerned about the health of the kittens. 'Perhaps the cat isn't getting enough from the scraps I've been giving her to provide enough milk,' he wondered.

'The kittens appear to have diarrhoea, that can't be right and the cat doesn't appear to be able to sort it either,' Mo thought. 'I don't have anything to give them though. I know, I'll take them to the Care Home. They'll know what to do.'

With that, he lined his rucksack with a few plastic bags and folded the duvet and squeezed it in, gently putting the kittens in one at a time. Satisfied that they were safe, he put his rucksack on and clambered down with their Mother slowly following.

He walked through the recreation park to the Care Home, where he had previously pushed Jennifer in her broken-down electric wheelchair.

He went around to the back door and knocked, relieved to see that it was Julie who answered the door.

'Oh, hello young man, nice to see you again. What can I do for you?' she asked.

Mo took the rucksack off and opened the flap.

'I have some kittens,' he said, showing her the inside of the rucksack.

'Kittens?' Julie replied in astonishment.

'Yes. But I don't think they are very well. I didn't know what to do.'

Just then the mother cat appeared. It strutted into the doorway, rubbing itself on Julie's leg and meowed.

'Oh, so you've decided to come home then have you Mary,' she said to the cat. 'Are these your babies?' she continued, looking at the bundle of kittens.

'You mean that she's your cat?' Mo asked, relieved.

'Yes. We wondered where she had gone. We thought something horrible had happened to her. But no! You clever girl. Have you produced these gorgeous kittens?'

Julie reached inside the rucksack and stroked the soft down covered kittens.

'They are so cute and cuddly. You say they aren't well?' she quizzed.

'They don't seem to be getting enough milk from their mother,' he clarified. 'And they've been very messy, if you know what I mean?'

'Oh well, we can soon rectify that. Come on in,' she said.

Mo entered the Care Home as invited.

'Where would you like me to put the kittens?' he asked, looking around.

'There's Mary's bed there,' Julie said, pointing to a cat basket. 'Please put them there.'

Mo did as instructed and gently lay the kittens down. Meanwhile, Mary padded around the room rubbing herself on Mo's leg as if to thank him, and then she joined the kittens in her basket.

'How come you've got them anyway?' Julie asked.

'I...I found them under a hedge. I thought they might be killed by a dog or something, so I brought them here,' he said, not completely elaborating the full extent of his involvement.

At that moment Sarah entered the room.

'Hello Mohammed,' she said, spotting him. 'What brings you here?'

'He's brought Mary and her kittens back to us.' Julie pointed out.

'Kittens! So, that's where she's been. Oh, how lovely,' Sarah said, kneeling to get a closer look.

'Mohammed says that they are not feeding from Mary very well, so he brought them here. I said we could sort that.'

'Well they are not supposed to have cow's milk. It will upset their digestive system. But for now, we can give them goat's milk and then I'll pop along and get something from the vets. I've got some eyedroppers that we can use.'

Sarah fished out three new eyedroppers and handed one each to the others.

The three of them took an eyedropper and kitten each and fed the kittens with some warm goat's milk, that Sarah had warmed in the microwave.

Mo selected the Tabby kitten, 'I have called this one Tom,' he informed the ladies.

'Oh, you've even given them names then?'

'Yes. The ginger cap one is called Abdul.'

''Why ginger cap?'

'It's because of the ginger fur marking over his head and ears.'

'Oh, OK.'

'And what's my kitten called?' Julie asked.

'He is Hassim.'

'Hassim?'

'Yes Hassim,' Mo confirmed

The kittens quickly cottoned on to the technique of sucking from the eyedroppers, while Mary got stuck into some cat food that Julie had put down for her.

'That's the second rescue mission that you've made for us. We ought to give you a job,' Sarah joked.

'Could you?' Mo asked earnestly, not realising Sarah was kidding.

'Well, I didn't actually mean…a real job. You're far too young and anyway I can't authorise employing you.'

'It would be very nice if you could though,' Mo added, thinking of having the means to pay his membership fee at Scouts after all.

'What about your schoolwork?'

'I will fit it in,' Mo lied.

'Well I suppose I could ask. Perhaps you could help the gardener, Chick, with a few odd jobs.'

'Yes, I will work very hard,' Mo assured them, enthusiastically.

After the kittens had stopped feeding, they were returned to the cat basket where again Mary joined them. All three cuddled up to their Mother and were soon asleep.

'Now the cats have been fed, I expect you could do with something to eat too Mo?' Sarah asked, already knowing the answer.

'Yes please.'

'A growing young man needs his food,' she said, busying herself to conjure up a large meal for him.

# Chapter Sixty-five

Unusually, Tom Bow had been given permission to have Jersey at home prior to going on duty at RAF Fairford, for a big military event.

He took her for a walk along the Gloucestershire way, which runs around the edge of the airport.

The dog was off the lead and enjoying sniffing a glorious collection of countryside smells, when suddenly she became excited about a scent that she was keen to track down.

After a few yards, and much to the Sergeant's surprise, the dog suddenly scampered up a tree branch that drooped down from an ancient willow.

'What are you doing up there you daft dog?' her master demanded. 'More importantly, how are you going to get down?'

Ignoring her master, the dog continued to frantically scramble her way up the branch and disappeared into the bole of the tree, barking excitedly. Its tail wagging like an unregulated metronome, beating out a frantic rhythm of joy.

'Come on down,' her master commanded. 'It's probably only a squirrel anyway and we haven't got time to go squirrel hunting.'

Jersey's head reappeared and looked down on the man, barking as if to say come on up here. Getting no response from her master, she disappeared again, her excited barking continuing to broadcast her joy.

'If you think I'm coming up there, you've got another think coming. Now come on down.' Tom ordered.

The dog continued to ignore her master.

'I know, I've got something that will attract your attention,' the man said, digging into his jacket pocket and pulling out a polythene bag of doggie treats.

He rustled the bag, exaggerating his actions to make it noisier. Immediately the noise caught the dog's sensitive ears and she came back into view again, still barking.

'Come on then,' her master invited, and held up the bag of multicoloured bone shaped treats.

The dog barked her approval of the offered treat but didn't move.

'If you don't come down, I'll leave you up there,' the man said, and turned to walk away.

The dog disappeared again as Tom carried out his threat...but only went twenty yards until he was out of sight of the tree.

'That ought to bring her down,' the man thought. But after listening for a few more minutes to the dog continuing to bark, clearly still excited by what she had found, the man walked back to the tree.

'That's it,' the man said tersely. 'Time to get serious.

Sergeant Tom dug into his other pocket and this time, took out a dog whistle, the one that he rarely used, and then only when they were on duty.

'I don't want to do this to you my friend, but needs must.'

He put the whistle to his lips and blew into it.

Immediately the dog stopped barking and became alert.

'Heel girl,' her master commanded.

The dog left the bole immediately and awkwardly slithered down the sloping branch. She ran to his side and sat obediently by her master's right leg, looking up to him, expecting to be given an important search job.

The man instead leant down and attached the lead to the dog's collar.

'Now what was that all about?' he asked her. 'You don't normally get so excited about squirrels, do you? You daft thing.'

'Come on, let's get on, otherwise we'll be late for lunch.'

As they walked away from the tree, the dog kept looking back, her tail still showing the excitement at her find.

Then she caught on to a new scent and started pulling the soldier along.

'I don't know what's the matter with you Jersey, but you're wearing me out.'

The pair went through the recreation park in double quick time, the dog almost dragging her master. When they got to the road, Jersey led her master to the right.

'No, that's not the way home. You daft dog! Come on you, this way, he said, dragging the dog away from a chance meeting that would have ended Mo's quest there and then.

# Chapter Sixty-six

Mo was now not afraid about being seen in public and had been cycling around the village, when he saw Angelina making her way home from school. Pulling up alongside, he surprised her.

'Oh, you made me jump,' she said

'Made you jump?' Mo asked puzzled.

'Don't bother,' she said tiredly, not wishing to go into explanations.

'Are you going to the park later?' he asked.

'Yes, are you?' Angelina replied, suddenly revived.

'Yes, if you are going,' he confirmed, enthusiastically.

'I need to go home first and change out of my uniform, and I'll be down there in about half an hour ok?'

'Yes, I will look forward to seeing you. Without causing you to jump,' Mo said trying to humour her.

'See you then,' she said, ignoring his attempt at humour.

Mo cycled back to the park and, after dismounting, leant the bike up against a wooden picnic table.

After half an hour Angelina turned up in ripped jeans and a blouse.

'You have ripped your trousers,' Mo observed.

'It's the fashion. That's what they are supposed to be like. It's all the craze these days,' she informed him.

'Oh, I see,' he said, feeling slightly silly. 'Who does the food gardens belong to?' Mo asked, changing the subject.

'Food gardens? What do you mean food gardens?' Angelina asked, puzzled.

'There, over there,' Mo said pointing. 'There is a line of them.'

'Oh, you mean allotments.'

'Allotments! What is allotments?'

'It's where people grow vegetables if they haven't got a garden where they live.'

'Oh. And you have lots of ground with no houses.'

'These are called parks, where everybody can go and enjoy doing things.'

'You are so lucky. Most of my country is dry and sandy. No rain means lots of dry ground. Not good for growing. Except of course, the poppies.'

'Poppies!' We have a special poppy day to remember our soldiers who died to keep us safe.'

'No, these poppies make much wealth for bad people. They are used for making opium.'

'But don't they use it in hospitals?'

'Yes, but not all. Some goes to drug gangs. Much money. Many fights. Many killed.'

'Oh, that's terrible.'

At that moment a group of other teens arrived with John Jones, their leader.

'Hi John,' Angelina said, acknowledging his arrival.

'What are you doing hanging around with that loser?' he said, belligerently.

'If you're going to be like that, then you can jolly well clear off,' she warned.

'Well you might like to know that the loser wears recycled clothes,' he said loudly, so everyone could hear. 'I asked my Mother about my cycling top with the logo on it. She said that she'd thrown it away in a clothes recycling bag. So how come that he was wearing it the other day?'

Mo shuffled uncomfortably.

'And what's more, that looks like another old top of mine too.'

Well, yes I did find the top in a bag of old clothes. But they were being thrown away,' Mo admitted awkwardly.

'So do you get all your clothes like that, out of the ragbag, tramp?' he continued, looking menacingly at Mo, and eliciting smirks of approval from his gang.

'Look, clear off John. Come on Mo, let's move,' Angelina said, standing up.

Mo followed her as she moved to a different table.

'Anyway Mo, ignore them. You were telling me about things in your country, poppies and drugs,' she prompted him.

'Yes, the Taliban capture people like me.'

'Capture? How awful.'

'They kidnapped me and forced me into a training camp. I had to do lots of shooting and to help to make suicide vests,' Mo confessed.

'Oh, that's awful,' Angelina empathised.

'And so I am glad to be here,' Mo concluded.

Unbeknown to both, John Jones was eavesdropping on their conversation.

'Wow, this guy is a terrorist,' he concluded. 'I must tell my Dad. He'll love it.'

As John got up to leave, he spotted Mo's bike leaning against the table.

'Here that's my bike,' he shouted. 'Where did that come from?'

'No, it is mine. I ride it here,' Mo replied, possessively, grabbing hold of the handlebars.

'You might have ridden it. But that's my bike. It was stolen from down the side of my house, a few weeks ago,' John Jones insisted, inspecting it.

'How do you know it's yours?' Angelina said, springing to Mo's defence.

'It was a Trek Marlin with a yellow frame, 21 gears.'

'Well I'm sure there's lots of them sold. It's not necessarily yours,' she continued.

'Yes it is because I put some red tape around the seat stem to mark the height. There look, it's there. I'm going to call the police,' he said reaching for his phone.

'No. Please. I find the bike by the bridge where people walk over the main road,' Mo explained.

'A likely story. We don't like thieves round here boys, do we?'

The newcomers surrounded Mo.

'Stop it,' Angelina appealed. 'Get away from him.'

But it was too late as John Jones threw the first punch at Mo.

Mo blocked several punches and tried to back away, but the others joined in and started kicking and punching him.

In the mayhem that followed, Mo was able to grab hold of John Jones around the neck and quickly put him in a strangle hold.

Mo was now angry. He saw red. His indoctrination in the Taliban training camp during hand to hand fighting with the repeated mantra of 'kill or be killed', kicked in.

'Get back,' Mo shouted at the others, who, seeing Mo's aggressiveness suddenly weren't so brave.

As Mo's assailant started to lose consciousness, Angelina, begged Mo to let him go. 'You're killing him,' she said. 'Mo let him go, let him go,' she begged.

Reluctantly, Mo let the strangle hold loosen and John slumped on to the grass gasping for air, holding his throat.

However, spotting an opportunity, one of the gang came up behind Mo and hit him on the back of the head with his fist.

Mo put his hands to his head and went down like a sack of potatoes and was on the edge of consciousness when the others found their courage again, moving in, and kicking him on the ground.

Despite her screams of protestation, the girl couldn't stop the onslaught, which only ended when Mo was clearly unconscious and unable to defend himself.

'You've killed him you maniacs,' she screamed.

'He shouldn't have stolen my bike, then should he? Let that be a lesson to you.' John Jones croaked, rubbing his throat.

The boy took Mo's bike and rode off with the others. Laughing as they went.

Fortunately, they hadn't killed him, and Mo came round quite quickly.

'Oh, Mo you're hurt. We need to get you to hospital.'

'No. No hospital.' Mo insisted painfully, sitting up.

'Your face is all bruised and you've got nosebleed. It might be broken.'

'I didn't steal the bike. I found it.' Mo insisted.

'Don't worry about that now. I don't know what to do,' Angelina confessed.

'It is OK. I will go back to my tree house and...'

'Tree house?' she repeated, what are you talking about? Are you hallucinating?

'I do not live at the army camp. I am living here in a tree.

'A tree!.

'What about your parents?'

'My family was all killed when my house was blown up,' he revealed.

'Oh, my god. All killed, how awful,' she repeated. 'Well in that case, you won't be going back to your tree in that state,' Angelina insisted. 'Look, I think my Mum is out at the moment. I reckon we might be able to sort you out at my house. Come on. I'll give you a hand to stand up. There, give me your hand.'

Mo struggled to stand.

'Ow. I hurt all over. My chest it is so sore,' he groaned, holding his ribs.

Well no wonder, they were kicking you,' she sympathised. 'They're animals. I've never seen them like that before. Come on. My house isn't far away.'

# Chapter Sixty-seven

Mo and the girl slowly made their way to her large four-bedroom house in a quiet cul-de-sac, half a mile from the recreation park. She had resisted the temptation to put a sympathetic arm around his shoulders, to help his painful progress.

'Wait here,' she said. 'I'll just check that Mum is out.'

Mo leant against the garden wall as the girl unlocked the front door and disappeared inside. Within a few minutes she reappeared. 'It's OK, nobody is home. Come in quickly, we've got some nosey neighbours.'

Mo groaned as he got his bruised body moving again.

'We'll soon have you fixed up,' she encouraged.

The girl led Mo into her house and closed the door behind them.

'I think the best place to sort you out is the bathroom, upstairs. We can flush all the bloody stuff down the loo then,' she said calmly, as if she patched up blooded teenagers every day.

Angelina led the way up the stairs. 'Can you manage?' she asked gently, as they headed towards the bathroom.

'Yes. If I do it slowly,' Mo whispered painfully, holding his aching ribs.

As they arrived in the bathroom, the girl invited Mo to sit on the toilet seat. 'Sit there while I get the first aid box,' she said, and left,

Mo looked around the small pristine bathroom, everything was clean, ordered and in place. It smelt of some sort of perfume. There was an electric shower over the large white bath, a sink and matching toilet. The floor was covered in some form of vinyl, which was just as well as his nose started bleeding again as he rubbed it. He panicked as some drops fell on the floor, wondering how to clean it up.

The girl came back, clutching a green plastic box which she rested on the sink, and opened it to reveal a well-stocked first aid kit.

'My Mum used to be in St John Ambulance and always keeps our first aid box stocked up. Now let's see. We'll clean you up and see what needs a plaster on. Let's have a look at your ribs first. Would you like to take your top off yourself?'

'Yes. I... Are you sure this is alright to be alone with me?' Mo said, feeling uncomfortable at her invitation to undress.

'Of course, I have a brother. It's no big deal. Now the top. Come on, so we can see what the damage is.'

As he lifted the top, the door suddenly opened and Angelina's mother, Helen, burst in to the bathroom.

'Dear god! What the hell's going on in here? she demanded.

'I...we...' Angelina stuttered, suddenly feeling guilty for her Samaritan act.

Frightened by the woman's sudden appearance, Mo dropped his top and stood up. He wondered if he should leave the bathroom and escape while he could.

'Who is he?' Helen demanded. 'What's he doing in my house?'

'Sorry Mum, this is Mo. He was set upon by John Jones and his gang.'

'You realise that I almost had a heart attack.' Helen told her. 'I spotted the bloodstains outside on the pavement and up the stairs. Angelina, I thought you or Paul had been hurt.'

'No, I'm Ok. It's just Mo here.'

'Who is he anyway? Why were they fighting? '

'He's a boy from Scouts,' Angelina blurted. 'They accused him of stealing John's bike.'

'I didn't lady. I found it,' the boy said quickly.

'Well that's for the police to decide.'

'Police!' Mo said, alarmed. 'I found the bike. Honest,' he reiterated.

'Well that's as maybe. In the meantime, let me see if you need to go to the Emergency Department for some treatment,' she advised him, calming down.

Helen examined Mo's injuries and assessed that he didn't need to go to hospital. 'It's only bruises. You're young, you'll soon get over them,' she said confidently.

'You don't get too much sympathy in our house,' Angelina informed Mo.

'He's Ok, don't fuss girl.'

'You mean apart from a set of nasty bruises on his rib cage, a cut to his scalp and intermittent nose bleed?'

'Yes, they're all minor. But I think you'd better go home now young man and explain to your parents.'

'That's just it Mum,' Angelina explained. 'Mo doesn't have a home...or parents.'

'What do you mean?'

'He's living rough... near the recreation field. In a tree.'

'What! Do you mean he's run away from home?'

'No...he's from Afghanistan...and...'

'An immigrant!'

'I came to the country to find my soldier friend.' Mo interjected. 'He said he would adopt me, if he could,' Mo explained. 'I am looking for him.'

'Adopt you?' You mean you are here illegally?'

'I have journeyed many miles from Afghanistan to find him. I have a photo.'

Mo pulled out, from his back pocket, the very crumpled selfie picture, that the soldier had taken of the three of them in hospital. He proudly showed it to the girl and her mother.

'He looks like this,' Mo said. 'That is his dog, that saved me from my house, which was blown up.'

'Oh my god! The girl and her mother said in unison. 'That's my Dad, my husband.'

'What do you mean? I don't understand,' Mo said, confused.'

'No! That is too much of a coincidence,' Helen said, in disbelief. 'So, you must be the boy that Tom has been talking about. The one that Jersey rescued from under the debris.'

'Yes. Sergeant Tom was my Scout Leader. He visited me in hospital, many times.'

'Oh my god,' Angelina exclaimed.

Then the 'penny dropped. 'You mean I am in the Sergeant's house?' Mo said in disbelief. 'I can't believe it!' the boy yelled excitedly. 'I have found you. I have found you,' he said, and hugged the pair. The stab of pain in his chest didn't detract from the overwhelming feeling of euphoria that he felt.

'Where is my friend, Sergeant Tom and Jersey?'

'They are on a training course in London today. Jersey must be reassessed from time to time to make sure she can still do her job effectively. She is there now. Tom will be so excited to hear about you though...I will call him later.'

'But, now a typical British welcome for you Mo. A cup of sweet tea is called for to help overcome the shock,' Helen announced.

'For all of us Mum,' Angelina added.

'By the way, where is the bike now?'

'John Jones has taken it home,' Angelina said. 'Hopefully, that will be the end of the matter.'

'Hopefully, no police either,' Mo thought. Although he would miss having the freedom of cycling around.

# Chapter Sixty-eight

John Jones pushed his reclaimed mountain bike down the side entrance of his house and carefully leant it against the wall.

He opened the back door, to be greeted by his father who was making a cup of tea in the kitchen.

'Hello son, I see you've got your bike back. That's good …Where was it?

'Some kid nicked it and had the cheek to ride it to the rec. I was going to call the police to tell them, but I decided he needed to be taught a lesson instead.'

'And by the look of it, you've had a bit of a lesson yourself.' Jones senior observed, seeing John's bruised and battered face.

'Yeah, but he came off worse. We sorted it,' the boy boasted, reaching into the refrigerator for a cold can of coke.

'I don't approve of vendettas. You should have called the police. Let me have a look,' his father said, examining the boy's injuries. 'You got any loose teeth?'

'No, I don't think so,' the boy said, running his tongue round his mouth. 'Lips a bit swollen though.' He rolled the cold can over his mouth. 'Ouch that smarts.'

'So, if he stole your bike, why would he bring it to somewhere where people would recognise it? Doesn't make sense,' his father rationalised.

'Perhaps he didn't know it was mine. He reckons he found it dumped by the bridge. I don't believe him. So, I gave him what for. Believe me. He came off worse,' he bragged, conveniently omitting the gang attack on the unconscious figure.

'Is he part of your normal park crowd?'

'Not really, he's only been there once before. Foreign looking kid. Although he speaks English, he's got a strange accent. He was the one who was wearing one of my tops that Mother threw out. Smells a bit too.'

'I wonder if he's one of the kids from the camp? Some of them have strange ideas about possessions too,' Jones senior observed.

'He was really vicious. I thought he was going to kill me at one stage. Angelina Bow stopped him from strangling me.'

'Heavens. Is he a big kid then? What's he like?

'About my height, I reckon. But very strong. Manically strong, I'd say' John exaggerated. 'He's mean looking too.'

'Sounds like it could have been much worse. You were lucky to get away with the few injuries that you got, then.'

'Anyway the most important thing that you'd probably be interested in is, that I think he's a terrorist,' John said, conspiratorially.

A what ? Have you had a blow to your head?' his father said.

'No, I overheard him talking to Angelina and he mentioned a Taliban training camp, shooting and suicide vests.

'What! You must have misheard.

'No. Honest.'

Now he'd got his fathers undivided attention he invented more lies.

When we were fighting, he had me in headlock and said something like, Ali Akbar. ...and something about another 9/11,' he lied, 'spicing up' his story.

'Really? 'He was probably trying to scare you.'

'Well he certainly did that. He sounded genuine. It was only when Angelina Bow called him off that he stopped trying to strangle me,' he reiterated. 'I reckon he's a trained killer sent in to murder someone important.'

'I think you've let your imagination get the better of you, young man. How old do you reckon he is?'

'Fifteen, sixteen maybe.'

'They don't send assassins that age.'

'Well I've read about boy soldiers. So why not? They might be doing it to get in under the radar and surprise people.'

'Unlikely,' his father said dismissively.

'Well you're the journalist. If it becomes a fact, just remember it was me that broke the story for you.'

'If, and it's a big if. If it's true. I'll remember, don't worry. But what about Angelina then?'

'She's been quite friendly with him and made him let me go.'

'So, she was on your side then? Isn't she the one you fancied at one stage?'

'Not my sort,' he lied, secretly jealous of her interest in Mo.

'So, he's her boyfriend?'

'Not exactly. I think they're just friends, mentioned something about scouts the other night. Anyway, they went off together after the beating I gave him.'

John withheld the fact that his mates had inflicted most of the damage to Mo when he was cowering on the floor.

'I wonder what school he goes to?'

'Don't know. It's not either of the ones around here.'

'Interesting. What if he isn't from the camp? I wonder. Now you come to mention it. I've heard rumours in the newsroom of a series of minor incidents.'

'What like?'

'Oh, stuff going missing from the allotments. Food bins messed with and charity bags rifled. Couple of incidents around the airfield too.'

'There you are Dad. Charity bags rifled. He was wearing my old tops. You're halfway to your exclusive.'

'Umm, I wonder if the CCTV at the Council Offices or the airfield has captured anything. Perhaps he's an illegal immigrant. Perhaps I ought to investigate,' Bert Jones mused, thinking aloud.

'Well you're the reporter. Perhaps you could ask the Bows too. They might be able to tell you something as Angelina is a close friend.'

'Good thinking young Jones. We'll make a journalist out of you yet.'

'If you get a large bonus, don't forget who gave you the story,' John Jones reminded his father. The teenager smiled to himself, 'If you mess with me kid, you're going to get burnt.'

Subsequently, John Jones took to social media and told his 'followers' about finding his bike and publicly accusing Mo of stealing it. He also hinted about Mo's 'terrorist' intentions and suggested that he was actively being investigated by a newspaper.

After he'd finished sowing the seeds of a scandal, John came back into the lounge to find his father still there.

'Oh, you still here. I thought you might be out investigating that kid?'

'Well I am in a manner of speaking. I'm working from home doing background work and writing up another story.'

'Well if that's all you do. I want to be a reporter when I leave school,. You've got a cushy life father.'

'Well it isn't always like this as you know. There are lots of times when I have to do unsocial hours.

'I reckon you shouldn't sit on the story for too long or someone else might get wind of it too,' John encouraged, wondering who would tap into his social media speculations and if it would go viral.

# Chapter Sixty-nine

Having rendered first aid to Mo in the confined space of the bathroom, the three of them went downstairs to the kitchen and had a cup of sweet tea each, as Angelina's mother had suggested.

When she had finished her tea, and satisfied that Mo was OK, Helen went upstairs to her bedroom and rang the emergency contact number that Tom had given her, in case of emergencies, whilst he was on the course.

Like most service wives, she considered herself a part time military widow and dealt with most family crises' herself, without having to involve Tom. This responsibility had, by necessity, made her a self-confident and unflappable person. So, whenever Tom was on a tour somewhere in the world, the family problem 'buck' stopped with her.

But Mo's sudden arrival was too big for her to manage by herself and needed his urgent involvement.

It seemed to take an age for the emergency contact phone to be answered and then, having asked for Sergeant Bow, another endless period before he finally came to the phone.

'Helen? What's the matter? It's got to be something urgent if you're calling me,' he said, concerned.

Helen couldn't hide her anxiety as she spoke. 'Tom we've got a problem.'

'Oh dear. Is it our Angelina? he asked.

'No. We have an unexpected visitor.'

'Unexpected...what?'

'Yes. An unexpected visitor.'

'What is so urgent about that?'

'You know the Afghan boy you told us about. '

'Which one?'

'The one you rescued with Jersey.'

'Yes. What about him?'

'Well, he's here.'

'Here! What! What do you mean, he's here?'

'Just that. He is in our home,' Helen revealed.

'How? Why? Surely there must be some mistake? Are you sure you're not being conned?' Tom suggested, suspiciously.

'No. Apparently, he's been living near here...near the airfield.'

'How? Has someone brought him over?'

'No. He told Angelina that he smuggled himself over here in the back of a caravan.

'So, he's an Illegal?'

'Yes, I guess so. So, what should we do? Report him to the Police?'

'No. Umm. Keep him there. The course is nearly over. I'll be home tomorrow.'

'We really ought to report him you know. We could be in serious trouble if the immigration people find out that we are harbouring an illegal.'

'Yes, I know... But we'll think of something...

'And he's been living in a tree house ever since.'

'A tree house! So, that's why Jersey got so excited near the airport,' the Sergeant revealed. 'Now it makes sense.'

'The boy has been looking for you,' she continued.

'Looking for me?'

'Yes. He said you were going to adopt him.'

'Adopt him!'

'Stop repeating everything that I say,' she said, clearly getting rattled. 'Did you say you would?'

'Well perhaps...when he was in hospital... after the bombing. Well his parents had been killed and I said....'

'Oh, you bloody fool! As a result of that, he's come thousands of miles to find you, so that you can adopt him.'

Anyway, how did he find us?

'He went to Angelina's Scouts.'

'Good for him. I told him about the international aspect of Scouting.'

'And Angelina has been going to some parties in the park and he turned up there too.'

'But how would he know she was our daughter?'

'At the time, he didn't. He got into a fight about a bike, and she brought him back here to render first aid on him.'

'Bless her. She takes after you for your kindness.'

'Yes well. He showed us the photo that you took of the pair of you with Jersey before you left Afghanistan.'

'So that selfie was a good decision after all,' Tom said, smugly.

'Anyway, stop blowing your own trumpet and come up with a decision to get us out of the mire. If we don't follow immigration rules, you know this will compromise your job in the army?'

'Let's...let's think about it. We don't want to make any rash decisions. I always thought that kid would make something of himself...and here he is. Well, I'll be blowed!'

'Don't let that cloud your judgement. We must report him.'

'Let's see.'

'I know your 'let's see'. This is serious Tom. If you won't do anything about it. Then I will.' Annoyed by her husbands 'laissez-faire' attitude, Helen hung up.

Tom smiled to himself, pleased that Mo had re-entered his life. 'Well, well, well. So, he survived the Taliban kidnap and subsequent air raid on the training camp. What's more he's travelled several thousand miles, confronted and overcome obstacles along the way. Good on you kid. I knew you had something about you.'

But, despite her threat, Helen did nothing and awaited Tom's return.

# Chapter Seventy

The journalist knew that the Parish Council offices and airport had CCTV and wanted to see if there were any pictures of the boy, or any evidence that this character was, indeed, up to no-good, as his son had suggested.

So, Bert Jones took a trip to the Parish Council Offices, on the pretext of writing an article on the nocturnal activities of local wild life.

'Yes, we've had reports from several allotment holders that they have had stuff going missing. Could be wildlife I suppose,' the official agreed.

Bert spent some time with the Parish council officials reviewing the night time CCTV footage.

'Let's have a look at that again,' the journalist directed. 'There look, it's just a fleeting image of a person jumping over the five-bar gate and going in to the allotments.'

'Not an animal then. Perhaps we've got a vagrant living around here. What should we do? Tell the police?' the parish official asked.

'No. they wouldn't be interested,' the journalist coached, thinking he didn't want to compromise his possible story.

'I suppose there's no real damage done. And none of the allotment holders are really losing a lot of produce,' the Official agreed.

'I'd say that the police are too busy to deal with minor crimes like this,' the newspaper man added, continuing to downplay the importance of his find.

'Yes, you're right. It's probably only a few spuds and carrots going missing anyway.'

'It doesn't have to be him taking the stuff either. He might have just been going to relieve himself.'

'Yes, that's a point. The toilets are locked at that time of night,' the official confirmed. 'Oh that reminds me, somebody has been using the men's toilet to do washing. I don't know who it is but when I went to lock up the other night, it sounded like a boy with a foreign accent.'

'Oh that might be a coincidence,' Bert lied, thinking her description tallied with his son's.

'The birds could well be having the produce after all,' Bert Jones continued.

'No, you're right. Let's leave it. If it gets worse, we'll do something then.'

'Is there any footage of the group of teens that gathers for a night time BBQ?' the journalist probed.

'No. I gather they go into the fenced off area for a bit of socialising. Unfortunately, there's no CCTV coverage of that area.

'Pity.'

'Well, you're not likely to get any wildlife in there either, as the youths make a lot of noise and it would scare anything away.'

'Not to worry. Thanks for your time,' the newspaper man said, leaving.

Using the same cover story of the nocturnal activities of local wildlife, the journalist then went to the airport offices and quizzed the security team there.

'Oh, we don't have any CCTV monitoring here,' he was informed. 'It's all done remotely by a specialist firm. They might be able to help.'

'Thanks. Where do I find them?' he asked.

'It's a central CCTV monitoring control near Birdlip. It's hidden away.'

'I'll find it, thanks.'

'Now I come to think of it, there have been a couple of instances that the fire team have investigated,' the security man recalled.

'Wildlife?'

'No, so you're probably not interested.'

'Try me, I might.'

'One was a fire in the field at the end of the runway. They seemed to think it was a vagrant's cooking fire. But they didn't see anyone though.

'Pity.'

'Oh Yes, there was something else.'

'Go on.'

'Someone was wandering around the other night. It was a cyclist on the runway.'

'A cyclist?'

'Yeah. It caused an aborted landing,' the security man said.

'Oh, that could have been nasty,' the journalist observed.

'Yeah, particularly as it was an emergency flight. A heart donor transport coming in.'

'That would have been a tragedy, if that had crashed.'

'The fire team again went and investigated but didn't find whoever it was though.'

'Do you think it could have been sabotage?'

'Who knows. But we've had no report of damage to any of the planes or hangars. And I know for a fact, that the local kids get up to stupid pranks when we're closed overnight.'

'Perhaps whoever it was couldn't do his planned mischief because of the unexpected flight.'

'He must have shat himself when that plane nearly landed on him though,' the security man laughed.

'I wonder if there is any CCTV of whoever it was?'

'Mmm, I think you're going to be unlucky. I'm not sure that the cameras cover that part of the runway.'

'Perhaps they could have been doing a recce for something?' the journalist said thinking aloud.

'Yeah, I suppose. But I think it's more likely that we got a vagrant looking for food.'

'Why do you think that?'

'The pub seems to think something, or someone has been messing with the food waste bins. They think food has been taken out.'

'Any chance that could just be animals?'

'Well, there's foxes and rats around there. That might tie in with your angle about wildlife though,' the security man suggested.

'Yes,' Bert said, thinking that the assumed vagrant story was what he was really after.

'Sorry can't help you anymore, I've got a flight coming in.'

'That's OK, appreciate your time.'

'A vagrant on a bike! That's the link then,' the journalist thought as he left the airport. 'He was riding John's stolen bike. So, it is the kid then. Bert couldn't contain his excitement having discovered this evidence. Ah ha, looks like I owe you some pocket money son.'

He then made his way to the central CCTV monitoring control hidden away in a remote Cotswold location.

Security notices indicated that the place was guarded by dog patrols and trespassers would be prosecuted.

Bert drove his car up to the security gates and showed his press id badge to the gate camera. He explained to the voice on the intercom the reason for his visit.

'I've just come from the airport and they tell me that you monitor their CCTV cameras.'

'I'm afraid I can't confirm or deny that,' the metallic voice responded.

'Well I gather there was an incident with a cyclist on the runway the other night, I just wondered if I could look at the CCTV for the airport?'

'Sorry, we need written permission from the airport management to give you access to their CCTV footage,' the officious voice declared.

'This could really be important,' Bert insisted.

'Sorry. Get me the authority and we'll see what we've got.'

Having had a previous 'run-in' about an article he'd written criticising the airport management, Bert thought it was unlikely they would grant him permission.

'I think I'll leave it, thanks,' he said.

# Chapter Seventy-one

After Angelina had pleaded with her mother to allow Mo to swap his tree house for a proper bed, he stayed overnight in the Bow's spare bedroom.

In turn, for allowing him to stay, Helen had insisted that he had a shower, washed his hair and wore some of their son's pyjamas. In the meanwhile, she washed his smelly bloodstained clothes overnight.

Mo, however, spent a restless night. For having spent many months sleeping outside and on hard floors, the bed was far too comfortable, and the house was too stuffy for him. So, despite the discomfort of his bruises, he dragged a sheet on to the floor. But every time he turned over, the pain from his fight injuries, jolted him awake. After tossing and turning most of the night, Mo eventually got off to sleep in the early hours.

When he eventually awoke, he was unsure of where he was. Then when full consciousness returned, he remembered he was safe in the Bow's house and going to see his Sergeant Tom later.

That thought spurred him on, as he groaned his way through getting dressed in his, now, clean clothes.

He went downstairs to see that Angelina, Paul and Helen were already at the kitchen table eating their breakfast.

'Good morning Mohammed,' Helen greeted.

'Morning.'

'Did you sleep OK?' Angelina asked, concerned about his bruised face.

'Not really. But I am OK,' Mo confirmed.

Would you like some breakfast?' Helen asked.

'Yes please,' Mo said, excited to have food put before him without having to scavenge for it.

'We have laid a place for you,' she said, indicating a vacant chair. 'Help yourself to cereals,' she added, pointing to a packet of Weetabix on the table.

Mo took four Weetabix and put them in to the bowl in front of him. He picked one up and was going to eat it, when Helen suggested he might like to have it with milk.

'Yes, thanks,' Mo said, embarrassed, picking up the jug and pouring milk over his stacked breakfast.

'My, you can certainly knock that back,' Helen observed, watching the bowl of cereal disappearing. Would you like some more?'

'Yes please,' Mo confirmed, shovelling in the last mouthful.

'Help yourself,' she invited, as three more Weetabix ended up in his bowl.

'When is Sergeant Tom going to be back home?' Mo asked, spraying Weetabix over the table.

'I would imagine sometime this afternoon,' Helen replied, trying to ignore Mo's bad table manners.

'Right, children. It's time you were on your way to school. Mohammed, you can do the washing up please,' Helen directed.

'Yes, I will do that, if you show me where everything is,' Mo replied, happy to repay Helen's kindness.

'Thank you for washing my clothes, they smell very nice now, 'Mo said.

'Well they were so dirty. I was surprised they didn't leap into the washing machine themselves.'

'I do not understand all the things that people say. Leap into the washing machine themselves?' he puzzled.

'Sorry, we do tend to talk in riddles sometimes,' Helen said. 'It just means that they were very dirty and could have been alive with lots of germs.'

'Oh!'

After Angelina had gone to school, Mo had a potentially long and boring wait for Tom Bow's return. So, Helen found him some chores to help while away the hours, including walking Shadow around the block.

'The walk will do you good. It will ease your aches and pains,' Helen suggested, seeing him out of the door. 'Don't go up by Angelina's school, just in case you bump into John Jones,' Helen warned.

'Ok. I will go to my tree house and get my belongings, if that's Ok,' Mo asked her.

'Yes, that should be Ok.'

Mo took the dog around the block, through the recreational park, past the scene of his beating and back to his tree house.

He tied the dog's lead to a branch while he painfully scrambled up into his nest in the bole of his tree house.

There he dug out his special possessions, the knife and flint the Sergeant had given him; his Scout neckerchiefs and woggles and other special things. Then he stuffed them into his rucksack.

'I will leave the duvet,' he thought. 'Perhaps I might need it again if the Sergeant doesn't want me after all.'

Stiffly, he slithered back down the branch and untied the dog.

'Come on Shadow, time to go home.'

He felt sad about leaving his tree house. He'd good memories of his adventure around it and having the cat and the kittens there too.

'Ah, that's it,' he thought. 'I shall go and see how they are. It's on the way back,' he said, talking to the dog. 'Now you must be a good boy when we get there and not bark at them, otherwise you will frighten them.'

He took the familiar route to the back of the Care home and knocked on the door. After a few minutes Sarah came to the door her hands covered in flour.

'Oh, hello Mohammed. Are you Ok? You look a bit battered, like you've been fighting.'

'Yes, I am fine. I...it was a misunderstanding about a bike, but I am OK,' he informed her.

'Sorry I haven't done anything about that job that we were talking about. I just haven't had the opportunity.'

'No, it was not that I came to see you about. It was the kittens. Are they OK?'

'Yes, they're fine.'

'Can I come in please and see them?'

'Well I'm right in the middle of preparing dinner and I'm not sure about bringing the dog into the kitchen.'

'Oh,' Mo said, feeling very disappointed.

'Ok but you'll have to be quick,' Sarah relented.

'Thank you.'

Sarah led Mo through the kitchen to a small corridor where Mary was lying with the kittens. She hissed and arched her back when she saw Shadow. But the dog paid no attention and merely lay down as if bored.

'See. They are OK,' Sarah said, showing him the brood. 'Look I must get back to the kitchen. Don't be too long. This is part of the resident's area.'

Sarah left as Mo knelt and stroked the kittens.

'It's OK Mary, Shadow won't hurt you or your babies', he said, stroking her back. Hello Tom, Abdul and Hassim, how are you all my friends?' he asked rubbing their soft downy coats.

Just then an electric wheelchair came along the corridor. It was Jenny, who recognised Mo immediately.

'What are you doing playing with those cats?' she demanded.

'Just saying hello, that's all,' Mo explained.

'No wonder you take a long-time mending wheelchairs. Well my wheelchair is working fine, with no thanks to you.'

' So I can see .'

'Have they taught you about batteries being square yet?' Jennifer said without stopping and disappeared down the corridor.

Mo left shortly after and met Helen near their house.

'Oh, thank goodness. Where have you been? I thought you were only going round the block.'

'I went and got some of my things from the tree house and I went to see my kittens in the care home. I am sorry if I worried you.

# Chapter Seventy-two

Angelina came home from school to be greeted by an overexcited Mo.

'What time is your Dad going to be home?' he gushed. I can't wait. It will be so great to see him again.'

'I'm not sure.'

'Oh, that's a car now, perhaps that's him?'

Mo ran to the front door for the umpteenth time that day, only to be disappointed again.

'No, it wasn't him,' he said, deflated.

'Don't fret, he'll be home soon,' she reassured him.

'Anyway, how was your day?' he asked.

'Well it was going Ok until someone told me about John Jones' post on Facebook.'

'What is that? Facebook?'

'It's something on the internet.'

'Oh,' Mo said, not really understanding about the concept of the internet.

'Someone, well anyone, who has access, can put anything they like on to the Internet for other people to read.'

'Oh, that is good then?'

'Not if it accuses you of doing something you didn't do.'

'What do you mean?'

'John Jones has told the 'world' that you stole his bike and what is worse, he says that you're being investigated by the newspapers for being a 'terrorist'.

'What! How can this be? How can he say things that are lies? It is not true. I found the bike.'

'I believe you. But I must tell Mum and Dad. They might need to do something about it, otherwise they might be prevented from adopting you, like you hope.

'Oh, this is terrible. What can I do?' Mo panicked.

'Don't worry. We'll talk to them. They'll know what to do,' Angelina said hopefully.


After several more 'false alarms', it was nearly five o'clock before the Sergeant finally came home from his training course.

Shadow heard the car before it had even turned into the drive and started barking.

'That's your master Shadow isn't it?' Helen said, talking to the excited canine and opening the front door. 'Stay,' she told the dog, holding on to its collar.

Mo, who had been in his bedroom brooding about what Angelina had told him, heard Helen's reassurance to the dog and ran excitedly down the stairs two at a time.

'Is it truly Sergeant Tom?' he asked her.

'Yes,' Helen confirmed, thinking that she'd be glad to shift the responsibility of Mo's welfare to her husband.

As Tom switched off the ignition and got out of the car, there was a race between the excited dog and an even more excited Mo.

Shadow won the mad dash. As the dog leapt up and down on Tom, barking its greeting, his master was instead looking at the advancing Mo.

'Mo, so it is you,' he confirmed, and enveloped the young man in a big hug.

Mo wept as he returned the hug. At last he had fulfilled his dream. All the uncertainty was over.

Those terrible experiences that he had suffered were now a thing of the past. He was with his Sergeant Tom, the man who had saved him. It was such a relief that he wept openly. All the tensions of the past months draining away in his tears.

Embarrassed by the boys emotions, Tom, with one arm around Mo's shoulders, got his case from the car and led him into the house.

They had just got into the house, when suddenly Mo realised, one member of his rescue team was missing.

''You are here, but where is my friend? Where is Jersey?'

'She's in the military kennels. I can't bring her home very often. Usually, only for special military circumstances,' Tom explained.

'Is she Ok?'

'Yes, she passed her re-examination tests, so we can carry on together, doing our job.'

'Oh good.'

'Yes, I was pleased too,' the soldier admitted.

'I'm so happy to see you,' Mo repeated, beaming at Tom.

'My, how you've grown. How old are you now?' the Sergeant observed, standing back and looking at Mo.

'I think 14 years, Mo replied, smiling.

'I see you're still wearing a friendship bracelet. Is it the same one that you made at one of our meetings?'

'Yes. It is cleaner now, since I have had a shower,' he said looking at Helen; who nodded her approval.

'Do I get a hug as well?' Helen asked, patiently waiting in the hallway, watching the joyous reunion.

'Of course,' the Sergeant said, planting a kiss on her expectant lips and enveloping her in an embrace.

'Mo felt a pang of great sadness as he recalled the greeting that his Mother used to give to his father at the end of his long day working in the fields.

'Cup of tea dear? Mo?' she asked them both.

'Yes, I'd love a brew, thanks,' Tom said, taking off his shoes.

'Yes please. I am getting used to drinking your tea now,' Mo added

The soldier and the boy followed Helen into the kitchen and sat at the breakfast bar, while she made the drinks.

'Now tell me about it. How the heck did you find me?' the Sergeant asked Mo.

Mo recounted his experiences since the Sergeant had left Afghanistan, including being kidnapped from the Red Crescent orphanage, escape from the training camp, his long frightening adventure across Europe and the Gangs in 'the Jungle'at Calais.

'You did this all alone?'

'No, my friend Abdul came with me...but...he...was killed trying to stow under a coach in Calais.'

'Oh Mo, I'm so sorry. That must have been devastating for you.'

'Yes, it was. I nearly gave up then,' the boy confessed, with a tear in his eye.

'But then you smuggled yourself into a caravan?'

'Yes. I was nearly caught when we got to Dover.'

'So, it was just by chance that you stopped here and met Angelina at Scouts and in the park?'

'Yes, and had it not been for her kindness giving me first aid, I would never have known either.'

'Oh my, what a story,' the Sergeant observed. 'And after all that, you made it and found me. So, how long have you been here?'

'I don't know, not many days.'

'Where have you been living?'

'I have been living in a tree at the edge of the airfield.'

'How have you eaten? Presumably you have no money.'

'I found lots of food in green bins and there are the gardens with no houses. There are many restaurants and supermarkets throwing away good food too.'

'I'm surprised that you haven't had food poisoning.'

'I used all my Scouting skills that you taught me,' Mo said proudly.

'You are a remarkable young man,' the soldier said, smiling. 'So, what are we going to do with you?'

The sergeant's question was the elephant in the room, nobody dared speak their thoughts.

Finally, Mo ventured his proposal.

'Will you adopt me, like you said you would?' Mo pleaded. 'I will be like your son. I will work very hard. I will bring in money.'

'It's not as easy as that Mo. Because you are here without permission. It is difficult,' the Sergeant explained quietly. 'Let's not make any swift decisions. Let's think about it.'

'Mo could be an exchange student from Afghanistan,' Angelina suggested, anxiously. 'They have country exchanges all the time at my school.'

'Yes, that might work for a short time, but I'm thinking long term,' Tom explained.

'So while you're here, it would be a good idea if you stayed in the house, Mo.' Helen added nervously. 'We don't want the neighbours asking awkward questions until we have a good story to tell them.'

'Dad, Mum. There is something else that you should know,' Angelina said nervously.

Mo was gesticulating for her to be quiet.

'Sorry Mo, I have to tell them.'

'What's the big secret?' Tom asked, looking at both of them.

'John Jones has posted on Facebook that Mo stole his bike and what is worse, he says that he is being investigated by the newspapers for being a 'terrorist'.

'Oh, my God,' Helen exclaimed. 'That changes everything. We can't wait any longer. We need to tell the authorities.'

'No hold tight,' Tom said quietly. 'Not everyone has access to his Facebook page and presumably there is no mention that he is here?'

'No. That's right,' Angelina confirmed.

'We need to discuss this further Helen,' Tom said picking up his case.

# Chapter Seventy-three

Despite her apparent friendly welcome, Helen was still livid with Tom and followed him up to their bedroom.

Tom misread her intentions and advanced on her passionately, only to have his hopes dashed as she handed him off.

'Come on babe, I've missed you,' he pleaded, trying to hug her.

'You've got to be joking.'

'What do you mean?' he asked innocently. 'What have I done now?'

'That boy, is what you've done.'

'What do you mean,' he said, finally backing away.

'So, you unilaterally decided to adopt him, did you?' Helen ranted.

'No I didn't...I said it...but I didn't mean it,' Tom admitted.

'Then you shouldn't have even thought it. Suddenly, we have a new addition to the family, and who is going to be left to look after him? Who's going to sort out his teenage problems while you're away playing soldiers? Muggins here,' she said, slapping her chest, emphasising her point.

'How was I to know he would take my words literally, and travel thousands of miles, risking his life through god knows what dangers?'

'His travel companion and best friend died in Calais trying to get here?'

'Yes, I know. That's a tragedy. But you can't blame me for that,' he said defensively.

'Well that could easily have been him. How would you have liked that on your conscience?'

'It was just a misunderstanding on his part...and I'm sorry. But, he's here now and we'll just have to deal with it. We can't throw him out on the street... I don't even know what we have to do if we were going to adopt him, anyway.'

'For Christ sake Tom what have you done?' she asked, sitting on the bed, shaking her head in disbelief.

'Nothing. I didn't mean for this to happen. Come on, the kid had just been through the most traumatic experience of his life. Can you imagine it? If it was one of our kids being blown up and losing the family? I was only trying to comfort him. What was I going to say? Son, you're on your own.'

'Well...I don't know,' Helen said, frustrated by the situation.

'I felt that I had to give him something positive in his life.' Tom said, passionately. 'A glimmer of hope in his cruel world. The kid had done nothing to deserve all that shit.'

'Well, us rowing isn't going to resolve it either,' Helen said, regaining her composure and going into planning mode. 'I'll make some enquiries, to see what we need to do.'

'Ok, thanks,' Tom said, relieved at the glimmer of a way forward.

'We can't be the only ones in this situation. There must be many other under age immigrants here.

Presumably, they are placed into care. But I don't know what happens after that,' Helen suggested.

Unfortunately, Mo had gone to his bedroom, which was next door to the master bedroom, and had been listening to the argument.

'So, he lied to me. He was never going to adopt me after all,' Mo realised.' I am truly alone. It was just as Abdul had warned me. What if the Sergeant doesn't want you after all?'

Mo's world was collapsing before his new life could even begin.

The atmosphere in the Bow household over the following week was depressing.

Helen made slow progress in her discreet enquiries about adoption and immigrant status. While Mo tried to come to terms with the possibility of having to leave the Bow family.

At the same time, Angelina was receiving a lot of verbal abuse at school from John Jones and his gang.

So, to improve everyone's morale, the Sergeant had organised a family barbeque on the patio and had taken his role as chef.

As the smoke from the sizzling burgers and sausages floated over them, Mo and Angelina were in quiet discussion.

'What's the matter Mo? You have lost your smile,' Angelina observed, as they were sitting waiting for Tom to cook the food.

'I must leave before they tell the authorities,' he explained. 'But where am I going to go? What am I going to do now? My dream is ended,' he said, dramatically.

'No! They won't tell anyone. They will find a way. We all want you to stay. Mum and Dad will do everything to get it sorted. Believe me,' she said sincerely and quickly kissed him on the cheek. Mo was taken aback. Embarrassed by her inexplicable gesture, Angelina quickly ran into the house.

To keep Mo occupied during the children's school hours, while he was off duty, Sergeant Tom took Mo kayaking on the River Avon and hiking in the Cotswolds; but while they were trying to think of a way to handle the situation, the matter was about to be taken out of their hands.

A large security operation was already being planned.

# Chapter Seventy-four

Bert Jones looked at the harassed Detective Sergeant across the desk, hoping that he had enough information to engage the policeman's interest.

'Keith, If I tell you of my suspicions, I want to be present at any subsequent raid and have an exclusive on the story,' the journalist insisted.

'Can't promise you anything until I know what we're talking about,' the policeman said, shuffling papers on his overloaded, untidy, desk.

'Come on, you can do better than that,' the journalist implored.

'I'll see what I can do. Go on then. Spill the beans. I'm all ears,' he said, distracted by a crime file that he was studying.

'It involves a possible terrorist plot.' Bert said, dramatically.' And covert activities by an illegal immigrant.'

'Sounds a bit dramatic. Where has this come from?' The policeman asked, putting down the file.

'I can't divulge my source. Just say, I've got reliable contacts,' Bert told him, hoping that his son's information was indeed reliable.

'You've got to do better than that Bert. You expect me to act on a journalist's hunch?'

'Call it intuition, if you like. Like you, I've had years of experience sniffing around our patch and I know, from a variety of different scenarios, that something isn't quite right here.'

'Go on, I'm listening, but I'm far from being convinced,' the Policeman added, unenthusiastically.

'Someone has been staking out the airport and nearly caused a plane crash the other day.'

'A plane crash! Go on,' the Detective said, sitting up in his chair.

'The airport fire team have also attended a fire near the end of the runway. They think that it's the spy's campfire.'

'And?'

'Surely it's worth investigating?'

'No. I can't do anything with that. Have you got more facts?'

'I think I can identify the possible terrorist too.'

'It sounds a bit sketchy to me. How can you identify this person?'

'Afraid I can't say. Journalistic privilege.'

'Yeah, right!' the policeman said, dismissively.

'As I see it, the high level of the national security status is a good indicator of world tensions. I think, at least, you ought to be tipping off MI5 that we have a possible terrorist plot unravelling in Gloucestershire.

'MI5!'

'Yes. We don't want to find out too late that there was another 911 brewing on our door-step and we did nothing about it. Do we?'

'I think you've been watching too many spy movies. It's probably just a homeless person.

'Could be an illegal immigrant.'

'If there is an illegal immigrant living around here, it doesn't mean that he is going to be plotting an act of terrorism.'

'No, but he could be,' the other added quickly.

'Just imagine the enormity of it if every 'illegal' smuggled into England in the back of a lorry, was planning to conduct an act of terrorism...' The police sergeant pointed out. 'It doesn't bear thinking about.'

'Ok, but within that large influx, there might be a few who are planning something nasty,' the journalist argued.

'Yes of course they might, and I agree that they wouldn't necessarily be on the Security Services radar but...'

'Precisely. But we could at least investigate this particular one. You could interview him. Find out what he's doing here. And you'd get the glory.'

'You said he!'

'Yes, I have my suspicions...rather intelligence,' he corrected himself, 'of who that certain individual could be. Certainly, I believe he is a person of interest.'

'Irrespective of your journalistic interest in the 'situation. You have a duty as a citizen to divulge all you know.'

'Yes, I appreciate that. That's why I'm here.'

'And if we acted upon it. You'd get...?'

'An exclusive.'

'I'm not convinced. If we haul this person in, I can almost guarantee what their story will be. The same as all the others.'

'Which is?'

'They are seeking political asylum because they are escaping from their war-torn countries and their lives are in danger.'

'And who could blame them?'

'No, I'd probably do the same, if it was me.'

'Tell me this then, if that's all they are doing, why is this person here, close to an airport? Can't you see some 911 parallels?

'OK...I'll have words with my Guvnor and see what he reckons,' the policeman agreed reluctantly. 'But don't hold your breath. He's got a lot on his plate at the moment. Wait here,' he directed.

But the Inspector was more than happy to believe that something might be afoot, especially as the suspect was close to an airfield, GCHQ and the Rapid Deployment HQ.

'I want you to contact MI5 and the Border Force and brief them about what you've been told.

I dare say they will take it on from there, but I want us to support them and make sure that there are no cockups. Do you understand?' the Inspector directed.

'Yes. Although I'm not convinced that he has got it right. I'd much prefer to do our own investigations before we send in the 'troops'.

'And if we are too late and something disastrous happens?' the Inspector challenged.

'It's a gamble that we'd have to take. At least we won't have egg on our face.'

'Either way, we're in the proverbial s h 1 t. If we don't act, then something does happen, lives could be lost. I don't want that on my conscience. No, I'd rather not gamble with people's lives, thank you.'

'Ok, you're the boss. But don't blame me if it's all a waste of time.'

'Just get on with it,' the Inspector said, angrily.

Keith Johns returned to his desk and the waiting journalist.

'Well?' the newspaper man asked, expectantly.

'Well it looks like we're going to go ahead. I hope for your sake that you've got your facts straight. It will be a costly exercise if we get it wrong.'

'Trust me. I stake my reputation on it.'

'Brave man. Let's have some details then about the suspect before I get in touch with the relevant people.

The journalist gave the Policeman the required information; including Mo's name, his association with Angelina Bow and advised him of his evidence about the airplane incident and scavenging in food bins.

'Obviously living off the land, to keep a low profile,' the Journalist suggested.

'Mmm, I think there was a report about milk missing off doorsteps too. Might be the same character,' Keith added.

'When do you think it will happen?' the newspaper man asked, excitedly.

'Give me a chance, I've got to get in touch with a few people and persuade them to take it seriously first. I'll let you know if or when it's going down, alright?'

'Great.'

'I hope you're a light sleeper because if it happens, it will be in the early hours.'

'What do you call early hours?'

'Usually between three and four in the morning.'

'Why that time?'

'The psychologists tell us that's the point when people are at the deepest part of the sleep cycle and are not thinking straight.'

'I can verify that, having attended a few early morning incidents for the paper.'

'Right, on your way then. Thanks for giving me a challenge. As I say, I just hope we're not going to be wasting our time.'

'You won't,' the journalist said. 'At least I hope you won't.'

Armed with the information the Journalist had given him, Keith Jones visited Shackleton Close. Using a story that he was seeking people's views on local policing, he established, through a very gossipy neighbour, that the Bow's had indeed got a lodger. A boy with black hair and brown eyes who spoke with a strange accent.

# Chapter Seventy-five

At 0330 the following day, a Police tactical firearms unit, backed by MI5 and immigration officers, surrounded the four-bedroom family home in Shackleton Close.

The assault group gathered around the front door, ready to storm in, once the heavy metal battering ram, known colloquially as the 'persuader', had knocked it down.

However, Tom, on a nocturnal visit to the toilet, had heard a noise outside and suspecting someone was messing around with the cars, surreptitiously pulled the bedroom curtains aside to peer out.

Beneath him, an eagle-eyed policeman spotted the movement of the curtain and immediately targeted Tom with his Heckler and Koch rifle. The marksman 'painted' Tom's chest with the red spot laser target finder.

Tom, used to being instantly alert, irrespective of the hour, knew immediately what the red spot dancing across his chest meant.

'What the hell,' he wondered.

'*TAC1 to TAC control*,' the Policeman called into his radio. We have been compromised. I have a suspect lit with my laser. He has his hands up.'

'*Roger that. All stations, all stations. We have been compromised. Watch out for any runners,*' the commander ordered.

And then other red beams joined the original one on Tom's chest and he understood what was happening, although he didn't understand why.

The soldier opened the curtains fully, put his hands back above his head, and stood motionless.

Helen woke up with a start, as the street lamp flooded the bedroom with light.

'What...what is it Tom?' she asked, waking from a deep sleep, frightened by the sudden disturbance.

'Don't worry Helen. But I think the house is surrounded by armed Police.'

'Oh my god! oh my god! What will the neighbours say?'

'Bugger the neighbours,' Tom spat. 'We've got a problem. I think they are looking for young Mo.'

'Why are they doing it in the middle of the night?'

'I don't know. Unless they believe that stupid kid's Facebook page, about him being a terrorist.'

With the element of surprise gone, the commander stood up and called through a loud hailer. '*Occupants of the house leave through the front door with your hands up. Keep three paces behind the person in front.*'

A powerful light was switched on to illuminate the front door.

While Helen woke Angelina and their son Paul, Tom woke Mo, who was sound asleep.

'Mo, Mo...time to wake up.'

Mo stirred.

'Mo, you need to get up now,' the soldier said firmly.

'But it is still dark. Are we going somewhere?' Mo asked, sleepily.

'It's the Police.'

'The Police?' Mo said, in alarm, suddenly wide awake.

'Yes, we have to go outside with our hands on our heads.'

'I will run,' he said, grabbing his trousers.

'No Mo. They have the house surrounded. And they have guns. They will shoot you, if you try to escape.'

Mo was in a quandary. His mind still fogged by sleep and frightened at the prospect of being confronted by the Police. Was his dream finally over?

The Taliban had told them, if the infidels caught them, his heart would be ripped from his chest while he was alive.

What other level of barbarity would he be subjected to? Would it be better to try and escape and be shot and killed or to allow himself to be captured and tortured?

'Come on. We need to go,' Tom encouraged.

In the end he allowed Tom to guide him down the stairs and they joined Helen and the two children by the front door.

'Dad, what's going on? I'm frightened,' Angelina confessed.

'It's OK. Nothing to be frightened of,' Tom reassured her, putting his arm around her. 'We have done nothing wrong. We shall be OK. Now, we must put our hands on our heads. Don't make any sudden movements,' he instructed.

Bert Jones had got the early morning call on his mobile from his police contact, Keith Johns, and quickly got dressed to witness the raid and subsequent arrests.

'Where are you going at this time of the morning,' his wife demanded, sleepily.

'I've got a tip-off of a raid on a suspected terrorist. Hopefully I will get the exclusive.'

'Oh, you and your stories,' she said, turning over. 'Be careful.'

'I will.'

He crept quietly down the stairs and got into his car and drove towards Shackleton Close only to be stopped at a Police cordon.

Quickly he dug his press pass out and showed it to the officer manning the cordon.

'You're going to have to park your car here and walk to the next cordon,' he was informed.


After a few minutes comforting his family, Tom opened the door. The commander repeated his order for them to *'leave with their hands on their heads.'*

Having been identified previously, two policemen, wearing full faced black balaclavas, came forward and handcuffed Mo and Tom.

'It's OK Mo, there is nothing to worry about, they will just ask you questions, that's all,' the Sergeant reassured him.

'No, they will beat me...and tear my heart out. The Taliban told us. If we are captured, that is what the infidels do.'

'No. I can assure you that will not happen. But you must not run away or fight them. If you do, they will have to use force to restrain you.'

Despite the Sergeant's calming words, it failed to slow Mo's racing heart.

After a quick 'pat down' they were separated from the others, loaded into a police van and driven away

Meanwhile, a distraught Helen, Paul and Angelina, were shepherded back into the house followed by two policemen and a policewoman.

'Why have they taken Dad and Mo away Mum?' Angelina asked.

'It's because Mohammed doesn't have the proper papers to be here, I expect' Helen explained, calmly.

'Oh, is that all. But he hasn't done anything bad or wrong,' the girl continued.

'No, I know he hasn't. I've been trying to sort it out too...but obviously not quickly enough,' Helen confessed.

'I bet that John Jones is behind this,' Angelina added.


Meanwhile, the journalist did as he was told and walked through the outer cordon but was stopped from progressing any further at the inner cordon.

'Come on, let me through,' he demanded. I've been invited to witness the arrests.'

'Sorry Sir. I've just picked up on the radio, that it's all over. The prisoners will be driving through here any moment.'

Just as he informed the upset journalist, they heard an approaching van. The Policeman lifted the incident tape and the van drove through with his blue lights on.

'Looks like you were too late,' the policeman informed the unhappy newspaper man.

'Damn. Do you know where they're going?'

'Police Headquarters I should imagine.'

'Well that was a waste of time,' Bert muttered, as he left the cordon on his way back to his car.

He drove across the other side of the city to the main police station, parked his car on the road nearby and made his way to reception.

'I'd like to see Keith Jones, please,' he asked the receptionist, showing her his press card.

'I'll try his extension,' she advised him. 'But I think he's on a job at the moment.

'Yes, I know. I was hoping to cover it,' the disgruntled journalist informed her. 'I thought he'd be back by now though. I'll give him a call on his mobile.'

'Ok, but I need to ask you to call him from outside, as I am on a break now, and need to lock up while I'm away.'

'If I must,' the disgruntled Journalist said, leaving the warm reception area. 'I'll call him now.'

But Bert soon discovered that in his haste to catch the action, that he'd left his own mobile at home.

'Damn! I shall have to wait until he comes back now,' he groaned

# Chapter Seventy-six

When they arrived at the Police station, rather than being charged by the custody Sergeant, they were released from their handcuffs and taken into separate interview rooms. Tom to one and Mo to another nearby.

After a few minutes alone, Tom was joined by a uniformed army policeman. The tough looking 'redcap' was red faced and obviously angry. He placed a tape recorder on the desk and switched it on.

'Interview started at zero four thirty hours with Sergeant Tom Bow. I am Captain George Bold, Military Police. I have been advised that you are in breach of immigration rules by harbouring an illegal immigrant,' he announced sternly.

'If you say so Sir,' Tom replied flatly.

'You are a serving member of her Majesty's armed forces,' he said dropping his thick frame into the chair opposite Tom. 'What are you doing having an illegal immigrant staying in your house?' the MP barked aggressively.

'And a good morning to you too,' Tom said, quietly.

'Look, I don't appreciate being woken up in the middle of the night to deal with a prat like you. So, don't try to be smart with me. Now, what's been going on?'

'I was on a posting in Afghanistan. A suicide bomber detonated a truck bomb that flattened half the neighbourhood, including Mohammed's house.'

'Mohammed?'

'The kid you are accusing me of aiding to be here.'

'Go on.'

'The explosion killed all of his family. My dog and I dug him out of the rubble. I knew the kid, he was a member of my Scout Troop and naturally I visited him in hospital. There was some confusion about me saying that I was going to adopt him.'

'What! you told him you were going to adopt him?'

'No. That was what he thought I'd said. But I didn't intend to. Obviously, that was a no-no.'

'No, of course not.'

'Anyway, it turns out that after I had finished my final posting, he eventually followed me over here.'

'You sure you didn't plan all of this?'

'No of course not. He's already gone through enough without me encouraging him to risk a journey like he's undertaken. For, not only has the kid gone through the trauma of the explosion, he was kidnapped from the Red Crescent orphanage by the Taliban, forced into a terrorist training camp, and survived an allied assault on the camp.'

'Yeah OK, he's been through hell, but that's still no reason for him being in your house illegally.'

'His parents, sister...and his dog were killed by the bomb,' Tom explained. 'He himself was injured and traumatised by it. He's only a kid and has travelled thousands of miles, so, when he turned up, what was I going to do? Tell him to sod off?'

Behind the interview room's two-way mirror, two MI5 officers were listening intently to the discussion, prior to interviewing Mo.

'Now, that's interesting about his stay in the Taliban training camp. So perhaps he was indoctrinated whilst he was in there then,' Detective Sergeant Chris Fence suggested.

'Come off it. I gather from 'intel' that he was only in the camp for a couple of weeks before the allied assault. What level of indoctrination could they do in that time?' Detective Sergeant Graham Hopson questioned.

'They could have 'sowed the seeds'. Perhaps he was already radicalised. Who knows who else he's been rubbing shoulders with and talking to on the way through Europe? Or in the camp at Calais?' Chris suggested.

'Have the plods completed checking out the kids hide away in the treehouse?' he asked.

'Yes, I think so.' The other said, reaching for his mobile.

'Did they find anything?

'Nothing except an old duvet.' Graham said, looking at the text that he'd received.

'What about at the Bow's house?'

'Battered old rucksack, Scouting stuff, a Bear Grylls fire flint, Swiss army knife. Nothing that would lead me to believe he was planning anything terror related.

They turned back to Tom's discussion with the Redcap.

'The kid was scared out of his wits. Could you imagine our kids doing that journey? Travelling thousands of miles overland from Afghanistan at his age? I can't,' Tom continued.

'As much as I recognise his determination to get here, that's not the point,' Captain Bold said dismissively.

'No! What is the point then?' Tom demanded, beginning to get annoyed with the unsympathetic Military Policeman.'

'The point is that you know, as a serving soldier, war is shit. Right?'

'Yes of course. I've seen enough dead and damaged bodies to know that.'

'Then you know you have to leave this sort of stuff on the battlefield. You don't bring it home,' the Redcap lectured.

'It's easy for you to moralise from behind an office desk thousands of miles away from the action,' Tom shouted. 'You weren't there dealing with raw emotions.'

'I don't have to be there to know what it's like, the MP said calmly. 'My son took his own life following his posting to Iraq. PTSD is a killer too.'

'I'm sorry to hear that...but you have to understand that I had no choice but to take him in. He was here, the kid was living in a treehouse. So, what else could I do?'

'As I say. In your situation though, there is no room for this type of sentiment.'

'No, but there is for humanitarianism. What about all the innocent orphaned kids caught in the crossfire of two warring factions? Traumatised little kids with limbs missing, because they wandered into an IED minefield.'

'All this is irrelevant. It doesn't excuse you failing to report the kid,' the Captain said, thumping the desk.

'I would have been letting him down,' Tom said, passionately.

'So, you think a raid by armed police in the middle of the night was better then?'

'No of course I don't. We were looking for the right procedure to adopt him...but somehow someone threw a spanner in the works before we got it sorted. I've got an idea who it might be and just wonder if they realise what they've done,' the Sergeant reflected.

'Well, don't be doing anything stupid that might make things worse.'

'No, of course I won't," the Sergeant reassured him. 'He's only a kid himself.'

'There is no point discussing this any further,' the MP concluded. When the press gets hold of this, you will have clearly damaged the reputation of the service that you represent. You will have dishonoured the rank that you are privileged to hold.

I will recommend that you should be reduced to the ranks and reported for the incident, which might also lead to a Court Martial. Good day to you, soldier.'

The Redcap picked up his tape recorder and left a bemused Tom.

'So much for acts of charity,' Tom thought.

# Chapter Seventy-seven

Mo was taken to another interview room by a WPC. But before he entered, Mo peered in apprehensively, fearing he was entering a torture chamber.

Instead, inside he saw a young woman in jeans and a jumper sitting behind a large table, several pieces of paper were lying in front of her.

'Hello,' she said, standing. 'It's Mohammed isn't it?' she smiled and shook his hand.

'Y...e...s,' Mo answered, his shaky voice displaying his nervousness.

Mo was suspicious to have been released from his handcuffs.

'Is this some form of psychological torture?' he wondered. 'Would someone come in next and hurt him?'

'Please sit down,' she invited, indicating a chair opposite. 'Would you like a cup of tea?'

'No, thank you,' Mo replied, fearful that it might be drugged.

'Yes, I suppose it's a bit early at this time of the morning, but I find it wakes me up,' she divulged.

At thirty-five Janet Folds had been working for the Immigration Service for fifteen years and her workload was increasing, year on year, as a result of floods of refugees escaping world unrest, hoping to start a better life in Britain.

As the numbers had risen, staff doing night duty had also increased. Tonight, it was Janet's turn to leave her husband in bed.

'My name is Janet,' I am an immigration officer. I have been asked to talk to you first before the security services come and have a chat. Do you understand?'

'The security services?' Mo repeated, fearful of what was to come.

'Yes. It's nothing to worry about. But they'd like to ask you a few questions, that's all. First of all, do you have any papers that allow you to be here in England?'

'No...I...I...crept into a caravan in France and escaped from the caravan when it stopped near Churchdown.'

'Have you subsequently tried to obtain any paperwork?'

'No. I have been keeping away from authorities. I was told in France that I would be immediately deported if I was found.'

'But you have been friendly with...'Janet looked at her paperwork, 'Um, the Bow family. In particular, Miss Angelina Bow, is that right?'

'Yes, she is my friend. I didn't know until she took me back to her house that she was the Sergeant's daughter.'

'The Sergeant?'

'The Sergeant who rescued me from my destroyed house.'

'Sergeant Bow?'

'Yes. The Sergeant who visited me in hospital and...'

'Well, I can see why you would want to meet up with him again. But unfortunately, there are rules about coming to England and you have broken them.'

'Does that mean I will be sent back?'

'Most likely, yes. That will probably be the final outcome.'

'Oh!' Tears welled up in Mo's sad brown eyes. All the struggles he had been through were going to be for nothing. He was going to end up back in Afghanistan after all.

Abdul and he had overcome those seemingly endless challenges of that impossible journey; avoiding robbers, Gang masters and the perils of overcrowded boats. Worse still, Abdul had lost his life in that coach accident. The dream was over. Now it had finally turned in to the nightmare that Mo had feared.

'How old are you Mohammed?'

'I am fourteen, I think.'

'Well, while you're here, we have a duty of care to look after you,' she added.

'What does that mean?' he asked.

'We'll find an arrangement, while all the legal proceedings are being done.'

'Will I be able to stay with the Sergeant? Mo asked hopefully.

'We'll see. 'I can't promise anything at this stage.'


At that moment the door opened and two men in suits entered.

'Sorry Janet. Have you finished?'

'Yes. But Mohammed is a bit upset at the moment,' she said, sympathetically touching the back of his hand. 'Do you want a drink now Mohammed?' she asked the boy.

'No. I'm alright thanks.'

'Ok. Well I'll leave you with these two gentlemen then.'

The boy swallowed hard, fearful of what was to come.

# Chapter Seventy-eight

As Janet left, the MI5 policemen sat down on the opposite side of the table facing Mo.

'Hello Mohammed. It is Mohammed isn't it?' A surly looking Detective said.

'Yes. That is my name,' Mo tensed, crossing his arms across his chest.

'What are you doing in England, Mohammed?' Chris Fence continued, fixing him with a withering look,

'I came to find my friend. The Sergeant Tom and his dog who saved me from my blown-up house.'

'Your blown-up house?'

'Yes.'

'How did it get blown up? Was someone in the house making a bomb at the time?' The detective probed, studying Mo's body language to assess the truthfulness of his answer.

'No. It was a suicide bomber outside.'

'Someone in your family? Did the bomb blow up prematurely?' he persisted.

'No. It was in a truck nearby.'

'So, what actually happened?'

Mo tensed, he had put the dreadful events of that day to the back of his mind and didn't want to revisit the tragedy.

'Take your time,' the other policeman coached.

'I don't remember too much because I was knocked out...but we were...we were sitting down to eat.'

'We? Who was we?' Chris asked coldly.

'My mother, father and my sister.'

'Nobody else?'

'No.'

'Go on.'

'My mother was just serving the food and there was a big blast outside. We knew it was a bomb. My dog jumped up on my lap and then the house fell down on top of us,' Mo sobbed.

'And the bomb was definitely outside?' Chris persisted.

'Yes. When they dug me out, they say that Nipper, my dog, had saved my life. But he was dead. After Jersey found me in the ruins of my house...'

'Jersey?'

'He is a search dog. He and Nipper used to play.'

'OK, carry on.'

'I was taken to the hospital with my sister, but she died.' Tears were now freely running down his face.

'OK, son, take your time,' Graham said gently.

The Sergeant and Jersey came to visit me in hospital while my injuries were getting better.

So, is that all?' Chris continued, leaving long quiet moments to allow Mo's nerves to get him to speak to fill the void.

'Yes.'

'Was your father in the Taliban? Is that how your house blew up?'

No. My father worked in the field tending his crop.'

'I suppose that was poppies was it?' the agent suggested.

'No, it was vegetables.'

'Are you sure? The terrorists get a lot of money from opium to buy guns.'

'Yes I know, but he just sold the vegetables at the market.' Mo said indignantly.

'I think your father was a terrorist and blew himself up making a bomb,' Chris persisted.

'No, he was not,' Mo shouted angrily, thumping the table.

'I need to verify what you've told us,' the MI5 agent said curtly, leaving.


'You mustn't mind him. He can be quite scary sometimes, the other MI5 agent, Graham, reassured Mo. 'Don't be afraid to tell me anything. You can trust me. This will be strictly between you and I.'

'Ok.'

'Do you have a mobile?'

'No.'

'Come on. All you youngsters have mobile phones.'

'No, I didn't have much money. But what I had, I used it to pay for our passages to the people smugglers.'

'So, where did you get your money for the trip? It must have cost a lot to buy your way here,' the agent suggested.

'My Uncle gave me his savings.'

'That was very kind of him.'

'Yes.'

'Why would he do that?' the policeman asked suspiciously.

'Because, instead of looking after me, as he'd promised his brother, my father, instead he sent me to an orphanage, and I was kidnapped by the Taliban.

'He obviously felt guilty then?'

'Yes.'

'OK, so when you got to England why were you living near the airport?'

'The caravan stopped near there.'

'The caravan?'

'The one that I smuggled myself aboard on in France.'

'Go on.'

'I didn't know where I was. But I jumped out when it stopped here. So, I slept under a hedge the first night and found a tree to get away from nosey dogs the next night.'

'But obviously, you had planned to be there?'

'No. I didn't know where I was,' Mo explained.

'Were you planning to find an airport for any reason?'

'I didn't know that there was an airport there until I woke up that first morning.'

'So, you're saying it was a pure coincidence that you happened to end up so close to where the Sergeant lived too?'

'Yes. I didn't realise that I was that close, until Angelina took me to her house.'

'Why did she take you to her house?'

'She was giving me first aid.'

'Why?'

'I had been in a fight with a local boy who accused me of stealing his bike. But I didn't steal it, I found it by the side of the road.'

'So you had a bike, and you were living right by the airfield! So was it you, that was seen riding on the airfield?'

'Yes...I... A plane was coming in to land and...'Mo confessed.

'So, were you going to deliberately cause the plane to crash?'

'No. I went on the runway because they don't usually fly at night.'

'What were you doing on the airfield then?

'I was seeing how fast I could ride.

'Fancied yourself as a Chris Froome, did you?' the policeman joked.

'Chris Froome?'

'Doesn't matter. Going back to the Sergeant. He must have said something about where he lived to you when he was in Afghanistan?'

'He might have. But I don't know anything about England. So it would not have meant anything to me.'

'So, you didn't know there was an airport close by to his house?'

'No.'

'Can you fly a plane? Have you got a license?'

'No. I have never even been in an aeroplane.'

At that moment Chris returned and sat next to his colleague.

'Sergeant Bow confirms that Mohammed's house was blown up by a suicide bomber. The guy had been shot by an Afghan army sentry,' Chris revealed, and glared at Mo, clearly rattled that his theory, that the boy's family were bombmakers, had been disproved.

'Do you know how to fly drones?' he persisted.

'Fly drones?'

'Don't play dumb with me kid. You know what drones are?' Chris scolded.

'The little ones that look like helicopter but with four rotors,' Graham clarified.

'No. How do they fly?' Mo asked.

'You use those hand controllers. You know, the ones you kids use for electronic games like Call of Duty etc.'

'Oh yes. I saw some of the soldiers with them. But we had no money to buy such things,' Mo told them. 'But we did meet a proper drone pilot.'

'What do you mean 'proper' drone pilot?'

'The one who flies the big drones, that look like planes.'

'Oh yes. And where did you meet them?'

'When we were going through France. She was an American, who gave us a lift in her car to Paris. We think she might have been the one who bombed the Taliban training camp. When we were rescued by special forces soldiers.'

'We?'

'Yes, my friend Abdul and me.'

'So where is this Abdul now? Is he hiding somewhere near here?'

'No. He was killed in France...hiding underneath a coach...he fell off an was...'

'I think I read about it,' Graham added. 'That must have been terrible for you?'

'Yes, it was,' Mo said quietly.

'Now tell me about this training camp. Did you have lectures?' Chris continued ignoring Mo's sadness.

'Lectures. What are lectures?'

'Did they tell you about the struggle with the evil Satan's country and how you must fight the infidel?

Mo hesitated and jiggled in his seat... 'No,' he lied. For they had actually been talked at about the terrorist ideology, but he didn't agree with their views and wasn't persuaded by their arguments.

Consequently, he withheld this bit of information so as not to undermine his chances of staying in the UK.

'We were only there for a short time before the camp was bombed. And we were constantly doing rifle drills and physical training.'

'Why?'

'They said we were not fit, and we needed to be trained for fighting.'

'Ok,' Chris acknowledged sceptically. 'Did you go to any meetings in Calais?'

'Meetings?'

'Yes, meetings with other immigrants to talk about bombs and things.'

'No.'


A moment Chris,' Graham suggested, and the two of them stepped out into the corridor.

'I don't think there's anything sinister about the kid. We're wasting our time here.'

'I'm not sure that he is telling the truth. Did you read his body language when I asked him about being lectured. He was obviously lying,' Chris revealed.

'Whether they did or didn't turn him, it's likely he will go into a deportation centre anyway.'

'Yes, I suppose you're right. If he was planning any mischief that will curb his opportunities anyway.'

'He says he hasn't got a mobile, so there is nothing that we can chase on that score either.'

'Ok, we'll leave him in the hands of the immigration people.'

'What about the soldier?'

'We'll leave him for the army to sort out. Last I heard he was getting a big bollocking from the Military Policeman.'

'I feel sorry for the kid. He's taken his life in his hands to come over and track this soldier bloke down and in the end, he is just going to be sent back home to where it all started.'

'Life's a shit and then you die,' Chris added and strode off down the corridor, leaving Graham to explain to Mohammed what was likely to happen next.

'Right, Mohammed, we are going to have words with Janet, the immigration officer now, Graham explained. 'As far as we are concerned you do not pose a threat and we will not be talking to you again. Do you understand?'

'Yes, thank you,' Mo said relieved, unconsciously removing his hand that had been covering his heart. 'Thank you very much.'

'Take Care Mohammed,' Graham said, closing the door. 'Hope it works out for you,' he thought.

# Chapter Seventy-nine

The MI5 people tracked down Janet in the building and told her of their decision.

'There's nothing that makes us suspicious of his intentions here. Likewise there is no indication that he is planning any devious activities ... other than the fact that he's illegal.'

'No, I didn't get that impression either. He is just a desperate young man hoping to start a new life,' she confirmed.

'We presume you'll send him to a detention centre for deportation anyway.'

'Yes, that's the current plan,' she explained. 'Unless we find that there are extenuating circumstances for him to stay.'

'OK. He's all yours then,' Graham said, leaving.

'Thanks.'

Janet went to the interview room where Tom had been blasted by the unsympathetic 'Redcap.'

Taking a seat opposite him, she introduced herself.

'Hi, my name is Janet Folds from the immigration service. I have been speaking to Mohammed and he has confirmed that he has no paperwork to allow him to be here.'

'Yes, you're right,' Tom replied, fixing her with a stare. 'He might not have the paperwork, but he certainly has courage and bravery. We are talking about a young man escaping the horrors of war... not a terrorist.'

'I agree and MI5 have just informed me that they are satisfied that he is not currently, a security threat.'

'Oh, that's a relief,' the soldier said. 'I never thought he was.'

'Yes, but he is here illegally.'

'Is there any other way that we can find to allow Mo to stay? Claim political asylum, uhm anything else he could use as a mitigating factor. Death threats on return, perhaps?

'Highly unlikely,' the immigration official said. 'There is, however, some sympathy to Afghans who were interpreters for the allies.'

'Well, that's it then,' the Sergeant said triumphantly. 'The boy did a lot of translating for me with some of the village elders. Perhaps that's the answer?'

'Perhaps. Although, he is a minor, and a child in the eyes of the law, our next step will be to deport him back to Afghanistan,' she informed him.

'Oh. Sod! We have been trying to find out how we can adopt him. But my wife has had no success.'

'I'm sorry to hear that. But clearly that is an option.'

'If...and it's a big if. If I adopted him would that... I mean, could he stay permanently?'

'Although adoption helps the system and Mohammed is a nice young man, it's a big decision for you to make with your family. You must remember the cultural differences might cause some...tension. You have to ask yourself; will he be able to fit in with your normal family life?'

Tom was wrong footed by her question. He had always assumed that Mo would just fit in. But she had sowed the seeds of doubt, now he wasn't so sure.

After all, he'd only known the lad occasionally as a member of a small Scout group. He hadn't actually lived with him in a normal family situation.

Was it fair on his family?...on Helen? As Helen had said, she would end up dealing with the day to day crises'. He needed to take the emotion out of his decision and really think this through.

The immigration officer cleared her throat and looked at the Sergeant, squarely.

'Look. As the deportation centre is currently overcrowded, I am quite happy for him to continue to stay with you while his case is being sorted out. How does that sound?'

'Well a damn sight better than at half past three this morning,' Tom conceded.

'Right, I will review his case with my colleagues and I'll be in touch soon,' Janet said. 'As there is nothing further to be gained from holding you any longer, I have agreed to let the pair of you go home.'

'Thanks,' Tom said, standing and shaking her hand.

'Mohammed is just next door,' she advised.

The soldier stepped out into the corridor and opened the door that she'd indicated.

When Mo saw who it was, his expression changed from dread to joy and he ran to him and hugged him.

'How did you get on Mo? You don't appear to have been beaten,' the Sergeant joked, trying to make light of their dilemma.

'The lady said I would be sent home,' he relayed emotionally. 'But she said that there was a lot of paperwork to sort out first,' he continued.

'Don't worry. I've told them that you can stay with us until things are sorted,' the soldier said, attempting to console him.

'And what will happen then?' Mo asked, looking at the Sergeant for some reassurance.

'We'll see,' his mentor said, deliberately not committing himself this time, until he'd spoken to Helen.

The mentally exhausted pair took a taxi back home.

# Chapter Eighty

Outside the Police station, as the news filtered out, a dishevelled Bert Jones was feeling very unhappy.

He had got up early to witness the raid, and had missed it. Worse still, he had been standing around mobile-less for hours, devoid of any snippet of information.

Finally, his police contact, Keith Johns, approached the disgruntled journalist.

'Right. So much for your terrorist theory. The kid is an illegal immigrant, that's all. Not a terrorist.'

Keith Johns briefly explained Mo's story as relayed to him by Janet Folds.

'Damn! That's my exclusive out the window,' the newspaper man cursed.

'My gaffer is after my blood too because of your, so called, hunch,' the policeman advised him. 'I did remind him that I was sceptical about it in the first place. But he still blames me,' Keith said, disconsolately.

'Well sorry about that. My informant was pretty convinced that the boy was up to no good,' Bert said defensively.

'That's another thing too. I assume it was your son who was your informant?'

'Well...errr...yes. He was actually,' Bert admitted, awkwardly.

'Well. In future, you can tell him to keep his petty accusations to himself.'

'Sorry. I acted in good faith for the public good.'

'Public good! Huh! What about the public purse? Do you know what that armed operation cost?

'No.'

'Tens of thousands.'

'Sorry.'

'You might like to get your son to remove his internet postings too, unless he wants to be sued for libel.'

'Oh dear, what's he put on line?'

'Only that the young man is a terrorist and that you uncovered the plot.'

'Oh God, did he? I haven't seen it. Sorry Keith,' the journalist apologised.

'Can I borrow your mobile, I've left mine at home.'

'If you must,' the Policeman said reluctantly.

Bert rang his son immediately.

Not recognising the mobile number, the boy answered cautiously. 'Hello.'

'John, it's your father.'

'Hi Dad. Have you got your scoop?'

'No. You got it all wrong. The police are telling me that you have put some libellous stuff on line.'

'I only put the truth on.'

'No, you made up the story. Now get it off before someone sues us.'

'But...'

'Don't, but me. Do it now. I will have some serious words with you when I get home. Now get on and do it.'

Fuming, Bert hung up on his son and handed the mobile back to its owner.

'Sorry Keith, sorry about that,' the journalist grovelled

'Goodbye Bert. Don't call us, we'll call you; unless you've got a real story.'

Bert Jones was furious with his son. He realised that his story, was not going to be the sensation that he had hoped for. Instead he was going to have 'egg on his face' by not investigating it thoroughly enough.

His already pre-prepared 'exclusive' report about a terrorist plot being defused in the early stages of planning, was going to be scrapped.

His hoped for 'scoop', was now going to be scaled down to a story about finding an illegal immigrant and it would be demoted to a few column inches. Not the frontpage banner that he had prepared.

'Even worse,' he thought, 'the editor is not going to be happy, as he'd held the front page for the big story.'

Frustrated by not having his phone with him, he had missed the deadline anyway, so he tiredly made his way home and rang the office from there.

After explaining to the editor about the real facts and eating 'humble pie', the vilified Bert was told to write a positive story to spin something out of his disaster.

'Here is what you are going to do,' the editor told the frustrated journalist. 'Buy the lad a mountain bike and get a photographer round there.'

As a result of the misleading information that he'd given his father, John Jones was grounded for a month.

# Chapter Eighty-one

Tom had been thinking about what the immigration officer had told him concerning Mo's cultural differences, and what would happen at home during his future postings.

'As Helen had previously said, would it be fair to leave her to cope with his teenage problems, while he was away?' he pondered.

'Other than adopting him, there were two other alternative options,' he decided. 'One; not to adopt Mo OR two; adopt him and leave the army,' - and based upon the vitriolic grilling he'd received from the Military Policeman, he might be pushed, before he jumped from the army anyway.

'But, if they didn't adopt Mo, what would happen to the young man? Would he end up being deported or left in an immigration centre waiting to be adopted by someone else?

He felt a great responsibility for Mo. He was very fond of him and having apparently given him false hopes that he would adopt him, perhaps he ought to 'bite the bullet'...On the other hand, he loved his job in the army too. What a quandary.'

Unable to come up with a clear decision, he took Helen and Shadow for a walk in the countryside to discuss it away from 'prying' ears.

'So, what shall we do about Mo?' he asked her.

'I've been ploughing through the red tape finding out about adoption and it's a quagmire of officialdom.

It's likely to take a minimum of six months; we've got to have assessments and medical examinations; got to find referees and go in front of a panel.' Helen revealed.

Then, when you've been given the green light to adopt, you have to get a court order.' Helen recited. 'No wonder people don't want to adopt, having to go through that rigmarole.'

'The only thing that is going for us, is that Mo cannot be cared for in a safe environment in his own country, although I'm sure some people will argue that. But the bottom line is that the adoption would be in Mo's best interests,' Tom enthused.

'Yes, I agree. What's more, he's a nice polite boy too. I do like him,' Helen confessed.

'But I'm concerned that, like you said previously, when I go away on a posting, that you will be left with the three kids...and Mo might not fit in.'

'Of course, he'll fit in,' Helen corrected him. Have you seen him with Angelina? They are good friends. And, if he goes to Scouts, he will make even more there. After all, you started him off on that Scouting road, didn't you?'

'Yes, I suppose I did. So, what do you reckon? Go ahead with it?'

'I think we'd be letting him down if we didn't, don't you?' Helen agreed. 'In that case, we'd better organise a party and tell him and the others that's what we're going to do.'

'Ok. It's a deal.' Tom put his arm around Helen's waist, looked into her bright eyes and smiling face and kissed her deeply. 'I love you,' he whispered, breathlessly as he hugged her tightly.

'I love you too,' she replied hoarsely.

# Chapter Eighty-two

The Bow's family subsequently had a phone call from a very embarrassed newspaper man.

'Hi. My name is Bert Jones. I'm calling from the County News. I understand that you have a Sergeant Bow living there?'

'Yes, that's my husband, Helen replied, puzzled.

'We...we...have picked up a story that a young Afghan boy has journeyed thousands of miles to track down his 'soldier rescuer'. Would that be correct?' Bert said, already knowing the facts from his police contact.'

'Yes, that's true, but don't forget Jersey the rescue dog who actually found him.'

'Oh, that's even better,' the journalist thought, 'everyone loves an animal story'.

'The paper would like to recognise the boy's courage by presenting him with a mountain bike. Would that be OK?'

'Yes, I'm sure it would,' Helen confirmed.

'I'd like to come over with a photographer and take a picture of the bike being presented and check the facts for the article, if that's Ok?'

'Yes. I'm sure they be delighted.'

The article which eventually appeared the following day was headlined

*'Afghan boy tracks down Hero Soldier.'*

*An army search dog handler has had an unexpected visit by an Afghan orphan that he rescued from under tons of rubble.*

*Sergeant Tom Bow and his arms and explosive search dog Jersey, rescued Mohammed from the ruins of his demolished home following a suicide bomb that killed the boy's family*

*At the end of the Sergeants posting in Afghanistan, the young boy travelled thousands of miles to track down and thank his hero.*

*This newspaper is so impressed with the courage and bravery of the fourteen-year-old that they have presented him with a mountain bike...'*

The Sergeant made special arrangements for Jersey to be released from the kennels for the photo shoot.

Subsequently, a picture of Sergeant Tom and Jersey with Mo sitting on his new mountain bike was featured with the article.

Along with the 'telling off' from his father, the picture of a smiling Mo on a new mountain bike further rubbed John Jones' nose in it.

But unbeknown to Tom, the newspaper article, generated another unexpected bonus too.

For when the army 'big brass' were advised about the positive publicity, they decided to let the Sergeant off with a warning, rather than pursuing the case for a more severe penalty as recommended by the Red Cap Captain.

# Chapter Eighty-three

'Mohammed, there is a visitor for you,' Helen said, answering the door.

'A visitor? I am not expecting anyone,' Mo thought.

'It's a young man,' she amplified.

As he got to the door, he stopped in his tracks. He was frozen to the spot in disbelief. He could not believe his eyes. There was a ghost, an apparition, in front of him.

'But you are...d...I am dreaming,' he stuttered, holding on to the door in shock.

'But Abdul, you are dead! I saw your body, after you fell off the coach.'

Nevertheless, ghost or not, Mo ran to him crying and hugged him tightly.

'How can this be that you are alive?' he blurted.

Abdul was in tears too, tightly clinging on to Mo.

'Abdul, still alive! Well I never.' Tom said, following Mo to the door. Despite his tough veneer, the soldier felt quite emotional as the pair hugged each other.

'My Impossible dream painting,' Mo suddenly said.

'What about it?' Abdul asked, puzzled.

'The white ghost was you, Abdul, not me. You have come back from the dead. I'm so glad my friend.'

'Well don't just stand on the doorstep. Do come in,' Helen invited. 'It sounds like you've got a lot of catching up to do.'

'Thank you,' Abdul acknowledged.

'How did you get here? Where is your transport?' Tom asked, looking outside.

'He had to go to the post office to post some letters.'

'Abdul, my friend. I can't believe it.' Mo sobbed, still holding on to his friend.

After a few minutes, when they had composed themselves, Abdul was able to explain how he had survived.

'Obviously, it was not me that fell from underneath the coach. There was someone else there when I climbed under. It was horrible when he fell off. I thought that I was going to go too, because my rucksack caught and dragged along on the road and I nearly lost my grip. Except my friendship bracelet, that you made for me, caught on something underneath and I could grab hold again. It saved my life.' Abdul explained, getting tearful. 'I still wear it,' he said, showing the multicolour paracord bracelet.

'But your rucksack! I saw your rucksack by the...by the person who fell off.'

'Yes, luckily the strap broke and it came off. Probably it was my bad sewing that saved my life,' Abdul continued

'Thank goodness,' Mo said, beaming.

'The back wheels went over him,' Abdul recalled dramatically. 'I felt the bump. And the horrible scream. I was so scared that I just held on even tighter.'

'I identified your rucksack for the police,' Mo explained. 'That's why we thought it was you... I left it there, but I saved your neckerchiefs. I have them upstairs.'

'Thank you.'

'So, did you get all the way to England under the coach?' Mo quizzed.

'No, it was so cold under there, I didn't think I would be able to hang-on long enough to get to England. So, when I was on the ferry, I moved and hid in a lorry instead.

It was a Downton lorry, which brought me to Gloucestershire, and I have been staying with some very kind people over by the lorry depot.

But what about you? How did you get here?' Abdul quizzed.

Mo explained about his journey in the caravan, the Scouts meeting, getting into a fight about the bike and finding out that Angelina, the girl who looked after him, was Sergeant Bow's daughter.

'But how did you know I was alive and living here?' Mo asked.

'It was in the newspapers. My new family told me about it and when I saw your picture in the paper on your new mountain bike, I couldn't believe it.

So, we found out your address and they brought me over here to see you.'

'We are so lucky. Many others don't find happiness here and we must thank your Uncle too,' Abdul suggested. 'Without his money, we would not have been able to make it.'

'No, you are right. We have already sent my Uncle a copy of the newspaper article through Sergeant Tom's friend Jeremy, in Afghanistan. He has taken it to my Uncle to let him know that I am alive and well in England.'

'We owe him so much,' Abdul said quietly, recalling that his life savings had given them their new life.

'Abdul we are having a celebration meal and I hope you will join us.' Tom advised him.

'Thank you, I will stay if I may.'

'I have to warn you though, I invited my mother,' Tom explained. 'She's a bit elderly and her mind wanders, but please be kind to her.'

'Helen joined Tom and held his hand. 'I have a special announcement to make.' Everybody went quiet and looked at the couple expectantly.

'Helen and I have started the official process to adopt Mo. He will become our adoptive son and Angelina and Paul's adoptive brother.'

Smiles erupted on everyone's face which melded into a group hug of happiness.

Just then the door opened, as Jennifer wheeled herself up the disability ramp. 'What's all this noise about?' she demanded.

'We're going to adopt Mo, Mother,' Tom informed the old lady.

'Mo! Who is Mo?' she puzzled, looking around. Spotting Mo, she said, 'Oh, it's you is it?!'

'Hello, Jennifer. How's your wheelchair now?' Mo asked.

'Oh you already know each other?' Tom observed.

'Yes,' Mo confirmed.

'Quiet,' the old lady commanded. 'You'll wake the kittens.'

'Kittens!' Tom looked at his Mother as if she'd experienced one of her delusions.

However, everyone craned their necks to see into the basket on the front of her wheelchair, and to their surprise there were three kittens with their mother lying quite contentedly on a blanket.

'My kittens,' Mo said, kneeling down to get a closer look. 'My, how they've grown.'

'Your kittens?' Abdul asked, joining him.

'Yes. Their Mother delivered them on my duvet when I first arrived. I took them to Jennifer's nursing home.'

'That's right,' she confirmed, 'and I've been given the job of looking after them by the staff. It's a very important job,' Jennifer explained. 'I brought them out for a ride,'

'I named one after you my friend.' Mo told Abdul.

'After me? Which one is it?' he asked, looking at the three cute kittens.

'It is the one with the ginger markings,' Mo revealed.

'Oh how nice,' Abdul cooed.

'The tabby one I called after Sergeant Tom.'

'I hope Jersey won't be jealous,' the soldier observed.

'And the one with the black cap I named after my Uncle Hassim who gave us his life savings so we could start a new and safe life here in England.'

'I have to tell you that Mo isn't any good as a wheelchair mechanic,' Jennifer interjected. 'Because when my wheelchair didn't work, he thought my battery was flat, rather than square.'

They all laughed.

## END

# Also by the Same Author
## Godsons - Counting Sunsets

Godsons – Counting Sunsets is a heartening story, charting the stubbornness of the human spirit to let the precious gift of life slip away without a fight to the bitter end.

Multimillionaire Geoffery Foster has been diagnosed with terminal cancer, and has irrationally swapped his luxurious Monaco penthouse for a single room in a Cotswolds hospice in Gloucestershire England.

Determined to maximise his remaining days and impressed by the selfless humanity shown by his hospice nurse, Andy Spider, Geoffery decides to redress his neglected Godfather responsibilities.

Together Andy and Geoffery embark on a journey to track down and improve the lot of Geoffery's three Godsons.

But will resolving the problems of childhood Meningitis amputee Tim, the alcoholic 'drop out' James and the abused husband Rupert, be too much for Geoffery's frail health.

Added to his challenges, a drunken and intimate wedding reception encounter with a former girlfriend comes back to haunt Geoffery as he also gambles with his life in the hands of a woman spurned.

Counting Sunsets becomes the abacus on which Geoffery records his remaining days.

Proving, *'It's never too late to be who you could have been,'* George Elliot.

# The Godsons Legacy

Andy Spider continues to be the glue that cements the three Godsons together as they expectantly await the release of their legacy from Geoffery Foster's will.

But surely even this pillar of society will be distracted from his task when tempted by the radiant beauty of Nadine.

Mesmerised by the exotic Monaco nightlife, his stoic resolve is weakened by lack of sleep and too much alcohol.

Pallbearers wearing Basques, Murder, Blackmail, Fear, Lust, a Motorway Crash, a runaway teenager and police Investigations are the unexpected consequences of Geoffery's legacy as he still controls their lives FROM BEYOND THE GRAVE.

The story is set in Gloucestershire England, near the beautiful Cotswold Hills

# The Godsons Inheritance

The three Godsons have to work harmoniously to place the final piece in the inheritance puzzle for the release of their legacy.

But the wayward Tim makes it a challenging exercise. His self-centred, bloody-minded arrogance means the whole intricate web of relationships is jeopardised. Will his heart bring him back in line or will he still be ruled by his head?

Meanwhile Rupert is continually in fear of his vicious megalomaniacal wife and James is clinging on to life desperate for a liver transplant.

Young army veteran Carrie is haunted by the trauma of active service.

Ben a young carer for his alcoholic Mother inadvertently opens up old wounds by looking for his father. Can fellow young carer Janie help or hinder Ben's traumatic life?

Andy is having a bad time in his personal life, haunted by a late night indiscretion and frustrated by having to coordinate the activities of the three Godsons.

The story comes to a dramatic and exciting conclusion, but is it the end. In this the third book in the Godsons series?

# Unexploded Love

A love triangle is already an explosive situation without the added complication of an unexploded bomb.

But the Luftwaffe's 1944 legacy of a large bomb exposes a burgeoning romance and throws together the three people in the love match.

Trapped in a collapsed hole with a ticking WW2 bomb for company, the love cheat's hope of escape is in the hands of the man he is cuckolding.

Will the frantic race against time succeed? Or will the husband take revenge?

The stark outcome can only be a blast from the past or UNEXPLODED LOVE?

# Gurney Leafmould –
# The Pied Piper of Calamity

With great DIY aspirations, there is nothing Gurney Leafmould won't tackle – but intent and results are poles apart.

For 'Do it Yourself' means upheaval when Gurney is holding the tools
This is a lively and humorous tale of DIY disasters created by Gurney, a hapless DIYer;

His calamitous CV includes house demolition and fire; a car blaze and a farm inferno coupled together with failed car maintenance and hospital chaos, which are all neatly wrapped in EU red tape. Not to mention a very delicate DIY surgical transplant.
Many wives and partners will recognise some of Gurney's 'attributes' in their own DIY champions.

Willing but incapable, he is a first class prat to his Mother-in-Law but to his long suffering wife, Gurney Leafmould is 'The Pied Piper of Calamity'.

Contains 'Adult Humour'

# Gurney Leafmould - The Ministry of Disruption

Gurney Leafmould was a hapless DIYer but is now legally restrained by an ASBO preventing him from undertaking any more DIY projects.

Unable to pursue his real passion, he turns to Journalism and proves he is good at it.

However, his decision to become an investigative Journalist has disastrous consequences when he stumbles on to a state secret, an organisation called the Ministry Of Disruption (MOD).

By subsequently joining this 'clandestine organisation', Gurney hopes to 'blow the whistle' on their activities and get a major news scoop.

He discovers that the MOD, which was created during WW2 as a guerrilla force to disrupt invading forces; is still active today and conducting disruptive training exercises.

So, if you've been held up in a traffic jam; been stuck at an airport, delayed on a rail journey, the cause of which you could never find out...then it's likely you have been an unwitting 'casualty' of an MOD exercise.

This is the second humorous Gurney Leafmould novel.

Lightning Source UK Ltd.
Milton Keynes UK
UKHW040950081219
354991UK00001B/58/P